Tori and Jace:

Trapped in his Love

Tori and Jace:

Trapped in his Love

Na'Cole

www.urbanbooks.net

Urban Books, LLC
300 Farmingdale Road, NY-Route 109
Farmingdale, NY 11735

Tori and Jace: Trapped in his Love

ISBN 13: 978-1-64556-512-3

First Mass Market Printing July 2023
First Trade Paperback Printing July 2022
Printed in the United States of America

10 9 8 7 6 5 4 3 2 1

Distributed by Kensington Publishing Corp.
Submit Orders to:
Customer Service
400 Hahn Road
Westminster, MD 21157-4627
Phone: 1-800-733-3000
Fax: 1-800-659-2436

Tori and Jace:

Trapped in his Love

Na'Cole

Song Lyrics Written By:

Lance Robinson & Na'Cole

First, I want to give thanks to the higher power. Without God and his glory, there would be no me. To my children, Nashira and Lance Jr., I love you two with all of me. You two are my life and the reasons I wake up every morning with the grind on my mind. To my love, Lance Sr., we've had a lifelong friendship, which led us to a seventeen-year-long relationship. I love you over and beyond the moon. To my mother, Ella, my little sister, Toni, and my big brother, Daniel, I love you guys so much. Our relationship means so much to me. Growing up, we only had us, and no one can take that away from me. To my beautiful friend, publisher, and mentor, Racquel Williams, I love you. Thank you so much for believing in me. You saw the potential in me when no one else did. I appreciate you so much. Thank you for taking me in as your little sister. Finally, my three bonus sisters, Iyisha, Carshina, and Tanesha, sistership through marriages and relationships couldn't make us any closer. I love you three as if we came from the same vagina. Lol. We are blood sisters for life.

This book is dedicated to all the lost girls and boys, the lost women and men who are afraid to speak their truth.

Prologue

They say pussy has a distinctive taste, depending on how well you take care of your body. If you provide for it, please it, and pamper it correctly, trust me, you just might be every man's main course meal. Personally, I love the taste of pineapples, and I make sure that it's a part of my daily meal. At all times, I need my baby girl to taste sweet. That shit will definitely keep a man coming back for more. Any man I've chosen to give a piece of my honey, my cake, my love land, my twat, my good old kitty cat is guaranteed to come back time and time again. The proof is *definitely* in the pudding.

Without even trying, I am able to nab a man. Do I want him? Maybe. I'm to the point now that I want to live, and how is that possible with a man on my heels every damn minute of the day? Don't get me wrong. Jace is the type of man every woman would want in her corner if they were into that love shit. I've never known what love is, so don't fault me for not appreciating a real man. He seemed to be sent down from Cupid himself, but the way Jace fell in love with me so soon was confusing.

Look, I know most women dream about getting married, having a family, going on trips, making love to the same man every single damn night, etc. Well, I've never been one of those types. I had too much to share with the world. Plus, growing up, I was always taught sharing is caring, and that is why I've chosen to give every man I felt was worthy a piece of me. I want to give you guys a taste of my life. I need everyone to get a glimpse into the life of a ho. Well, I wouldn't necessarily call myself a ho per se, though I do enjoy sex. Google.com calls it a "sexual addiction," but I disagree. I don't absolutely need to fuck. For me, sex is therapeutic. It heals all pains and heartaches.

I sometimes use sex just to get through a long, stress-filled day. For the love of sanity, it's a part of nature, although I haven't always taken advantage of what God has blessed me with. When the time was right, I did take full advantage. The power of a woman's honeypot is undeniably something else. Pussy will have a man doing all types of dumb, belligerent shit. Trust me, I know . . . Flips hair. I will fuck your daddy and your uncle. What does N.W.A. say? Fuck the police. Yes, love, I will fuck their ass too if the price is right. If my grades in school are on the line, my teachers can get it too. I really don't give a fuck. If that means getting my way, I'm down for it.

Every woman reading this should know what the power of a woman is. It's self-explanatory. I really don't want to expose the power of the P-U-S-S-Y because there may be a couple of men lurking, but all you women catch my drift. Ronnie said it best in *The Playas Club*, and I quote, "*You got to use what you got to get what you want.*" Trust me. I'm down to do it all, and I know how to get *exactly* what I want. They say everything that glitters isn't gold, and eventually, I will find that shit out the hard way. My sexual urges and desires will get me into a bunch of bullshit. Some shit I may not know how to handle, but I'm hoping to survive. If not, just know I'm not going out without a nut or without giving you my story. I'll skip through my many nights of pleasure as a kid because I understand reading sexual things about a child is weird. I know that some people may not be able to stomach certain obscene and graphic shit. So, without further ado . . . Welcome to my world.

Chapter One

"Mirror, mirror on the wall, who is the most beautifullest of them all?" Tori said to her reflection as it stared back at her. She stood in her most natural state. Hair curly and wet as it hung down to her shoulders, she stared into the mirror, hoping for a response. When she didn't receive the affirmation she wished for, she frowned and recited the words again. "Mirror, mirror on the wall, who is the *prettiest* of them all?" she said, thinking she would somehow get a response if she used a synonym.

Tori found herself talking to the mirror every single morning. Although she knew her parents loved her, she also knew her looks weren't worthy. No one in her life ever called her pretty or beautiful—not even lovely. So, she found herself looking for validation from her own reflection.

"Mirror," Tori said in a sad, almost whiny tone, "you don't think I'm pretty?"

Tori was no idiot. She was actually very smart, and she knew she controlled her reflection. So, she knew if the mirror wasn't speaking, then the pretty and beauty just weren't there. Tori twisted her lips and bit down on her inner cheek. She wanted to cry aloud, but she was used to the disappointment of not being one of the beautiful girls. She placed her ponytail holder onto her curly wet 'fro and took a seat on the toilet lid.

OK, so I'm ugly, she thought to herself. "I mean, I have to be. Mama doesn't tell me I'm pretty. Papa doesn't tell me I'm beautiful. The other kids treat me badly, and Jace won't even look my way."

It was the start of eighth grade for Tori, and she figured she'd begin to look a little different by this time. To her, she'd always been an ugly duckling. With all the superficial people in L.A., Tori could never feel comfortable in her own skin. She knew she would never be good enough. Still, she felt that she would become like a fine wine with time. Instead, here she was, almost in tears over the way her skin and her facial features looked.

Tori lived in Los Angeles, California, where everything, and everyone, for that matter, seemed to be so shallow. If you weren't skinny, light-skinned, with straight teeth and pretty hair, you just didn't belong. She was the opposite. Tori wasn't your typical L.A. girl, although she was a native. Her skin was highly melanated, and her hair had nappy coils. Her body type was skinny and lanky, making her look awkward. Tori had the perfect set of teeth, and her eyes were the color of amber. She was stunning. She just couldn't see it. Her eyes hid behind a pair of thick bifocals that made her look overly nerdy. The stereotype of what "pretty" should reflect had impacted Tori's self-esteem.

Knock, knock, knock.

"Tori Savanna Givens, you are going to be late for school. Hurry up," Mrs. Givens announced.

Tori cleared her throat and sighed. She had to make sure her pain couldn't be heard when she responded.

Knock, knock.

"Tori, did you hear me?" her mother asked.

"Yes, Mother. I'll be right out," she finally responded.

It was time to get her day and the school year started. There was absolutely no turning back. Tori was determined to get through this school year without any faults. When she finally made it to school, she felt the jitters in her stomach.

"New Year with the same people who treated me like crap," Tori said as she walked into Hollenbeck Middle School.

The only thing that had Tori excited and smiling on the inside was seeing Jace, the boy she had the biggest crush on. She couldn't help but watch him and follow his every move. Tori was only 13 years old, but her 13-year-old vagina tingled every time she saw him. Only having the opportunity to be in

Jace's personal space back in the sixth grade because he was failing math, Tori longed for the opportunity to present itself again. She remembered
walking past her math class and hearing Jace tell
their teacher, Mrs. Redd, that he didn't understand division and fractions.

*"So, what's going on, Mr. Doss? You are really
falling behind in math. Are you studying, or are
you just looking online for the answers?" Mrs.
Redd asked, not letting Jace get a word out. She
knew his type so well. The popular boy in school
who feels he can get through life without any
real skills besides making silly young girls do his
grunt work. "Are you making these little girls do
your homework for you?"*

*"No, Mrs. Redd. I've been studying. My parents
don't play. I just don't understand the work," Jace
said as Tori moved closer to the classroom door.*

*"Well, to pass the sixth grade, you absolutely
must pass math. There is no way around it."*

*"I know, and that's why I came to you, to see if
there is anything you can do . . . or any makeup
work I can do. My mother is going to murder me
if I fail."*

*"I don't know, Jace. You don't seem serious
about school, and I don't have time to help a student who is only throwing himself at my mercy*

for sympathy. Regardless of whether you pass, I will still get paid," Mrs. Redd said, looking at Jace as his head suddenly hung low.

Tori silently peeped her head into the classroom and saw the hard time Mrs. Redd was giving Jace. At that moment, Tori decided she was going to help him. The following day, she mustered up all the courage she could to approach Jace during lunch. Tori was a little bit on the shy side, so, of course, she had to prep herself for this big event. Then, after the prepping, she had to pep talk herself all the way over to his table.

"Hi, Jace," Tori said as she approached him and his crew at their lunch table.

"Hey, what's up?" Jace said shortly. He briefly looked up at Tori before turning his attention back to his conversation, quickly dismissing her.

Tori knew he wasn't talking about anything serious. She heard him mention something about one of her fast classmates who apparently let him finger her the night before, so she decided to continue with her proposition.

"Umm, Jace," she said nervously while fixing her glasses and tucking imaginary hair behind her left ear, "I realize you've been struggling with the math lesson." Jace's head snapped in her direction. He looked up at her, into her eyes, and instantly, her glasses fogged up. She was so hot and afraid. Her body began to drip with sweat.

She couldn't believe she was actually approaching Jace, and he was looking into her eyes.

"Nah, baby girl, wrong person," he stunted. Tori's eyebrows furrowed. This wasn't the same Jace that sat in Mrs. Redd's class not even twenty-four hours ago in tears over his grade.

"Well, if you need help, I will tutor you—"

"No need. I'm good on the tutoring, but thank you for offering," he said.

Tori walked away. She knew he needed her, and in due time, she knew he would be taking her up on her offer.

"Aye," Jace yelled across the room as he ran up to her. "What's your name?" he asked as he smiled and reached out his hand.

"Tori," she said shyly. She took his hand into her sweaty palm and shook it.

"All right, Tori, let's meet up and get this tutoring going."

Tori agreed. She was happy she didn't let her shyness get the best of her. She would've for sure missed this opportunity. She had to step up and volunteer her services. Tori couldn't see Jace fail. She needed to be able to secretly stare at him in every class they occupied together. However, after being tutored by Tori in the sixth grade, Jace hadn't uttered a word to her. Still, she lusted over him, drooling whenever she saw him. In her mind, Jace was a god. Tori wished she had a friend or friends to confide in about her feelings.

Jace was always the man. Even in kindergarten, the swagger he possessed just dripped from his entire being. Tori needed him in her life. He would be the person to expose her to the finer things.

Tori walked down the hallway thinking about the so-called good old days. That was then. As she snapped back into reality, she realized this was now, and her life hadn't changed.

"Blackie, black, black," Tori heard a girl yell out as she made her way through the halls, attempting to get to her sanctuary, the place where she found the most solace . . . the girl's bathroom in the very last stall. Tori decided she wouldn't respond. Instead, she kept her head down and walked as quickly as possible.

"Look at her little scary self. Nappy head, scrubbing pad head," another girl spat.

Tori ran in the direction of the girl's bathroom, almost in tears. One would think she'd be used to this by now, but being teased in school still hurt her feelings. As soon as she rounded the corner, she bumped right into Jace. To Tori, he was so gorgeous, a beautiful boy. She knew that he would grow into a beautiful man within the next couple of years.

"Sorry," Tori said with tears pouring down her face.

"It's cool," Jace said. "Aye, are you OK?" he asked, but Tori kept it moving.

She couldn't face him. She didn't know how, especially in her current state. Snotty nose, red eyes, and ashamed to be who she was. Hell no, she wasn't OK, but she wasn't about to give Jace this part of her. The part that made her feel like a basket case. The days she tutored him, she always tried to look her best, but he never really acknowledged or paid attention to her. She did her best to look pretty for him, considering they were only 11-year-old sixth-graders at the time. Tori did whatever she could to catch this boy's attention. They'd spent an hour together, Monday through Thursday, for two months straight. Tori gave Jace lessons in math, and Jace unknowingly gave Tori wet dreams. How could she cry in front of him?

Every day, Tori made sure her ponytail was nice and neat. She made sure her glasses lenses sparkled, her clothes were OK, and her smarts were on full display. Confidence was key, and right there, at that moment, all confidence was gone with the wind. She ran into the bathroom over to her favorite stall. Tori slammed the door behind her and cried her pretty little eyes out.

"Mirror, mirror, on the wall—fuck you."

After that day, Tori begged her parents to transfer her to a different school. She let them in on her being bullied for years. Her parents wanted to speak with school officials to get an understanding. However, they knew that wouldn't do anything to better things for her. So, they transferred her, and that was the last time Tori had any type of interaction with Jace for years to come.

Tori had always been a go-getter in every sense of the word. Growing up in an African and American household, she was raised to always exceed in everything she set out to do in life. Her parents, Mr. Larry Givens, a California native, and Omeiha Jahja Givens, a South African immigrant, had always displayed to their daughter what hard work and dedication consisted of. They made sure she understood the great payoff her life could receive if she stayed focused.

Tori's parents worked seven days a week, owning an independent, successful cleaning service. Their money was long, but they were only willing to give Tori the minimum necessities. They lived by the Bible and didn't believe in spoiling their child. "Spare the rod, spoil the child" was an everyday motto in their home.

She grew up amongst the middle class, but her parents never gave her the illusion that life and material things would be handed to her. With her mother living in a small town in South Africa most of her life, then later immigrating to the States in her teenage years, she never allowed Tori to slack on her studies. Education was not a privilege for her mother, and money wasn't always available. Because of that, Tori always had to work for whatever she wanted outside of what Mr. and Mrs. Givens gave her. As an only child to two rightfully strict parents, Tori went through life submissive and respectful. She knew neither parent would hesitate to punish her severely. Graduating elementary and high school as an A-average student had Tori right on track with everything her parents demanded of her.

Everything her parents envisioned her to do growing up, Tori tried her best to fulfill their every wish. Nonetheless, she had a few internal demons she battled alone daily. By the age of 11, Tori grew curious about sex when she had her first wet dream. The feeling was something different. It made her feel good. The unbelievable rush of an orgasm made her want more. However, the wet dreams weren't happening as often as she would've liked. Soon after, Tori began exploring her own body by masturbating. Whatever she could get her hands on to insert within her walls, she used them.

She was ready for sex early, but she was too shy to approach the boys. The only boy she had ever approached was for tutoring purposes only.

Her looks did not add up when it came to getting a boyfriend. She couldn't compete with the light-skinned, slim, good-hair students that occupied her grade school and high school. But for Tori, looks weren't everything. School was her number one priority, Monday through Friday. Math, English, and science were why she'd never missed a day from school. Tori was weird in that way. Fashion and popularity weren't number one on her list. Most kids hated school, and their favorite pastime was gym, lunch, and recess. However, those three periods were the worst for her. During those times of the day, Tori would be pushed, kicked, tripped, and talked about so badly. The other students couldn't understand why she was so different. Her dark skin made her an easy target, and instead of Tori defending herself, she would exchange the emotional pain for physical pain.

She never thought what she was doing to herself was something bad. Whenever she pleased herself, it always seemed to relax her, relieving her daily tension. Tori didn't realize she was setting herself up for failure with a soon-to-be addiction that she wouldn't be able to control.

By the time she turned 14 years old, she had met her best friend, Amelie. She was someone Tori was able to confide in. Finally, someone to tell all her deepest, darkest secrets to.

Chapter Two

The sun settled suddenly, and Tori found herself in a daze, reminiscing about the day she reconnected with her fiancé, Jace. Her life back then was typical. She followed a strict routine and made sure her last days at UCLA went by without any distractions. Months before that day, she found herself having plenty of wet dreams about him. In college, she vowed to stay on top of her shit and not give in to the many temptations she knew would be somewhere lurking.

Tori decided she would be like Ray Charles, blind to all the bullshit. She threw herself deeply into her studies, not allowing any man in. Tori focused on walking out of UCLA as a woman with self-control on her résumé. But when she saw her future man, Jace, walking around campus, all that self-control shit became null and void. She knew she had to have him. Tori knew God hadn't put them in the same atmosphere for nothing.

She hadn't seen him since leaving her middle school back in the eighth grade, and it was no shock to her that he looked even sexier seven years later. He was more than a woman could ask for. Jace had it all, and it showed. He was a good-looking man with swag and money. And with him being a college student, Tori knew soon enough he would have a degree under his belt as well.

Tori had managed to save herself for so many years. She had no idea what a man felt like, but seeing Jace made her entire yoni water for some reason. Tori was determined to give it all to him. However, this time, she wasn't bold enough to approach him. He was still the man. He was still popular, and all the women on campus were like a permanent fixture on his arms. Everyone knew Jace was destined to be something great, including Tori—especially since he had a brand-new hot song out that repeatedly played on the school's radio station.

From the day she saw him again, Tori envisioned herself being a part of Jace's team one day soon. And on this day in particular, during her last year at UCLA, she was given that opportunity.

It was a typical day on campus. Tori sat Indian style in the grass while studying for her math test, trying her best to focus and not seem as thirsty as the other women. Looking up from her book, she spotted Jace walking, accompanied by a few groupies. Squinting her eyes with an exasperated expression on her face, Tori just stared, wishing she was the girl on his arm. It was as if they were staring at each other as Jace walked in her direction.

Shit, I think he sees me staring, Tori thought to herself. *Tori, blink. Stop staring at him,* she urged herself. Taking in a deep breath, she hurriedly rolled her eyes down toward her book. After seeing a smile creep onto Jace's face, she knew she was busted. Jace and the two women were on the verge of walking past her when suddenly, he stopped walking in midstride, looked down at Tori, and nodded his head coolly. He smiled. He spoke to her without words, and Tori found his arrogance intoxicating. Now standing at six feet and three inches tall with a toffee complexion, toffee-colored eyes, a short Caesar haircut, and an athletic build, Jace was the sexiest man walking this earth in Tori's eyes. His "spruceness" was something she wanted to get next to, but she was afraid she would be rejected.

"Hi," she said shyly. She instantly felt her nipples poking out and peeking through her shirt. Her body became hot. Her nerves were getting the best of her. She couldn't believe she'd just spoken to Jace. Looking back down into her advanced calculus book, she smiled, beating herself up on the inside.

Hi? That's all you had to say was hi? Huuuhh? Tori Givens, you get on my nerves with all that shy shit. You keep that shit up, and he will realize who the hell you are. You must be trying to scare this man away. You've been praying for this day, and the only thing you could think to say was hi? Tori placed her pencil into her mouth and tapped softly on her bottom front teeth. It was a habit of hers whenever she became nervous or uncomfortable. She had to find something to occupy her thoughts.

She just knew that one day soon, she would belong to him. She would take over his body and expose him to the life of a woman with nympho tendencies. Never would she press because she knew what her parents expected of her. They wanted her to complete college first before jumping into a relationship. However, they had no idea of her sexual urges. In all honesty, Tori could've taken or left the relationship. She didn't mind maybe one day falling in love, but at that moment, the only thing on her mind was hot, steamy sex.

Jace stared at Tori. Her shyness was noticeable. He chuckled and mocked her.

"Hi," he said, smirking.

He excused himself from the beautiful women that clung to him and walked closer to Tori. She almost fainted. She couldn't believe this man . . . a man from her past . . . This man, the man she'd watched for months now, was standing right in front of her, preparing himself to engage in a conversation with her.

I guess I'm one of the pretty ones now, Tori thought, smirking inwardly. Jace knelt to her level while balancing on his toes. He took her hand into his and kissed it.

"Chocolate is my favorite thing to devour on a nice day," he said smugly. He left nothing to the imagination, and it took everything in Tori not to blush. "What's your name?" he asked.

"Ummm . . ." Her words were caught in her throat. Jace had her choked up. The difference several years made. Tori looked like a brand-new girl. She didn't look like the throwback blackie, black, black. That much was obvious, considering Jace's approach. "Me?" she asked. Tori was so unsure of herself.

"Yes, you," he said, licking his lips.

"Uhhh," she said. She took a deep breath and smiled shyly. "I'm sorry."

"Fuck it. I'ma just call you Mocha," Jace said, chuckling at Tori's nervousness. "Mocha, your parents blessed you with so much beauty, and I would love to get to know you," he said honestly. He had an agenda. Tori would be another notch on his belt by the end of the night.

Tori brought her bottom lip into her mouth. She had an agenda of her own. She was ready to skip all the talk and get straight down to business. *So, you don't know my name, Jace? Oh, don't worry. As soon as I put this pussy on you, just know*

you won't be able to stop saying my name, Tori
thought to herself. She was always trapped inside
her mind thinking but never sharing her thoughts.

"Thank you," Tori said aloud. Her heart fluttered
as she continued to stare down into her book,
pretending to study.

"Do you mind if I take a seat next to you? My
ankles and shit starting to fuck with me," he said,
drawing a giggle from her lips.

OK, he's polite or whatever. I like that, Tori
thought to herself.

"Yeah, sure. Take a seat. I don't own the grass."

"Oh, she speaks," Jace said, chuckling. "You
don't have to be shy around me, baby. So what
are you studying?" he asked, flipping a page in her
calculus book.

*Yes, I speak. I suck, and I fuck. Don't let this
shyness fool you. I'm that bitch,* she thought to
herself. But it was all lies. All her erotic thoughts
were just that . . . thoughts. Tori wished she *was*
that bitch. Although she'd pleased herself on many
occasions, she was still a virgin. She'd never had
actual sex with a real man. Instead, she was big on
toys, porn, and other foreign objects.

"I'm studying for a math test," she said, finally
looking Jace in his eyes.

When she did, she was instantly sucked in. It
was almost like being hypnotized. His beautiful
eyes made her wonder what type of man he was.

She needed to know if all her wet dreams were for nothing or if she had masturbated with purpose. Every time she fucked herself, she always imagined being in the throes of passion with him. Tori stared into his eyes, studying them, unable to escape his brown pupils. Jace licked his bottom lip. The two looked corny as hell sitting in the grass, staring into each other's eyes. But there was something about this entire moment that had them both mesmerized.

"I hate math, man," Jace said, chuckling. He lifted Tori's book from her lap and read the cover. "Advanced Calculus . . . That's what's up."

"Math is my favorite subject," Tori replied.

"That means you're smart as fuck," he said.

"Yeah, I do have a high IQ and GPA, but I'm sure that is not what guys like you look for in a woman."

"How do you figure that?"

"I don't know. I'm just an outsider looking in, but I have noticed the type of girls you hang around."

"Damn . . . You're one of *those* types." He smirked.

"What types?" she asked.

"You're judging me before you even get to know me. I can fuck with a smart woman. That'll just force me to step my intellect up a little. You see how I just came with that big-ass word," he said, and they both laughed.

"Well, excuse me." She smiled.

Jace and Tori sat outside on the grass, talking for the next two hours. She shared her story of being an only child in an African-influenced home. She told him about how she had to follow the directions and routines of her mother. However, she never touched on her elementary school and high school days. Instead, she kept certain things on a need-to-know basis.

Tori was 21 years old, but her parents still took care of her and pretty much ran her life. She explained that since being allowed to move on campus, she felt a sense of freedom. Also, because she was an upperclassman, she didn't have a roommate. She instantly threw out hint after hint. Tori was ready for Jace, and she wouldn't let up.

"I'm tired of living up to my mother's standards, and I'm sick of following the rules, you know?" Tori explained, and Jace nodded his head in agreement. "My mother, she's so harsh. I honestly understand. She grew up in South Africa. Her life wasn't beautiful rainbows and sunshine, so I get it. But damn, she's very critical." As Tori talked, Jace sat on the side of her listening, soaking in all of her insecurities, shortcomings, and vulnerabilities. "I plan on changing a lot of things. I'm an adult, and it's time I take care of myself—"

Jace looked over at Tori and gripped her face, turning her focus and gaze onto him. Tori removed her face from his grasp as she frowned.

"I hear you, baby. Trust me, I understand." He cut her off in mid statement. "You're grown, and grown women do grown things. One day, you'll break away from under your mother."

Jace was tired of talking. He didn't sit next to Tori to hear her long life story. He was ready to fuck her and leave her where she stood. Pussy wasn't hard to come by for him, but he wanted her. He always noticed her around campus, toting her big-ass economics, psychology, physics, and statistics books around. Jace didn't doubt she was a smart girl, but she was one of not many he had yet to smash.

"It's getting late. Let me help you to your room," he said.

The two sat talking for so long that the sun was now setting.

"Yes, of course," Tori said. Jace stood and held out his hand, helping Tori to her feet. He brushed the dust from the back of her shorts, copping a free feel. "Thank you."

"No problem. It's too many crazies out there. You need a real man to help you get safely to your dorm room." They both laughed.

"A real man, huh?" Tori asked shyly. She grabbed onto his arm and felt his biceps. That was her way of copping a free feel too.

"Hell yeah. I would've said a real nigga, but I try not to use such vulgar language in front of pretty women," Jace said while picking up Tori's books from the grass. He placed her math books onto his forearm and cradled them as if they were a baby.

"I've heard the word 'nigga' a time or two. There's nothing vulgar about it. Honestly, I find the word empowering depending on how you use it," Tori stated. The two walked side by side as they walked to the dorms. They both looked comfortable as if they'd been friends their entire life.

"Hahaha, you gon' have to explain this shit to me." Jace chuckled.

"OK . . . Well, basically, a word that was once used to tear us down in the past is now used to embrace one another. We turned something that was once negative into something so positive. It's a word we as Black people can use to show each other love. We own that shit. It's all ours."

"OK, OK, I hear you. I like your take on that."

"I mean, it's not a word I use personally, but I don't mind it as long as you're not using it in a way to degrade someone. I love positive vibes." She laughed.

"I suppose. Don't worry, though. A nigga don't do that degrading shit. I'm a vibe within itself."

"Yes, Jace, you are definitely a vibe. Speaking of vibes, I heard you can sing or whatever." Tori smiled. She wanted to hear his voice because she'd listened to a couple of songs he'd produced played on campus. Yes, his vocals were laid on the track.

However, his vocals weren't doing enough justice to the songs; she could barely hear him. He wasn't the lead singer, and they were studio recorded, meaning they were already mixed to sound good. Tori wanted to hear Jace's voice up close and personal. She wanted to hear him in his rawest form—uncut, unedited, and not watered down.

"You know your boy do a little some, some. My forte is producing, though. There's something about those instruments and shit. I can't get enough of it. That's my passion, and one day soon, I'ma be a big deal," Jace explained.

"You're already a big deal. I heard two of your songs hit the billboards."

"Yeah, my shit up there. Right now, they're holding down the twenty-fifth and sixty-third spot. Nothing major. My music ain't at number one yet, and I was only the coproducer on both songs."

"No big deal? Are you serious, Jace? That is such a *huge* deal considering you're new to the industry and still in college. Don't downplay your talents. Anyway, can I hear you sing something? I love me a good old love song," she said.

"Yeah . . . I got you."

Jace cleared his throat, preparing to serenade Tori's ears and heart. First, he created the beat using his lips and tongue to start the instrumental to "Sweet Lady" by Tyrese. Then holding his teeth tightly together, he imitated the bass. Next, pushing air from between his teeth, Jace forced out the sound of the high hat. Next, his deep baritone brought out the chorus of the song.

"*Be my sweet lady . . .*" He held the note. "*I want you to be my lady. Ooohhh, bae.*" Jace played around with his voice, smiling as he brought Tyrese's song to life. "*Sweet lady, would you be my sweet love for a lifetime?*" He sang the entire chorus on key as Tori smiled from ear to ear. He wasn't sure if he was singing the words correctly, but he knew his voice was on point. Raw and uncut, Jace sang as they walked.

However, he didn't want to give Tori the wrong impression and make her think he was asking her to be his lady. So Jace continued to sing and snap his fingers, making sure his counts in between the notes were correct. He had to stay on beat while he finessed his way into Tori's little wet spot. Tori bobbed her head, feeling the way Jace made her heart smile. The way he stayed on beat and in tune, she knew this song was handpicked just for her. She felt it in her heart.

He moved his fingers and head with the melody of Tyrese's lyrics. "*I never really seen your type, but I must admit that I kinda like.*" After that part, Jace abruptly ended the song.

"A'ight, that's all I'ma give you for now," he said as they reached Tori's dorm. "Well, looks like we made it safe and sound."

They stopped in front of the door and turned to look at each other.

"Looks like," Tori said. "You sounded amazing."

"I know," he said cockily. "Well, thank you for allowing me the chance to walk you home and giving me your take on *niggas*," he said aloud, and they both laughed.

Jace walked closer to Tori and grabbed her face. He bent down slightly and kissed her lips. She didn't flinch. Instead, she kissed him back. They stood in front of her building, kissing for a while, and after pulling back, Tori felt light-headed. She also felt herself becoming moist. She knew she needed Jace in her room.

"Thank you for walking me, Jace."

Distraught, Tori turned and walked away, leaving her books behind purposely. She knew he would soon realize she left them behind and would come searching for her. She ran through the lobby's double doors, giving Jace a chase. He would have to hunt her down to return her property.

Jace stood, looking confused. He looked down at his arm and noticed he was still holding her books. Quickly, he began walking toward the double doors. *She about to have me in this bitch looking thirsty as hell with her fucking books in my hands. She definitely about to give up some pussy,* he thought to himself as he walked through the doors toward the security desk.

"Yo," Jace said, clearing his throat.

He set the books down on the security desk and frowned slightly. The security guard had his head down, staring into his phone, so Jace tapped on the desk.

"Aye, my mans."

"What's up, Jace?" the security guard said, finally looking up and seeing Jace's face.

Jace knew at that point he couldn't turn back. Considering one of his classmates worked as security, he knew he couldn't leave her books and just be done with it. Plus, he knew he wouldn't have a problem getting up to Tori's room now.

"What's up, bro?" They shook hands. "Aye, I'm looking for . . . Shit, I forgot shorty's name." He thought about it. Jace couldn't remember Tori's name to save his life, and that's probably because she never told him, so he played it safe. "I'm looking for Mocha's room," he said, calling Tori by the name he'd given her earlier. To him, that had to be her nickname because her skin was so chocolate, and she looked too good to be called anything less.

"Mocha? Shit, we ain't got nobody in this building by that name. Matter of fact, let me look. Maybe she's new, and I haven't been informed yet."

"Nah, she ain't new. Damn, what *is* shorty's name?" Jace opened Tori's calculus book, and it read: *Tori Givens, Dorm C, Room 305. Please return if found*. He smirked. That was definitely a sign from God. "Tori . . . Shorty's name is Tori," Jace said.

"Oooh, Tori Givens. She just went up. Just take the elevators to the third floor. It's the third door on your right."

"Tori Givens? Damn, why does shorty's name sound so familiar?" Jace said under his breath. "A'ight, bet," he said to the security guard. He picked up the books and made his way to Tori.

Jace decided to skip the elevators and took the stairs instead. He ran for the pussy, skipping every other step as he ascended the stairs in a hurry. When he reached her door, he bit down onto his inner jaw and played with his chin a little. Deep in thought, Jace stood there thinking about what he would say. He was never nervous when it came to sex, and that's because every woman he'd ever been with threw the pussy at him. He never had to stalk it or hunt it down.

"Tori fucking Givens. I know her from somewhere. A nigga just can't put his finger on it. Fuck where you know her from? We can figure all that shit out later. She knew what the fuck she was doing leaving these goddamn books behind," Jace coached himself. "Here, baby girl, you left these behind." He practiced his words. "Hell nah. That shit sounds like some old creepy sugar-daddy-ass shit." Jace laughed. He stood with one fist up, ready to knock. "Yeah, I think you might be needing these soon. Nah nah nah. That shit sounds lame as hell." Jace put his index finger and thumb to his face, squeezing the bridge of his nose. "Fuck it and fuck these books. So be you, my nigga. Shorty wants you to bend her ass over."

Once again, Jace lifted his fist to knock, but before he could place his fist on the door, Tori opened it. She stared at Jace with a smirk on her face. She knew, sooner or later, he would be at her front door. Tori was dressed in an oxford grey Champion sports bra and a matching pair of bikinis. Jace's jaw almost instantly dropped. His fist was still stuck in midair as he breathed heavily. Tori grabbed his shirt, pulling him into her tiny dorm room. He followed her in, finally dropping his hand and placing it to his dick and balls. Jace held on to his erection.

Tori backed herself up against the wall and smiled, holding on to the middle of his shirt. She pulled him to her and felt the hardness of his dick on her leg. She looked into his eyes and smirked. He came right on time. She had just stepped out of a quick shower, so the day's smolder and mild musk were both washed away from her body.

Jace took Tori's bottom lip into his mouth and kissed her. He grabbed a handful of her ass and rubbed it. A few seconds later, the two were coming out of their clothes. Somehow, her math books ended up on the floor. Jace's clothes were scattered across the room, and they both were in bed naked, making love. Jace took Tori's virginity, but not her innocence. There was nothing innocent about her. She was ready to get fucked from the first day she laid eyes on her very first pornography tape. She'd been penetrated a time or a thousand before, but never by a man. Tori was already obsessed with masturbating. When they were done, and Jace left her dorm room, she would fuck herself again. Finally, she'd gotten a taste of real dick, some "OK dick." Jace had the type of sex that'll make a bitch fall in love, and that's not what Tori wanted. However, the monkey that constantly hung onto her could only be relieved of its duty after some great sex and a good one-on-one session with herself.

"Go deeper," Tori said.

"Mmm mmm mmm . . ." Jace's voice moaned out as he pulled back. He felt himself reaching his peak, and that was something he wasn't ready for. "Fuck," he said under his breath. He looked down at Tori, and she wore a look of annoyance on her face. "Damn, Mocha. Why didn't you tell me you were a virgin? You tryin'a make me fall in love?"

"Who said I was a virgin, Jace?" she retorted, staring back at him.

At this point, she was irritated. She'd always wondered what Jace was packing ever since the sixth grade. And after seeing all the women on campus on his dick, she knew he had to be fucking, fucking. He had to be banging bitches' brains out.

"I know what virgin pussy feels like. I felt it when I first got up in you," he said. "I need a break. You gon' have all the niggas laughing at me if they find out I couldn't please yo' cute ass properly. I swear to God you got a nigga ready to bust."

Tori smirked. She decided the conversation was over, and she would take control. She didn't need a break. Jace had her hot and ready. Tori used her weight to roll on top of him. No one would've ever thought this was her first time when she slammed her body down onto his loins. Over and over again, Tori bounced her body up and down on Jace's. She rode him like a real cowgirl, and she didn't let up. She needed to feel like a real woman, and her first official ejaculation that a man brought from her body was just what the doctor ordered.

Jace lay there, arms wide open, watching Tori take control. Her face was commanding, and her eyes looked straight ahead as if she had an out-of-body experience. Emotionless and expressionless, she had her way with him. He allowed her to do her thing and bring them both to a nut. She did not disappoint. Tori leaned down and slowly rolled her hips while Jace held on to her ass. He knew at any second that his seeds would be spilling.

"Fuck me, Jacey. Fuck me."

"Mocha, slow down. Goddamn," he moaned, but Tori was in control.

"Grab my ass," she told him.

The feeling Jace got from Tori's demanding words as well as her sudden personality change, turned him on. He wanted to fuck her, but the way his cum was set up, he couldn't oblige her request, so she fucked him. She rode the fuck out of his dick, making his toes curl as his face created a sexy mug.

"Damn, Mocha." He held on to her waist.

Jace announced his orgasm, and Tori announced hers too. She was ready. As soon as Jace felt his body preparing to release, his dick expanded triple times in size and thickness. He filled up Tori's walls with every inch of him. Soon after, Tori moved her ass on Jace's erection as they both climaxed.

After getting her cherry popped for the first time, Tori needed a long, hot shower. It was much needed after her sex session with Jace. She wanted the sex to last a little longer, thinking maybe she would've been the one to tap out first. However, Jace ended up being the one who couldn't hang. Tori knew her middle would be a little too much for him to handle. Being a virgin at the age of 21 was rare, and she was sure it'd been a very long time since Jace felt anything close to tight pussy.

After their sexual encounter, she allowed him to stay the night, and it was by force. Although Jace

was the man with the ladies, he never got too tired
and just fell asleep. However, after being with Tori,
he quickly fell into a deep, peaceful slumber. This
was a first for them both. This wasn't how she
imagined her first time would be. She preferred
a long night of rough fucking and afterward, cud-
dling up alone with her pillows. And that was *after*
she'd kicked the nigga out. But she didn't want to
disturb him. She figured she would let him sleep
off their previous sexual bliss, and in the morning,
fuck him again.

Chapter Three

Buzz, buzz, buzz, buzz.

The following morning, Tori grimaced as she felt around for her buzzing cell phone. Her eyes remained closed as her hand reached in the direction of the noise.

"Huuuhh," she said aloud, frowning. The sound of her alarm was irritating. Tori had a whole attitude. She was so exhausted from the night before, feeling like she'd just fallen asleep only minutes before.

"Just five more minutes," she screamed. Still, her alarm didn't listen.

At this point, she was ready to say fuck school and her calculus test, which was worth 40 percent of her grade. When she finally located her phone, she quickly shut off her alarm and sat up groggily. Without looking, Tori felt behind herself searching for Jace, but he was no longer there. He had crept out of her dorm room in the wee hours of the morning while she slept. She turned around and shrugged her shoulders, not really pressed about Jace deciding to leave without informing her.

"Let's get this test over with," she said, picking herself up from the bed and getting dressed.

This test was going to confirm her hard work and dedication. All she ever wanted to do was make her parents proud. Maybe then she would get the love and attention she longed for. Tori was truthfully the perfect daughter. Mainly because she pushed all of her sexual urges to the back of her mind and made school her number one priority. This final test would earn Tori bragging rights and help her leap into adulthood. A successful one. Being an obedient daughter came with its perks at the end of the day.

Twenty minutes later, she took her usual ten-minute walk to her calculus class, dragging her feet as she shuffled through the grass. She knew her teacher, Professor Davis, would be waiting on her. He was a little creepy and a pervert. Most days, she hated going to his class. His flirtatious remarks toward her were a bit much at times, and today, Tori was not in the mood to deal with his bullshit. She dreaded sitting in his class, but she put on a brave face. This was her last test, and soon enough, she wouldn't have to deal with creepy-ass Davis anymore.

Tori walked into her class unnoticed and took a seat in the back. She sat and listened to her teacher's quick lecture before he proceeded with the calculus test.

"Good morning, class," Professor Davis said. "We're just waiting on one more student before we begin. If I could have you all turn your books to chapter 56 and take a quick glance, it would be much appreciated," he announced. Before the students could follow his directions, Tori spoke up.

"There's no need for that, Professor. I'm here," she announced. "We can start."

"OK, class, you heard her. Let's get started." Professor Davis smiled. He liked Tori as a student. In fact, she was his favorite student. She seemed to brighten his day with her always on-point answers and her willingness to help tutor other students. "Put everything away. The timer will start in two minutes, and you will have an hour to complete your test. If you finish early, you may bring your test to the front and leave," were the last words Tori heard him say before she picked up her pencil and began.

Tori sat looking down at her papers, filling out her scantron sheet, correctly answering every question. She didn't miss a beat; she was smart as hell and a pro when it came to the subject at hand. It took her twenty minutes tops to complete most of her test, and when she got to the final two questions, she thought about them for a while, realizing they might be trick questions. Sleepiness took over her vision. However, she continued to push through. Finally filling in the last two bubbles, Tori gathered her belongings and figured she would lay her head down and rest her eyes for the rest of the allotted time.

She heard him say, "All right, class, put your pencils down," and she quickly sat up.

Tori wiped the sleep from her eyes and stretched. The classroom was now empty except for Professor Davis. She felt a little confused. She was wobbly, and her body felt unsteady. Tori placed her books into her backpack as Professor Davis approached her with the biggest, creepiest smile on his face.

"Is everything OK?" he asked.

"Everything is fine. Why do you ask?" Tori lifted her book bag onto her desk and began zipping it. She'd fucked up falling asleep and being left alone with Davis.

"I mean, it's not like you to sleep in my class. You must've had a long night."

"No, I didn't have a long night." Tori chuckled, feeling a little embarrassed. She'd most definitely had a long night, but that wasn't something she wanted to discuss with her teacher.

"Are you sure?" he asked, lifting Tori's test from the desk. "From what I can observe here, you have done a great job with your answers. I figured maybe you were up all night studying." He winked. "But you do know I have to take twenty-five points off your test because you were sleeping in my class."

"Really, Professor? OK, I admit, I did pull an all-nighter. This was the most important test to me." She lifted her scantron sheet. "And as you said, I did an excellent job."

"I agree. From what I can see, you answered every question correctly, but you know the rules, Ms. Givens . . . unless you're willing to take me up on that date I've been asking you about."

She knew it was coming. Davis was a young, 35-year-old college professor. He'd seen many young, beautiful girls on campus during his five short years at UCLA. However, Tori was one of a kind. He'd been trying to take her on a date since the beginning of the semester. Tori stood.

"Are you blackmailing me, Professor?" she asked with a smile as she turned on her charm. She walked into the professor's space and grabbed his dick. "I have something better than a date. Those twenty-five points will kill my perfect GPA, Mr. Davis, and I know you wouldn't want to do that to me." Tori's voice became seductive and teasing. It was almost as if she were a different person.

"Nah, I'm not blackmailing you, Tori. You can easily say no. I just see something I want when it comes to you. We don't have to fuck. I'm just asking for a harmless date."

"You see, Professor, I would rather fuck. I don't do dates. You're not my man, and a student-teacher relationship wouldn't look right. Wouldn't you agree?" She squeezed his manhood even harder. He rubbed his chin with one hand and grabbed hold of Tori's ass with the other.

"I never knew you were so aggressive, Tori. How about I give you what you want, and you give me what I want?"

"How about I just give you a taste, and you give me an *A*?" she said. She released his dick and grabbed hold of his tie. "I know you want me. We can just cut to the chase and get right to it. Let me feed you this pussy, and, in turn, you make my grade look perfect." Bashfully, Davis smirked and reached for Tori's hand. Gripping it, he bit down on his bottom lip. "I promise to give you the best you ever had."

Tori had never known herself to be so aggressive either, but Jace woke up her inner confidence. He'd introduced her to the gift of womanhood. Her essence was something she never tried to control a man with, but today, she had no choice. With Davis, she had to use what she had to pass his class. She had the upper hand and the power . . . The power of pussy, that is.

"Pussy comes a dime a dozen, Ms. Givens. I want so much more than that," he stated, honestly. He was an experienced man. However, he hadn't experienced anything like her, and Tori knew this for a fact.

Tori couldn't see herself giving him more than just a quick lay. Her grades were the most important thing to her. Aside from her sexual urges, she was trying to kill two birds with one stone . . . her twenty-five points and some dick.

"You don't think men come a dime a dozen too, Professor Davis? I stay with a bunch of niggas at my doorstep," Tori lied, trying to make herself sound interesting. She even took it upon herself to use the "N" word, figuring she'd sound hip. "So, let's stop these games." Tori sat on her desk and opened her legs wide, exposing her neatly shaven vagina lips. "This pussy right here is top-notch. Trust me."

Tori removed her hands from Professor Davis's tie and went straight for his belt buckle. She quickly and effortlessly dismantled it, pants button, and zipper.

He placed his hand on her thigh and moved his way slowly—and lustfully—up her leg. His fingers were like bloodhounds as they sniffed and guided themselves to Tori's tantalizing pussy. He rubbed her softly. She smiled, and so did he. Then he removed his hand, slipping it from underneath her dress. He brought his fingers up to his nose and sniffed.

"Shit, I smell like water," Tori said, winking.

"Yes, love. You do." He put his fingers in his mouth and licked them. "You taste like water too," he announced.

"I know. And if you don't enjoy it, I give you permission to take away *fifty* points," she said cockily. Tori already knew he would more than likely fall in love with what she had in between her legs, especially since she'd only had one other man inside of her.

"Confidence, I like that. But I've had plenty of pussy in my day. So what can you give me that I haven't had before, Ms. Givens?" He slipped his index and middle finger back into Tori's tight center, then moved closer and pecked her on the ear. His breath was warm, and his rapid finger movements turned them both on.

"You may have had more than you could probably handle. However, out of your 35 years of life, I know you've never experienced anything like *this*," she said seriously as Professor Davis's pants fell to the floor. "This pussy right here is worth an *A+*," she said honestly.

Tori pulled down the professor's underwear, and he wasted no time inviting himself inside her welcoming walls. Just as Jace had done, Davis guided himself into Tori, taking his time. He held on to her as she wrapped her legs around his waist. Both of their bodies shook with excitement and pleasure. Her pussy was so tight that it took everything in Davis not to go crazy inside of her. She trembled slightly when he suddenly forced his way in, ultimately hitting her spot. Tori didn't expect Professor Davis to have her body trembling the way he did. To her, Davis was like the ugly side nigga who only got pussy when he paid for it. He wasn't even close to being her type. Honestly, he was nobody's type. Professor Davis was short, chubby, his legs were shaped like a *V*, and he sported glasses. He was a little too nerdy for her. However, that perfect *A* grasped her attention.

Tori's body shuddered every time Davis dug into her. She held him around his neck and bit down on it to stop herself from moaning out loud. *Mmmm, if he weren't so fucking fat, I would've put it on him in a different setting. I definitely would've taken him up on that date, but ugh, hell no.* Tori held on to the professor even tighter, and when he got comfortable enough inside of her, he pumped faster. She helped his movements. Tori squeezed Davis's ass and guided him deep inside. He wasn't afraid to fuck shit up, and he wasn't afraid to drive Tori crazy. This was the type of sex she expected from Jace and not from her unattractive teacher. Nevertheless, she was not complaining. Tori showed him how much of a team player she was by returning his strokes with a few intense strokes of her own.

"Ms. Givens . . . Throw that pussy, baby," he said softly into her ear.

Tori threw it at him; she had to live up to her promise. Her middle was tight, juicy, and barely tampered with. Right there in her calculus class, she fucked her teacher on the desk. There was nothing she needed to do to make him come. Tori kept her eyes staring straightforward, appearing almost in a trance. Her face was expressionless and emotionless, but the feeling Davis gave her insides was gratifying.

Davis pulled out of her, helped her down from the desk, and bent her over. He gave Tori eight hard, long strokes as she gripped the desk with her bottom lip balled up into her mouth. Tori closed her eyes. She felt the tingling sensation of her orgasm coming. She felt Davis's erection expand, and soon after, they both ejaculated. Davis left Tori's entire insides soaked. She stood and turned to look at him. In silence, she loosened his tie and took it from around his neck. Then she cleaned herself. She stared at him the entire time, silently taking her time wiping his little ones from in between her legs.

"Was that worth all one hundred points?" Tori asked as Davis stood dumbfounded with his private part still erect, pointing directly at her. Davis couldn't get his words together to form an answer, so Tori took that as a yes. She fixed her dress and smiled as she neatly folded the tie.

"Thank you, Professor." Tori smiled. "Do you mind if I take this as a little souvenir?" She stuffed the tie into the side pocket of her book bag. "Professor?"

"I'm sorry, Ms. Givens. Yeah, no problem. You can have it." He pulled up his pants.

"Can we exchange phone numbers? I mean, I would still love to take you out on that date whenever you're free."

"No, Professor, this was a one-time thing. If anything, you can email me," Tori said as she walked toward the classroom door, and Davis followed behind her.

"Shit, I tried." He chuckled.

"So, my grade will be perfect?" she asked.

"Yes, of course. A deal is a deal, Ms. Givens."

"I appreciate you, Professor." Tori pinched his cheek before she made her exit. She knew that once she glanced at her grade, it would be everything she asked for.

Chapter Four

Because it was such a beautiful day outside, before Tori went back to her dorm room, she made a pit stop. She walked toward the wide-open grass area to do her usual chilling in the sun. Although the test she'd been studying for was done and over with, she figured she would continue her daily ritual. Walking over to where she'd studied every day for the past couple of months, she passed a crowd of people standing in long lines. She stared at them, trying to understand exactly what the hell was going on. Finally, she stopped walking and stood in place, scoping things out. There were four tables lined up side by side, and every folding table had at least fifteen people standing in each line waiting their turn to approach the beautiful men and women that occupied them. Tori squinted her eyes and tapped the nearest student on her shoulder.

"I'm sorry to bother you, but what's going on over here?" she inquired curiously.

"No bother at all. They're handing out applications for summer jobs," the young lady said, smiling.

"Oh, OK. These lines are so long, I thought they were passing out free money or something," Tori said, giggling. "Do you know what type of work they're hiring for?"

"Here," she said, handing Tori a flyer. "Here's the job info. These papers have been hanging around campus for some time now. From the description, the job sounds pretty easy and interesting."

"Flirty Girls Anonymous?" Tori frowned. "What is this?" She laughed. "Are they even allowed to solicit on campus? This sounds like a strip club or a hotline for horny old men."

"I don't know, but whatever it is, I'm down. Do you see the pay? It's $600 a week. I don't give a damn. If I have to, I'ma shake this ass until I can't shake it no more. Or sell this pussy until it old and worn out." Both women laughed. "Nah, but seriously, it says it's an office job, so how much harm could that cause?"

"I guess you have a point." Tori shrugged. "Well, before you leave, let me know how it goes. I'll be sitting over in the grass reading this book." Tori showed the girl the novel she had in her hand. "By the way, my name is Tori." Tori stuck out her hand.

"Aja. Nice to meet you, Tori, and will do."

Tori walked away and took a seat in her usual spot underneath the tree. She leaned back, making sure she was facing the walkway. For whatever reason, Jace weighed heavily on her mind. Although she'd not even an hour ago had sex with her teacher, she couldn't miss the opportunity to see the man who'd taken her virginity only the night before.

It would've been ideal to go home and bathe first, but because she and Jace did not exchange phone numbers the previous night, she had to catch him on campus. She knew soon enough he would be walking past her with a couple of bad bitches on his arms. *Men ain't shit,* she thought. Sitting back, she waited to see him.

An hour later, Tori had read six chapters from her novel, and that was how long it took Aja to come back with some information about the job. Tori closed her book and stood when she saw Aja approaching her. She smiled, dusting off her dress as she waited. Aja's face was complemented with a huge smile of her own, so Tori had to assume she scored the job.

"Wow, girl, I am so sorry. That was a long-ass line," Aja announced. "Buuuut . . . It was well worth the wait." She flexed her eyebrows, moving them up and down.

"I see the huge smile on your face. So, does that mean what I think it does?" Tori asked. "Hold up.

Let me prepare myself for your news." She laughed.

"Well, if you're thinking I got the job, then, yes, you are thinking correctly."

"Oh, wow. So, just like that? Right on the spot? That's what's up," Tori said.

"Yeeeesss, girl. They were so nice too. I'm ready to work."

"So, what will you be doing?"

"Office work, answering calls, talking to customers about their needs, and possibly getting them comfortable enough to continue to do business with the company."

"Their 'needs'?"

"Yeah, I'm excited. I can't wait."

"Sounds interesting. Congratulations, Aja."

"They're still looking for candidates. You should go try your luck." Aja smiled and handed Tori a card. "If not now, at least think about calling them. Shit, $600 a week with incentives. You can't beat that."

"Yeah, that does sound good, but kind of too good to be true."

"Well, I don't know about you, but we're grown, and living off Daddy's money is pretty much over with for me. So, I have to do what I can. I can't keep fucking these Hollywood-ass niggas for money and a meal. I'm only 21, and my pussy feel so run through," Aja said, being honest. "Here, give me your phone number. I start my new job in two weeks. So, let's stay in contact, and I'll let you know what this job is really about." She handed Tori her phone.

Honestly, looking at Aja was like looking into a mirror. Their features were so similar. From their beautiful eyes to their full, pouty lips. Even their chocolate skin.

"OK. Sounds like a deal. In the meantime, if you ever need a meal, call me." Tori put her phone number in Aja's phone. "I live in the dorms. Building C, room number 305." She handed the phone back and prepared to leave. She decided she had waited long enough to see Jace, and he still hadn't shown up. She was tired at this point. Admittedly, Professor Davis had worn her out a little.

"All right, girl, I will definitely do that."

On cue, as soon as Tori and Aja parted ways, she spotted Jace from afar, speaking in what seemed to be a deep conversation on his cell phone. She smiled while staring at him, and he smiled back. But instead of him stopping to hold a conversation with her, he walked past her. Jace looked to be on a mission. Still, he could've stopped and acknowledged her. Tori followed him with her eyes and head, then waved at him as he went by her.

Damn. Really, Jace? You fuck me, and then

say fuck me? Tori thought to herself. She scowled and grabbed her belongings from the grass. She was fuming. She couldn't believe Jace had played her to the left. Deciding she wasn't going to make a fool of herself, she walked away in the opposite direction.

Chapter Five

Jace was on a moneymaking mission. He was already the man on campus, and now, it was time for him to come up in a major way. His walking past Tori without acknowledging her was not intentional. But the phone call he was on was very important. As he went by her, he smiled with his phone glued to his ear as he spoke with a music exec named Big Percy from 290 Record label. Somehow, a couple of his tracks fell into the hands of this famous, powerful man. He was like a Suge Knight of his time. Big, light-skinned, and feared by most, he was feeling everything he heard, and he was willing to pay Jace substantially to be part of his team. Big Percy was ready to sign Jace to a ten-song production deal, which would be completed within two years.

Jace wasn't sure how his name reached so high up on the totem pole, but he wasn't complaining. Nothing was official at this point. It was only something to consider. What Big Percy was offering him is what he was working his way through college to

achieve. By the grace of God, as soon as college was
a done deal, he would be living his dream, doing a
job he was passionate about with a nice $5 million
in his bank account. He figured he must be a big
deal if huge music execs were reaching out to him,
and this was a duty he planned to take seriously.
Although he'd just really met Tori, he planned to
take her to the top with him. He used to watch her
the same way she watched him, and he knew she
was a good girl. He deserved the perfect woman,
and she deserved a man that was on the come-up.

"Sounds good. I don't want to confirm anything
just yet, especially not over the phone. I'll get with
my attorney, and together, we can figure some
things out," Jace said.

"Cool, cool. You don't want to pass this opportunity up, my man. I'm willing to offer you 5 mil
for these ten songs. I heard you're a hot commod-
ity over there at UCLA. Somehow, I came across
a song you produced, and, real shit, I was im-
pressed."

"Aw, man, gratitude. I appreciate it. Look, I'll be
graduating next month, and after that, I'm all the
way in. Then I can focus more on writing and shit."

"A'ight, my nigga. I'll be in touch then. Is there a
number I can call your attorney on so that they can
look at these contracts in the meantime?"

"To be honest, I don't have an attorney yet,"
Jace announced. "But as soon as I get everything

situated with graduation, I'll definitely be looking for proper representation. Then after that, I'll hit you up," Jace said excitedly. He wanted to dive right into this once-in-a-lifetime opportunity, but he didn't want to be stuck in a contract if he later decided 290 Records wasn't the music home for him.

"Look, Jace, I don't want you to sleep on this opportunity, so I'ma go ahead and hook you up with the perfect entertainment lawyer. I got you. The nigga owes me a couple of favors. I'll contact him and send him over the contracts. That way, by the time you graduate, he'll be contacting you," Big Percy said, and Jace thought about it.

The shit sounded too damn good to pass up, so he wouldn't let it slip through his fingertips. He agreed, and Big Percy had Jace's contract drawn up before they disconnected the call.

"Aye, we need to come up with a new name for you too."

"Damn, I never thought about calling myself anything other than my real name." Jace put his fingers to his chin. "Hmmm . . . 'Jacey on the Beat' when I produce, and 'Jacey' when I do a feature. What do you think?"

"Hell yeah, that'll work. Jacey on the Beat it is."

"A'ight, Big Percy. Let's make some fire-ass music."

Click.

Chapter Six

"Tori . . . Tori . . . Wait, wait . . ."

Tori lay in bed sleeping comfortably, and all she could envision was a caramel-complected young woman in the nude. Tori saw her lips pressed against the other woman's southern lips kissing, pecking, licking, and teasing her until she yelled out Tori's name. The young lady had an appetizing body. Her thin but thick-in-all-the-right-places figure was definitely something to feast on, and Tori took full advantage. Her skin was soft and blemish-free. Tori rubbed her right hand up and down her victim's body as she let her tongue take control. "Tori, please," the woman moaned, and her back arched. Grabbing Tori's hair and wrapping her legs around Tori's shoulders, Amelie thought she would gain control. However, Tori had that control button on lock.

"That's how you wanna play it?" Tori took time out to say before she turned the heat up another notch.

She grabbed Amelie's clit in between her teeth, knowing the clitoris was the most sensitive part of a woman's vaginal area. Tori murdered it— fucked it with her whole mouth. Sucking on her, Tori showed Amelie she wasn't to be fucked with. Tori wasn't letting up until she knew Amelie was sorry for trying to test her. Tori didn't know the meaning of the word stop. She created the rules when it came to an orgasm, and whatever it took, she was going to do it. Tori pulled on Amelie's pearl while simultaneously fingering her. She knew Amelie was ready to come when she heard her screaming her name once again. Amelie's legs loosened and shook uncontrollably.

"Tori! Tori!" Tori felt a subtle push to her body. "Tori, wake your ass up."

She heard a voice. Caught off guard, Tori slowly rubbed on her clit as she dreamed about her best friend.

"Girl, what the hell are you doing?" Amelie asked, and Tori's eyes slowly began to flutter open.

"Huh?" Tori said groggily. Her body felt a little unstable as she came to.

"Huh, my ass. Why the hell haven't you been answering your phone?"

Tori's nostrils flared as her attitude came to the forefront. Her perfect wet dream was now ruined, and in that instance, she wanted to murder whomever this rude bitch was. She knew the familiar voice, though. Her vision was still blurry, but she knew Amelie was the rude bitch in her room.

"Amelie, why are you here?" Tori asked. She snatched her cum-glazed hand from her yoni and tried to sit up, but before she could, Amelie tackled her. "Get yo' heavy ass up."

"You scared me, bae. I've been calling your ass for hours. I thought somebody or something killed your ass." Amelie straddled Tori and kissed her lips. Tori grabbed Amelie's ass, kissing her back passionately while feeling on her entire body. "I love this side of you. I wish we could let the world see us just like this," Amelie said.

Tori simpered. Although she loved her best friend, she couldn't see herself in a relationship with another woman. She fantasized about Amelie on many occasions, but they never took things further than just kissing.

"Nope, what we share is just between us. God didn't create us to be in a relationship with the same sex. I want kids one day and possibly want to marry the person I decide to have kids with. So stop doing this shit every time we see each other," Tori said.

Amelie caught a quick attitude and attempted to remove herself from Tori's body.

"Where are you going?" Tori held on to her waist.

She leaned up on one elbow and stared at Amelie's mug. Then placing the fingers she'd just pulled from her vagina into Amelie's mouth, Tori watched her frown turn into puckered lips. Amelie slowly sucked on Tori's fingers.

"I'm sorry if what I said bothered you, but that's how I feel."

"I understand, Tori, but I can't help my feelings. Especially when you sit and tease me like this. But you know I love you no matter what," Amelie said.

Tori knew Amelie truly did love her, and her feelings were mutual. They were best friends, and it had been that way since high school.

"We need to talk," Tori said, allowing Amelie to get up. Amelie stood and took Tori's hand into hers.

"About?" Amelie asked. Tori chuckled but didn't respond.

"Come on, get up. Your mother called me. She's been looking for you too."

Tori sucked her teeth and sighed. "I'ma call her back." She sat up and motioned for the bottle of Patrón Amelie brought with her. "Let's take a couple of shots first," she suggested.

"Let's do it." Amelie grabbed the bottle and two plastic cups from her bag. "Bless the bottle."

"Bless the bottle? What does that even mean?" Tori asked, and Amelie smacked her lips. She opened the liquor and poured them both a shot.

"You know what blessing the bottle means. But you know, you been acting like a real square lately," Amelie said.

"Amelie—"

"Fuck all that. Here's to an everlasting friendship. My bestie boo. It's a Tori-and-Amelie thang."

"I'll drink to that."

The women put their cups up to their lips and quickly downed the liquor.

"I love you, friend."

"Yep," Tori said while pouring herself another shot. It wasn't in Tori to wear her emotions on her sleeves, and she wondered how long Amelie would love her after this news.

"Yep? You could never just say it back. I understand that your family never showed you much love."

"Shut up. You don't know what you're talking about. You're overstepping."

"Whatever, Tori. Anyway, what's new?" Amelie asked and took a sip of Patrón.

She knew exactly what she was talking about when it came to Tori's emotions . . . or lack thereof. They'd known each other since high school. Amelie remembered when she had to bring Tori something to eat because the Givens were too busy building their company. She even remembered Tori sharing with her how the only way she could get through her long days was by masturbating. Amelie helped Tori suppress her urges, but at the same time, she played on Tori's weaknesses. Amelie had gone through it all with Tori, but she respected her wishes and changed the subject.

"This is what's new." Tori showed Amelie the card she'd gotten from Aja earlier that day. "I'm thinking about applying. I need me a real job to get me through graduate school," Tori explained.

"Flirty Girls Anonymous? You trying to be a call girl or some shit?"

"No, this is an office job. I know my funds are about to run out really soon."

"Why you say that? Your parents will support you as long as you're doing well in school. I wouldn't worry about a job right now. Here. Take a sip." Amelie placed her hand underneath Tori's chin and fed her the liquor.

"I'm doing great in school. Well, I'm doing well enough to keep the funds rolling in. But what I want to tell you, I need you to be a real best friend and listen. So what I'm about to tell you is . . . whew," Tori said, smiling and licking her lips.

Amelie poured herself another drink and quickly drank it down, preparing herself for Tori's news.

"OK, I'm ready. Tell me."

"So, it's this guy . . ." Tori smiled and blushed. "I lost my virginity last night to this beautiful man." She blurted out, "It wasn't planned, but it happened, and I really enjoyed it. Don't be mad at me."

Amelie sat with her mouth wide open. She wasn't jealous at all. She knew how Tori felt, and as long as she was willing to give her attention, Amelie was cool.

"What?" Amelie said excitedly. "Girl, how was it? I can't believe your reserved self let a man in."

"Well, I let him in, but not *all* the way in. You know that part is hard for me. It was good, though," Tori said. "What's crazy is I've known him almost my entire life. I tutored him in the sixth grade. Then after I transferred in the eighth grade, we lost contact," Tori said as if she and Jace were old friends. "I hadn't seen him until a couple of months ago."

"Oh, so you been holding out, huh?" Amelie asked.

"Not holding out, but it wasn't important. I'm glad you didn't beat my ass after hearing this because I know how you feel about me."

"Of course, I know I have to put my feelings to the side and be a real friend. I love you, Tori. Just don't let him separate us. Promise?" Amelie stuck her pinky finger out, and Tori intertwined their pinkies together.

"Promise."

Chapter Seven

Sometimes promises are made to be broken. In Tori's case, she was willing to break all promises to get what she wanted. After finally opening up to Amelie about Jace, she made the conscious decision to get drunk enough to take things to the next level with her. Why not live her best life? The women sat on the bed and threw the shots back repeatedly. By the time they had reached the bottom of the bottle, Tori was ready to take Amelie all the way down.

Tori stood and walked to the bathroom. She needed to relieve herself first. The Patrón had her bladder on full, and her head was spinning. She was tipsy, but she wasn't drunk. She sat on the toilet, looking around the small space. The more she looked, the more it seemed like the walls were closing in.

Boom, boom, boom.

"Tori, hurry up. I gotta pee too," Amelie announced.

"OK, I'm coming out now." Tori wiped herself and stood. She looked around for a towel to clean herself up with. Although she didn't plan to let Amelie please her, she still wanted to smell her best. After locating a towel, she ran it under the warm water and gently washed her private area.

"Tori," Amelie yelled with a slur.

"Calm down. Dang," Tori slurred. She fixed her clothes and reached over to the shower caddy, searching for her trusty bullet vibrator. As soon as she located the vibrator, the bathroom door swung open.

"I tried to give you some privacy, but, dammit, I have to pee." Amelie pulled her clothes down and covered the toilet seat with nothing but ass. Tori laughed and concealed the vibrator.

"Hurry up. I have to show you something."

Tori exited from the bathroom and wobbled back over to her drink. She placed the adult toy underneath her pillow and waited for Amelie. Three minutes went by. Then Tori heard the toilet flush. A minute later, Amelie opened the bathroom door.

"We should go out tonight. I'm feeling lovely as hell, and I'm ready to shake this ass on a fine-ass bitch. Hell, why not? You don't want me."

"Really, Amelie? Let's lie down for a minute. After that, we can go search for a party," Tori said, and Amelie pursed her lips together.

"Girl, you know your ass is not about to go out and party." She laughed. "Sounded good, though."

Amelie walked over to Tori's bed and flopped down. She scooted next to Tori and lay on the pillow, on her back, looking up at the ceiling as Tori lay beside her looking up as well. They were both deep in thought, thinking about life and what was in store for their futures.

"You ever think about where you will be in the next five years? Shit, 26 is closer to 30 than it is to 19."

"No, I don't think that far into the future. You're the one who's doing big things. You're getting your degree in mathematics. You have a five-year plan. I don't."

"Yeah, but it's never too late to better yourself."

"I know, but five years from now isn't really important to me."

"It should be."

"Whatever." She smacked her lips. "What is *your* five-year plan, Tori?"

"I see myself married with children. There are so many handsome men in college. Every day, I walk around this campus envisioning what life would be like with a man who has just as much ambition as me."

"Oh, so that's why I don't have a chance with you? I don't have enough ambitions for you?"

"Shit, Amelie, don't start. That is *not* what I'm saying."

"I know, Tori. Calm down. I was only playing," she said. "I get what you're saying, but I've never been into the male species. I love women. It's too bad you won't let me show you how *I* get down."

"You want to show me how you get down?" Tori asked. She sat up and leaned into Amelie. "Show me how you want to be a better woman."

Tori grabbed Amelie's leg and pushed it to the side. Kissing Amelie's neck, she put her hand up Amelie's shirt and fondled her breast.

"Show me you have dreams and goals." Tori made her way down Amelie's body. "If you can show me that, then I'll show you how *I* get down."

Tori pulled Amelie's shirt up and slowly licked her, twirling her tongue around Amelie's nipples, one by one.

"I want to show you." The sound of pleasure fell from Amelie's lips, followed by slurred words. "Shit, Tori, that's my spot."

Tori didn't respond. She just continued to make her way south. She wanted to give Amelie everything she'd been asking for. Tori had plans to give her this one night of passion and get back to their friendship afterward. When Tori's lips and tongue touched Amelie's stomach and navel, they

were both startled by a couple of knocks at the
door. Tori sat up and looked down at Amelie. She
debated on answering. Tori had no friends besides
Amelie, and her only friend was laid out right in
front of her like a buffet ready to be eaten. *Who
the fuck is this knocking at my door? People can
be so rude. Whoever this is could've at least called
before showing up. This probably isn't meant
to happen*. Tori just let them knock. They would
eventually go away. She had a mental conversation
with herself. Her mind told her to do the right
thing, especially since she wasn't expecting any
company to begin with. The two women tried to
ignore the soft knocks. Tori continued kissing
Amelie's body, but they both became irritated
when the knocks got louder.

"Just get the door. It might be important,"
Amelie said, and Tori sighed.

She climbed from the bed, fixed her clothes,
walked the short distance, and opened her door.
She swung the door open wildly, ready to go off.
Caught off guard, she stood there baffled. Tori
couldn't believe who was standing in front of her.
On the inside, she was beaming and happy. But her
facial expression displayed anger and annoyance.

"Bae, who is that?" Amelie asked, shaking Tori
from her trancelike state.

"A friend," Tori quickly responded and stepped out into the hallway. She stood with her arms folded across her chest, awaiting an explanation.

"What's up, Mocha?" Jace said.

He stood there in the hallway dressed up, looking handsome as ever in a pair of black slacks and a matching black polo shirt. His hair was nicely cut and faded. Tori looked at him unimpressed while trying not to blush. Jace played her earlier that day. She wanted to curse him out and call him every name except the one his mother gave him, but Tori knew she couldn't. She had willingly given her innocence to a man she didn't know. He wasn't the same ole Jace she barely knew in grade school.

"You don't look so happy to see me."

"I'm *not* happy to see you. I saw you earlier, and I know you saw me too, but you walked right past me like you didn't know who the hell I was—like you didn't just take my virginity the night before. Like this pussy didn't satisfy you."

"Nah, Mocha, it wasn't nothing like that. Honestly, I saw you, but I was on an important business call. I got some exciting news today," he said. "Look, I don't want you to feel like last night meant nothing to me because it did. I know we're just getting to know each other, but you've been on my mind heavy since I left your room this morning. That shit ain't normal for me."

Tori couldn't help herself. She blushed. "Really?" she asked. "Wow, no one has ever admitted to thinking about me except my best friend."

"That's surprising, Miss Mocha."

Tori sighed. She knew his little complement was fake as hell. "You had me falling asleep in my calculus class."

"In Professor Davis's class?" he asked.

"Yes, in his class."

"Damn. That's twenty-five points off your test. My bad, Mocha." Jace licked his bottom lip. "How can I make it up to you?" he asked.

"It's cool. I have it all under control. I took care of it, and my grade is fine." Tori winked.

"I still feel bad. Professor Davis is a tough nigga and a fucking pervert. I caught him staring at a couple of students' booties once. The only way his creep ass would've fixed your grade is if you gave him a little pussy." He chuckled, and Tori tried to grimace discreetly. *How did he know?* "I know you didn't give that nigga what belongs to me." He paused as Tori stood there at a loss of words. "I'm just fuckin' with you." He laughed out loud.

"I would never fuck with his perverted ass. I'm one of his best students, and he didn't want me to fail, so he left my grade alone. But he made me promise I wouldn't tell anyone. He didn't want anyone to think he was playing favoritism."

"I feel you." His lips displayed a half smirk.

"Seriously," Tori said, and he waved, then came closer to her.

"I see you have company. How long will she be over?"

"Yeah, my best friend is here. She's going to be over for a while. Why? Do you want to come in?" Tori asked, and Jace chuckled.

"I wanna do more than just come in." He grabbed Tori's face. "I wanna lay you down." Their lips touched, "and tell you about my important day."

"Mmm, you want to lay me down? Well, I don't mind doing it standing up." Tori welcomed Jace's suggestion. She was on the same page he was on. Making sure he knew that, she kissed his lips and said, "There's a restroom around the corner. You wanna go?" Tori got straight to the point.

There was something about Jace that brought out her innermost sexual thoughts. When Jace broke through the barriers of her virginity, her alter ego emerged as well. Sex for Tori was nothing. At this point, she was willing to fuck anyone at the drop of a dime. She'd saved herself for twenty-one years, and she had a lot of making up to do now.

"Hell yeah, let's go!" Jace agreed.

He picked her up, bypassing the other dorm rooms, and rushed her into the small space. Then he twisted the lock, making sure no one could enter. He placed Tori on her feet, and she took control.

Aggressively, Tori pushed Jace up against the wall
and grabbed his face. She sloppily kissed him,
sticking her tongue into his mouth as she sucked
on his lips. Jace grabbed her ass and rubbed it. He
allowed her to take control while he lay the back
of his head up against the wall, enjoying her take-
charge attitude. They felt each other up, lusting for
the feeling of delectation. Tori made her way to
Jace's print with her hand and rubbed it.

"Damn, you ain't playing," he managed to say.

"I don't have time to play. I want you," she responded, determined to reach a moment of relief.

The thought of how this small restroom had
them so close together had Tori feeling carnal
and desirous on the inside. She couldn't believe
the man she'd dreamed about for months—fuck
months—she'd crushed on this man for well over
ten years, and now, he was entangled in her web
of sex and sin. Tori wanted to give Jace the power.
She wanted to let him take control of her body. She
just didn't know how.

After a few minutes of kissing and fondling, Jace
decided he would go the extra mile. Tori wasn't doing enough, so he picked her up and wrapped her
legs around his waist. Tori held on to him, and
Jace serenaded her mouth with his tongue. Next,
he pinned her up against the wall. With her legs
still wrapped around him, he grabbed both of her
hands, holding them to the wall. Then he licked

her from her lips down to her neck, finding the perfect spot to leave his mark, sucking and biting her.

At this point, Tori moaned aloud. Her vagina yearned with desire. Her pussy lips salivated and dripped. The feeling of not being in control when it came to someone who wasn't her parents made her feel free.

"I *need* you," she moaned. "Jace, I want you."

"I need you too," he murmured.

He unwrapped her legs and slowly began to unbuckle his pants. Tori watched as his huge bulge and boxers came into view.

"Tori!"

Boom, boom, boom.

Tori heard her name, followed by a few knocks at the door. They both jumped, and she grabbed her chest while Jace buttoned up his pants.

"Shit, I forgot all about Amelie," Tori whispered. "She cannot know I'm in here with you."

"Tori, are you in there?"

"You want me to answer?"

"No, just be quiet. She'll go away soon."

"Tori, are you in there? With a man? I can hear your voice."

"Damn," Tori said, leaning her head into Jace's chest. "She's going to kick my ass."

"Why would she do that?" Jace asked as he looked down at her.

"You wouldn't understand," she explained. "I'm in here, Amelie, but I'll be out in a few," she shouted.

"Yeah, all right, bitch. Did you tell that nigga, whoever the fuck he is, you were about to fuck me before he came knocking?"

"Damn, you get down like that?" Jace asked, and she shushed him, placing her finger to his lips.

"Please, Amelie, stop. I'll be out in a second."

"Stupid, ho. I'm going home," Amelie said. Tori took a deep breath.

"So, where were we?" she asked. There was no shame in her game. She was ready to let every bit of her juices flow. Jace stripped her down and sat her on top of the sink. Her entire ass hung down into the basin while she waited for him to penetrate her. Tori opened her legs wide, damn near doing a split.

She leaned her head back and balled her lips up as he slowly stroked her.

"Jace, please don't take your time with me," she whined. She finally let her guard down when it came to sex and moaned. That slow penetration shit was for the fucking birds. She needed this man to fuck her brains out. There wasn't enough room in the small area for her to take control like she had done the night before, so she had to tell Jace exactly how she wanted to be pleased.

"This shit too good, Mocha," he moaned, whispering in her ear. "I gotta take my time in you. I don't want to fuck you. I want you to feel the same shit I'm feeling." He continued to move his hips back and forth. His dick hit Tori's middle softly every time he entered her.

"I feel it," she whispered. "I feel you," she assured him in a whisper. "But I want more, Jace. I want you to kill it," she told him honestly.

"Let me have my way. Let *me* take control. Let me take my time," he responded.

Tori tried to talk her way into being in control, but Jace had the upper hand. Although Tori may never admit it, I will go ahead and say it. He had her feeling so good, but it wasn't enough. She wanted her middle split in two. She *needed* to come immediately, but his slow movements turned her off.

"Please, Jace, just fuck me," she begged.

He looked down at her, noticing her face showed displeasure. "I need *all* of you," she whispered.

Soon after, Jace took hold of her legs, forcing them over his shoulders.

"Jacey!" she yelled his name. She couldn't help it.

Her legs felt like cooked noodles under his grasp, but that was nothing to her. Tori controlled her vaginal muscles and took hold of Jace's erection. *That's* when he got a little aggressive. He finally gave her what she wanted, positioning himself to rock her entire world. For the next twenty seconds, Jace fucked Tori fast and hard. The feeling of Tori's juices threatening to rain down on him while she gripped his back had Jace biting his bottom lip.

"This what you wanted, right? Is *this* what you like?" Jace asked.

"Yes," she screamed.

Chapter Eight

I love it when he calls me that shit . . . "Mocha." Jace just doesn't know what that name does to me. Makes me feel so erotic, like a stripper or even a porn star. Mmm . . . All the things Jace had woken up in me make me hot every time I think about it. I was already giving myself all the pleasure I thought I needed before he came along. But after the feeling Jace and even Davis gave me, I realized everything I was missing.

So, I know what you're thinking, and I intend to answer every single question you may have. I'll start from the beginning with Jace and me. As you can see, I fell for that man, and I fell quickly. It wasn't intended. Sometimes, shit just happens. I wasn't sure if what I felt was love or not at that point because I'd never experienced love before. Not even with my parents, seeing as though they were never really around.

Jace's personality was everything. He had "superstar" written all over him. That fact didn't mean anything to me, but me pulling a guy of his caliber was something to boast about. His looks grasped my attention from the beginning. Jace was a pretty boy and sexy. If there was a type to be had, he was it. I just knew he didn't notice me because of my dark, ugly skin. I was a kid back then, and I didn't know the value of my melanin, but now I know better.

When he first spoke to me in college, I knew for a fact he did not remember me. He treated me as if I were a new person in his life, and I reciprocated that shit. I had to figure out a way to slide in that "Oh, you don't remember me from such-and-such shit." I fell in love with the attention, so I let it be. His sex wasn't much to brag about, but he knew what he wanted, and he came to claim his prize. I gave him what he needed, and in the midst of that, I finally became a real woman. Us being intimate was *not* by chance. The night was so beautifully warm and calm that we being brought together as one would happen regardless.

I thought it was going to be a night of good, rough fucking with him, but, of course, he didn't live up to those expectations. There was still something about him that I wanted to get to know on a deeper level. I couldn't place my finger on it, but it was a real fucking mystery. But in due time, it was realized. I wasn't looking for a man at the time. I would've much rather been out in these streets living my best life. But Jace had awakened something within me. Maybe it was a sexual beast. I knew if I could fuck once, I would want to fuck repeatedly.

I was personally chasing after an orgasm. Sex was like a drug, and I needed to feel that same euphoric feeling I felt the very first time I had sex. So, the next day, I had to take Professor.

After Jace and I fucked in a public bathroom, we went back to my room to talk. I swear I was becoming a wild child. If my parents ever found out about any of this, they would undoubtedly disown me. I lay on his chest, and he wrapped his arms around me. Jace broke it down to me how he had this five-year plan to become a beast in the music industry. I was honestly happy for him. He explained that when he walked past me earlier that day, he was on the phone with a very important person. The nigga's name was Big Percy. Big Percy would help him advance in his career once we graduated. He didn't go into details, but I knew it was a big deal from the way he sounded. We were only a month and a half away from walking across the stage, so things quickly took off.

As I listened, I was in awe. He had his shit together. It's kind of crazy how I just talked to Amelie about a five-year plan, and here comes Jace telling me about his. He told me he wanted to make me his girl. He couldn't see himself continuing to fuck around with too many women. He even placed a gold chain around my neck with his initials, JD, on it. I looked at it and asked if he was sure about all of this. He was giving up so much for a girl who wouldn't be able to love him properly. He expressed to me how he was beginning to feel drained of all his sexual energy because of the many women he'd smashed. Then shit started to make sense to me. He wanted to keep me at his side, and he knew that if he were in a relationship with me, he wouldn't have time to be with other women. I was slightly interested, but it was a lot to think about. Things were moving a tad bit too quickly. I first needed to talk to Amelie so that she wouldn't be upset with me. We were best friends, so she would be my excuse not to jump into a relationship with him.

"Jace, are you sure about this? You don't think we're moving too fast?" I asked.

"Considering the business I'm about to enter into, life will *always* move fast for me, baby. I've never seen myself with just one woman, but there's something about you. Plus, I need a woman at home bearing my babies, my legacies. I don't want to be a nigga out here just fucking and impregnating bitches . . . I mean, having children with a lot of women. I need to lock you down. I don't want no one else to have you," he said, and I believed him.

I lay there taking in his cologne and every word he spoke. He wanted me, and I considered it. Plus, me living off the Givens's money was soon coming to an end. What Jace's motives were, I didn't know. Maybe he had no motives. Maybe my pureness and him knowing there weren't many women out there like me had him willing to break all his rules. Jace just didn't know the thoughts that ran rampant in my mind.

"Well, let me talk to Amelie. I need to make sure she and I are good." I tried to find every excuse not to give in to him. We'd only had sex twice, and from what I could tell, Jace had no direction in the bedroom. Of course, I hadn't had many sex partners, but I knew how I wanted my body to feel when I had sex.

"You fuckin' her or some shit?" he asked.

I sat up and looked into his face. My hand rested up against my dorm bed. He was all lit up and glowing. I saw the excitement written all across his face, but he needed to pipe down because I knew for a fact, I was a little too much for him to handle alone.

"No, I'm not having sex with her. She's my best friend. I left her kind of hanging earlier. I need to make sure she's OK," I said.

Afterward, Jace and I sat talking for another hour, just getting to know each other. He asked to meet the Givens, and I wasn't feeling that shit, especially not before graduating college. I asked him if we could hold off on meeting my parents until after the summer, and he reluctantly agreed.

"That's cool. I have a lot of shit going on right now. I'm going to the next level, and I want to take you with me, but I'm going regardless of whether you're rocking with me." He grabbed my waist and continued. "I wanna make sure your parents are cool with everything."

Ooohhh, shit. That was all I needed to hear. Shit, fuck Omeiha and Larry. My new boo was taking me to the top with him. Me and my little purple baby, my vibrator who *always* goes with me.

"I'm rocking and rolling," I said giddily.

"I'm glad to hear that shit." He grabbed my face, pulled me back down to him, and kissed me. I looked into his eyes as he placed his warm lips to mine. "I got a song I want you to hear," he whispered, lips still pressed to mine. "Not right now, though. I gotta get back to the crib. When I bring you over to meet my peoples, I'ma let you hear it."

I honestly couldn't wait. I've gone back and forth with myself. I didn't know if Jace was really what I wanted. He seemed so pure and genuine but couldn't fuck worth a damn. I knew that if we decided to be together, I would cheat on him. Huuuh, a rock and a hard place, to say the least.

We wrapped up our conversation with that last request. I walked Jace to the door, and one last time that night, he kissed me. This time was more passionate. His body pressed up against mine. His lips and tongue finessed mine. Afterward, I called

Amelie. She and I agreed on a meetup later that week. After that, I did the only thing I could think to do. I pulled my vibrator from underneath my pillow and gave myself a nice bedtime exploitation.

Now, on to Professor Davis. There honestly wasn't anything about him that piqued my interest besides a perfect A. It was my fault I fell asleep in his class, and everyone knew that if you fell asleep in his boring-ass class, points would be deducted from your grade. He dangled that shit over my head. He fucked with my emotions on purpose. Davis just knew that a date was bound to happen, but hell no. What the fuck did I look like? Plus, the most popular nigga on campus . . . Yes, I said 'nigga.' Anywho . . . The most popular man on campus was now checking for me. I would never date the likes of Davis. Everything about him made my skin crawl, especially after I fucked him. I just couldn't understand why he couldn't take shit for what it was. I thought all men loved sex. I thought they all would prefer pussy over a dumb-ass, simple-ass date. The dick was great. It honestly felt better than what Jace delivered, but I was not interested in him at all.

You may be wondering what happened with Professor Davis's tie. Well, long story short, I used it as a little leverage. I knew he would try to play me and still press me about a damn date. Like I said before, when it comes to pussy, men will do some dumb-ass shit. Why was he so educated but so damn dumb? He left me in possession of a tie with his *and* my DNA. I would hold on to that free ride for the rest of the semester.

A week after our little "encounter," Davis continued to harass me. Like any other sane person, I threatened to have his ass locked up if he didn't stay the fuck away from me. He thought his little stick had some power to it. Although he had some good dick, it wasn't good enough to catch a chick like me slipping. I did consider maybe going one more round with him in the back of my mind, but I digress. I had a new man, Jace, and I was trying to see what having a man in my life was like. However, I realized that if Jace and I were going to be a thing, I would have to cheat on him from time to time.

If Davis were smart, though, he would've waited to submit my grades, but he didn't, and even if he did, I still had evidence of our coition. He'd been pushing up on me too hard. I swear if he didn't stop that shit, then he would spend the next five years of his life in jail . . . for rape. Don't worry; I stashed the tie in a very nice, cool place. All the evidence is kept out of sight and out of mind in a tamper-proof evidence bag. Maybe it's in a safe, or maybe it's in plain sight. Who knows . . .

Chapter Nine

If life were a love song, for Tori, it would have to be something old school like "Something in My Heart" by Michel'le, or maybe "Somebody Loves You, Baby" by Patti Labelle. However, Tori never really emphasized love. She'd never thought about it.

When Tori thought about life in the past, it was always work hard, get good grades, masturbate a little, and everything else will fall into place. Nowadays, all she thought about was sex. She wanted it all the time. But the sex she was currently receiving was not what she desired, even though Jace was such a sweetheart. Tori really appreciated his attempts at lovemaking. If that were something she was really into, he would've been the man for the job. But she would've much rather gotten dicked down every night, skipped the emotions, and even the foreplay. It had only been three weeks since she'd started dealing with him, and already, she was on the prowl in search of a new victim. It was crazy how after sampling one piece of dick, she was ready to sample many more.

Sitting down on her bed with a pen in her hand, she scratched off everything she'd accomplished over the years from a piece of paper she had on the bed. School being number one, securing the bag that was almost in her bank account was number two, and becoming the queen of busting several nuts was yet to be determined. Putting her pen to her lips, Tori looked up and stared out the window, thinking about her next move. She looked at the trees that brushed up against her window and knew she had one hell of a day ahead of her.

"*Grrrr*," her voice grumbled. "I don't know why I scratched that shit off. I don't even have the money yet. Duh, dummy." Tori took her pen and wrote some words next to her scribble, grimacing. "Secure the Givens's bag," she said while smiling as she rewrote the words.

Days before, Tori and Amelie agreed to meet up and have a little lunch today. She sat and thought about the conversation she needed to have with Amelie. They hadn't spoken since the night she had sex with Jace in the bathroom. Tori was sort of embarrassed. Plus, she felt terrible for doing Amelie the way she did. So, she had been dodging her for about a week now. But she knew that if she wanted to remain best friends with the only person who'd ever been there for her since they met, she needed to go ahead and have that long-overdue talk with her.

Sighing, Tori lay back on her bed. Before she dressed, she decided she would call her parents. She picked up her phone and dialed their number. The phone rang a few times before going to voice-mail.

"Hey, Mom." Tori sucked her teeth and blew out air before deciding she wouldn't leave a voicemail. She erased it and then hung up. Sitting up, she dialed the number again. With the phone pressed to her ear, she listened, allowing the phone to ring until the voicemail picked up again.

"Hey, Mom, this is Tori. I was just calling to check up on you and Dad. Call me back when you get this message. I love you," she said. Before she could disconnect the call, her other line beeped. Tori looked at her phone and saw Mama and Papa on the screen, so she clicked over.

"Well, look who has decided to call her parents," Omeiha said in her almost nonexistent accent. She'd been in the States for so long that her English was almost perfect.

"Hey, Mother. I'm so sorry I haven't been in contact. I've been so swamped with school and stuff," Tori explained. "Finals have had me bent out of shape," she said, silently smirking.

"That's no excuse, Tori," Omeiha said as if she and Tori spoke regularly. Before college, Tori barely ever saw her parents.

"I know, Mom. I will do better. How is Papa?"

"Your father is OK. He has been worried sick about you. You know how nervous he gets when we haven't talked to you in a while. But your father and I will let your noncontact go for now. There are more important things to be upset about."

"What? Upset? Wait, what happened?"

"Don't play crazy, Tori." Her mother didn't hold her thoughts or feelings in. She always spoke her mind, especially when it came to Tori. "I spoke with Amelie the other day. She told me about your new guy friend."

"My new guy friend?" Tori played stupid. "I don't know what Amelie's talking about. I don't have any new friends."

"I'm not stupid, Tori." Omeiha's accent was now thick and angry. "Why would Amelie tell us this if it's not true? You know what's at stake if you defy us."

"Yes, of course, Mother, I know what's at stake. Amelie is lying." Tori sighed and rolled her eyes. She felt her anger building. Now, she was more than eager to meet up with Amelie. The nerve of her to get in her feelings and tell her parents about her. "Look, Mother, I'm 21, and me having a new friend, or friends, for that matter, is nothing I have to lie to you about."

"Are you talking back to me, Tori?"

"No, but this is *my* life, Mother. Even if I decided to have a male friend or two, that is *my* decision to make. But Amelie is lying."

"Ooohhh, so you control your own decisions now? Your father will hear about this." *Click*.

Tori rolled her eyes and set her phone down. In the back of her mind, she just knew that Amelie fucked up her money. She stood and made her way to the bathroom to meet up with Amelie's back-stabbing ass. She wanted to stand her up for the snake shit she pulled, but in so many ways, Tori understood. Amelie was in love with her, and her actions were entirely out of spite. Tori couldn't blame her friend. She knew that one day soon, she would have to become an adult and stand up to her parents. However, today just wasn't the day. She picked up her Victoria's Secret Crush perfume from the bathroom's organizer and sprayed it between her breasts. Then she rubbed her fingers up and down, spreading the sweet scent around. She lifted her JD chain and smiled.

"Yeah, bitch, I got a new man," is what Tori wanted to say to her mother, but instead, she brazenly spoke those words into the mirror at her reflection.

She opened her legs and sprayed her inner thighs. Tori's nostrils involuntarily flared. She stared at herself, wishing Omeiha in her presence.

"Don't try to pretend like you give a damn. You and your husband have ignored me my entire life. That little-ass money you're holding over my head is *my* money. I deserve it, controlling-ass winch."

Tori looked at her reflection menacingly. She waved her hand at the mirror and proceeded to get dressed. "If Amelie fucked this up for me, I'm going to kill her."

Tori put on a pair of denim knickerbockers, a plain white V-neck shirt, and a pair of gold sandals. Today, she decided to go with a thick, beautiful, curly 'fro and some gold sunglasses with dark tints to hide her dismay.

No shade, but she planned to have Amelie's and her conversation behind the hidden vision. She wasn't about to show Amelie any respect after the little spat she just had with her mother. Tori exited her bathroom and walked over to her wallet. She checked it to make sure her ID and the credit card Daddy and Mommy provided her were still inside. She needed a strong drink to deal with Amelie's shenanigans. She prayed all the funds were still intact and not restricted. If they were restricted, this brunch would be on Amelie's dime. She grabbed her keys from her nightstand and made her way to the front door.

"OK, Miss Tori, get it together. I should've used my vibrator before this shit."

Tori leaned her head back and moved it from side to side. She closed her eyes and unlocked her door. She twisted the doorknob . . . right before hearing a knock.

"Who is it?"

"Aja," her new friend said. Tori quickly opened her door. "Hey, Tori. How are you?" Aja pulled
her hair behind her ears and stared down at the
ground, avoiding eye contact with her.

"Hey," Tori said, confused. She put a delicate
hand to Aja's shoulder, concerned.

"I didn't mean to pop up unannounced, but you
did say whenever I needed food, I could come
to see you." Aja fidgeted with her hands. "I'm
starved." Aja looked up, forcing a smile. Almost
instantly, her smile turned into balled, trembling
lips.

"Yeah . . . yeah . . . Come in." Tori looked at Aja
with furrowed eyebrows. "Is everything OK?"

Aja walked in, and Tori closed the door. She
looked a mess, and Tori didn't know how she could
help her. Aja didn't look as if she came over for
food. She looked more like she was looking for a
safe haven. Aja was a beautiful, dark-skinned girl.
She and Tori could've easily been mistaken for
sisters because their facial features were uncannily
alike. Aja was five foot nine with a body to die
for. She was a typical, dark-skinned L.A. girl. She
blended in well with all the segregated, skinny,
well-kept Black girls. Her hair was jet black and
pressed bone straight. Even her pupils were similar to Tori's.

When Tori first met this girl, she couldn't help
but notice how beautiful she was. But today, Aja

looked as if she'd been through hell and back. Her appearance was disheveled, and her body movements, the way she seemed trembly, were a bit erratic.

"No, everything is *not* OK." Aja broke down. "Tori, I can't believe this just happened to me," she said.

"Wait, Aja, calm down." Tori grabbed her arm and led her to a chair in front of her desk. Aja took a seat, and Tori knelt in front of her. "What happened?"

"That damn job," Aja began. "I started that job last week, and everything was going fine."

"OK, so why are you crying?"

"I worked from home accepting inbound calls for their call services. Pretty much having sex, but nothing was physical. I was warned not to do it, but the money was calling me, and I needed the extra cash." Aja wiped her nose.

"You were warned not to do what?" Tori asked inquisitively. She was still debating calling the services for a job herself, so she needed to know just what the hell had Aja so shaken up. "What you're saying isn't making sense. What did you do?"

"I was warned not to ever meet up with the clients. I had clients calling me from all over the world. One of my clients decided he would fly into the city, and we would do our own thing. Then he raped and robbed me, Tori." Aja broke down.

"Oh my God!" Tori stood and went into her bathroom. She got Aja some tissue and brought it back to her.

"I can't believe I fell for the bullshit." Aja took the tissue from Tori's hand and blew her nose. "He promised me $2,000 and ended up getting me for five hundred. Now, what am I going to do?"

"I don't know, Aja. Maybe go to the police? I mean, I don't know exactly what you would tell them, but maybe they can track down this person's phone number he called you from."

"I don't know. I was told not to meet up with anyone. I don't want to lose my job. I need the money."

"Yeah, I understand, but you have to decide what you want to do. I can't make those decisions for you," Tori said as nicely as possible. "Look, let's think on it. I'm sure we can come up with something. In the meantime, if you're looking for a meal, I was on my way out to eat. You can tag along if you would like." Tori brushed Aja's hair down with her fingers, then helped her up and hugged her.

"I can eat. Thank you, Tori, for everything."

"I haven't done anything special. Just being a shoulder to lean on. I understand sometimes life happens."

"Well, thank you for being a shoulder to cry on." Aja smiled and rubbed Tori's new necklace. "JD?"

"Yeah, Jace gave me this. Cute, right?"

"You and Jace . . . You guys are a real couple? Like, you're not just one of the chicks he smashed? Y'all go together?"

"Yeah, why? Is everything OK?" Tori asked.

"Yeah, everything is fine." Aja chuckled nervously. "Thanks again, Tori. I appreciate this."

"You're welcome. Just stop meeting up with these weird-ass men, and everything will be OK."

"Agreed," Aja said. "Do you mind if I use your washroom really quick?"

"No, I don't mind. Go ahead."

Aja stood and made her way inside. She closed and locked the door before quickly pulling out her phone and dialing a number. When there was no answer, she decided to call a couple more times, back-to-back, and still no answer. She sat on the toilet pretending to piss while Tori stood on the other side looking at her clock.

"Is everything OK in there?" Tori asked.

"Umm . . . Yeah, I'm finishing up now. My stomach was killing me." Aja flushed the toilet and walked out.

"Are you ready?" Tori asked.

"Yeah, come on. Let's go."

The women walked to the front door. They were now ready to meet up with Amelie.

Chapter Ten

Jace sat down and leaned back on the over-sized grey suede sofa. He put a weed-filled blunt between his lips, puffing slowly as he lit it up. He focused his sights on the small fire while it danced around for a couple of seconds and the aroma of weed filled the room. Then he grabbed his phone and played a track he'd recently laid down for a hot new R&B song. He had plans to present this song to Big Percy when they finally met up. Jace removed the blunt from his mouth and inhaled the thick smoke.

He bobbed his head to the soft, bumping beat. Then he listened as the guitars came in and then the high hat. The shit he created was something like a throwback classic vibe. A sexy little love song was what he'd planned to write to this beat. Jace put his hand to his chin and mumbled as he moved his hand, trying to come up with some beautiful words to place with this lovely instrumental.

"Let me come inside your world (yeah, yeah), diamonds and pearls," he rambled on.

He cleared his throat and warmed his vocals. Jace did a couple of runs with his voice and looked down at his phone. He saw an unknown number as his cell came alive on his lap. Jace quickly silenced it and decided it was time to get serious. He went all the way in. He cleared his throat once again, watching his cell as the number called him for the second time.

"Who the fuck is this?" Jace said to himself and silenced his phone. He put the phone on *do not disturb,* deciding to call it back after his studio session was over.

He took another pull from the weed and brought his notes up on his cell phone. It was now time to write down some shit. Some heartfelt shit. Pen to pad, Jace got his words off. The blunt had him taking off. The words flowed effortlessly. The beat had him feeling all mushy inside, so he laid that soft shit down.

"If I could, then I would love you for a lifetime (yeah, a lifetime). I'm done chasing behind those skirts, 'cause, baby, you're my lifeline (yeah, my lifeline). If I had to die today, just know that for you, I laid my life down. (Girl, I gave you my life.) Don't you ever discredit a real man with real intentions of loving you and giving you the life you have now. Ooohhh, ooohhh, yeah, yeah, yeah, yeah. Sing it for me; say!"

Jace wrote that verse with little old Mocha in mind. He spilled his feelings onto the screen of his phone. His fingers typed rapidly as the words came to him in abundance.

"I'm giving you a lifetime of love. If it's not good enough, then show me how to love. With you, it could never be fuck love. You're my lady; you're my baby, so don't play me."

"Now, let me lay this shit down on the track. Tori gon' love this shit," he said aloud as he stood and made his way into the booth with his weed as his wingman.

Forty-five minutes later, Jace's phone chimed, signaling he had twelve voicemails. He quickly let the voicemails be until he finished getting his words on the track. Jace was in his zone. He placed the professional headphones on his ears and looked at the words one last time. He felt like Ginuwine at the beginning of the *So Anxious* video. He told the engineer to start the track, and the instrumental began to play through Jace's headphones.

Buzz, buzz.

"Aye," Jace said into the mic, "cut the music." He motioned his hand as he spoke. The buzzing of his phone had thrown him off. He looked down at his phone. The number wasn't familiar, and it was a little different than the number that called him before. However, he was curious to know who'd been calling his phone. He settled into the booth and placed the headphones back onto the stand. He debated on answering, but something in his heart told him not to, so he let that call go to voicemail as well. He silenced his phone and gave the engineer the thumbs-up. Then Jace listened as the track began to play.

"You ready, Jace?" the studio's audio engineer asked. Jace put the blunt to his lips, taking in the high. He blew it out and coughed. Then clearing his throat one more time, he went to the lyrics he'd just written on his phone.

"A'ight, I'm ready. Run that shit back."

Chapter Eleven

Tori and Aja took the twenty-five-minute drive from the dorm to the restaurant in complete silence. Tori had so much to say to her best friend that nothing else occupied her mind but the words she'd planned to get off her chest.

Where is the loyalty, Amelie? You know how my parents are is what she thought would be her first words. Tori's eyes were still hidden by her dark shades, so she knew her thoughts and irritation were covered. She felt that maybe Amelie's intentions were good, but she couldn't be sure.

Both women stared straight ahead, focusing their attention on the traffic. They both admired the sun that glowed so brightly throughout the entire city. Today was the perfect day to be out shopping on Rodeo Drive or skinny-dipping and living life at the beach. But in Tori's world, today was the perfect day to give Amelie a piece of her mind. The clearing of Aja's throat finally brought Tori back to the present. She looked over at Aja and smiled.

"Are you feeling better now?" Tori asked.

They sat idle at a red light on Sunset Blvd., awaiting the opportunity to pull over to the nearest curb and park. Although Tori needed to have a serious conversation with Amelie, she didn't think twice before inviting Aja to brunch. It was just a natural reflex to offer a little help to this girl who was clearly in need. Tori gripped Aja's hand firmly and smiled.

"Yeah, I'm OK now. Although I was bamboozled out of all that damn money, I'm just happy I still have my life."

"That's the spirit. I knew you wouldn't be feeling down for too long." The light finally changed, and the women drove across, parking in the nearest open spot.

"I'm down, but not out is how I look at it. I've been through worse shit," Aja stated.

The women got out of the car. Tori stepped on the curb and grabbed Aja's hand. They walked together, making their way to El Compadre Mexican restaurant.

"Oh, I forgot to tell you that we're meeting up with my best friend. Well, my almost *ex*-best friend," Tori said. She pulled her shades down slightly and looked at Aja. Aja returned her glance.

"I wish you would've told me earlier. I don't want to impose," Aja said as she used her free hand to pin her hair behind her ear.

Tori pushed her glasses back with her index finger and focused ahead. The women looked like supermodels. Naomi and Tyra didn't have a thing on these two. Their hips moved as if they were on a fashion runway.

"You're not imposing. She's cool, and her name starts with an A like yours," Tori said, and they both laughed. The women released hands as they approached the door to the restaurant, and Tori, being polite, held the door open for Aja.

"Thank you, madame." Aja smiled and walked in. Tori entered behind her. Her eyes locked with Amelie's. Amelie smiled and waved Tori over.

"Come on. There's my friend right there."

Almost instantly, Amelie's smile turned into a frown. She was confused about who this third wheel was walking on the side of her best friend, grinning and shit.

"Hey, Amelie." Tori walked over, and Amelie stood. Amelie mugged Aja, bewildered at how much she resembled Tori. "Give me a hug." Tori grabbed her friend and wrapped her up in her embrace. She decided to play nice friend because she saw the confusion on Amelie's face. Tori decided the shades would be removed, and she was going to be cordial after all.

"Tori," Amelie said, breaking their embrace, "who is this?" Amelie's face still displayed a look of indignation. The way she felt on the inside was something she just could not pretend and be fake about.

"Oh, this is—" Tori, on the verge of introducing the two, was immediately cut off.

"Aja." Aja stuck her hand out for a handshake. "Nice to meet you, Amelie." Amelie frowned again and stared at Aja's hand as if it had shit on it.

"Anyway . . . I thought you and I were having lunch today. And why does this girl look like you? Your father had some extra kids we didn't know anything about?"

Tori grabbed Aja's still waiting hand and pulled it down.

"Amelie, don't be a jerk. Aja, pay her no mind," Tori said. The ladies stood having a stare-off. The tension was thick, and Tori felt it. "Come on, ladies, let's take a seat."

"I don't think I have an appetite anymore," Amelie said, still mugged up with the stank face.

"Well, at least have a drink or two. It's on me. Well, that's if you didn't fuck things up for me, Miss Petty."

All three ladies took a seat, and Amelie called the waitress over.

"I started without you, but you can pay for this one too," Amelie said.

When the waitress finally arrived, she took their orders: three margaritas, an order of chips with salsa, and pico de gallo.

"So, Aja, how did you meet Tori? Are you fucking her too?" Amelie asked in a serious tone.

"*Really,* Amelie? No, we're not fucking. I told you already we met on campus," Tori said, not wanting to talk about Aja's business.

"First of all, simmer down. Second of all, you didn't tell me anything. And third, how did y'all meet on campus? I need to know everything since you took it upon yourself and invited her. Especially after you stood me up for that Jace guy and then had me here waiting on you for over an hour."

"Wow," Aja said, smirking. "You seem a bit aggressive." She smiled, not feeling bothered or intimidated by Amelie.

"There is no 'seem,' sweetie. I'm very protective. I don't know you, and we had this date planned for some time now," Amelie said honestly, looking Aja up and down.

"It's not a big deal. Tori and I met while I was standing in line for a job. Tori asked me for information about the job. After receiving that much-needed info, I gave it to her. I later told her that I was tired of fucking men for money and how much I needed this job. She offered to help me out from time to time, and the rest is history. Explanation enough?" Aja asked.

"You didn't have to explain that to her, Aja," Tori said with a voice full of regret.

Amelie sat baffled. She wanted to apologize, but she couldn't form the words.

"It's OK. Hopefully, I gave you enough information to be comfortable with me," Aja scoffed. She stood and excused herself. "I'll be back, Tori. I have to use the ladies' room."

"OK." Aja walked away, and Tori stared at Amelie. "You always stirring up some BS. Why did you do that to her?" Tori scolded her friend.

"Well, you know how I am. Don't bring no random people around me. *I'm* your only friend. These other people are just wannabes. Especially that fucking Jace. You promised me that you wouldn't let him come in between us. You've been with him for what, three weeks now, and this is the *first* time I'm seeing you?"

"You need to calm down with all that possessive stuff. Jace hasn't come in between anything. I like him, but it's not that serious."

"I can't tell. You left me all hot and bothered. Then come to find out you were in the bathroom with him, probably fucking him while I lay across your bed waiting for you to fuck me."

"Keep your voice down, Amelie," Tori said, using her hand to emphasize her words. "Even with that being said, you know I'm not into women. And that didn't give you the right to call my parents and mention him to them. That was for me to do, Miss Shady Boots. In all honesty, I came here today to give you my ass to kiss. When I called my mother, and she mentioned your name, I was beyond pissed the fuck off. Are you trying to ruin things for me purposely?"

"You're right. I was just upset. I'm sorry, best friend," Amelie said, giving Tori a genuine apology. Amelie allowed her anger to get the best of her, and for that, she was so sorry.

"Yeah, yeah. There's gonna be a lot of ass-kissing before I accept your apology." Tori pursed her lips together.

"OK. Well, stand up and bend over." She laughed.

"Amelie, go to hell," Tori said, watching as Aja came strutting back toward the table, seemingly in a better mood.

"I needed that. My bladder feels much better," Aja said.

The waitress walked back over to the table and set their drinks and chips down. After she walked away, the women chilled out. The afternoon was still young. Why keep the atmosphere tense? Why not get to know one another a little better?

"So, I want to be the first to say I'm sorry if I offended you earlier," Amelie said.

"That was not an apology, Amelie."

"I accept your apology, and I understand. There wasn't any ill will on my behalf. Tori offered me a meal and a good time, so I couldn't decline it," Aja said. "I didn't know my meal would possibly be

in human form, though." Aja smiled seductively.
"You're looking pretty tasty over there, Amelie.
How tall are you?"

"I'm about five four. Why?" Amelie responded.

*What the fuck is going on? Are you serious
right now, Aja?* Tori thought to herself. That little
comment threw Tori for a loop. She sighed and
looked at Aja.

"I love the feistiness in you. It's fitting. You short
women are the sexiest when you're upset." Aja
openly flirted, and Amelie couldn't do anything
but blush. Tori looked at Aja with surprised eyes,
and then she looked at Amelie out of the corner of
her eye, waiting to hear some disrespectful shit.

"I'm flattered. I know my personality is ev-er-ry
thang," Amelie said. She sat back in her seat.

Lifting her alcoholic beverage, Amelie put the
straw in her mouth and twirled it around with her
tongue. Now, it was Tori's turn to be jealous. She
looked back and forth between the two women,
trying to dissect the entire situation. Tori was
thankful the tension dissipated; however, she
didn't appreciate her best friend and her new
friend flirting. Hell, she didn't even know Aja was
into women.

"Yes, most definitely it is," Aja responded, leaning forward and placing her bottom lip between
her teeth.

"So, you like feisty?" Amelie asked, and again, Tori looked at her, baffled. "Well, you ain't seen shit yet."

Amelie flirted back as she set her glass down, and her pressure rose. Aja was just her type because she resembled Tori so much.

"Where are you from, Amelie?" Aja leaned forward. "You can't be from L.A. You remind me more of a Compton girl."

Amelie laughed. "Hell no, I ain't from no square-ass L.A. This Black girl shimmer is Compton all day. That's where all the fly girls reside, baby," she responded.

"Do show and tell." Aja chuckled. She raised one eyebrow and winked her eye.

At this point, Tori had heard enough. She didn't meet up with Amelie for this bullshit. They damn near fucked weeks earlier, and just that easily, Amelie was on to the next. Fuck the fact that Tori had a whole man, and fuck the fact she wasn't feeling Amelie like that. Tori didn't like the thought of the two women having her in common. She knew the type of woman Amelie was, and with her just getting to know Aja, she didn't want her best friend getting tangled in some bullshit.

"Are you two serious?" Tori stated, breaking the two from their lesbian, I-want-you-bad conversation. "What happened to you two hating each other?" Tori's attitude was apparent.

"I don't hate her. I think she's kinda cute . . . or whatever," Amelie said while smiling.

"Or 'whatever'?" Aja asked, and Amelie smirked.

"Naw, baby, you *are* cute. Well, cute is for puppies. Baby girl, you are sexy."

"Oh my God, can you two stop?" Tori said, laughing.

"OK, I quit. Let me give my best friend a little bit of my attention. We can fuck . . . I mean 'talk' later, Aja."

"Yeah, Tori, it's all about you right now. It's your world, baby girl," Aja said. She placed her straw in her mouth and drank her entire margarita. "So, how did you nab that fine-ass nigga, Jace? I see you about to be on the come-up. You don't even need that little phone se—"

During Aja's rant, Tori cut her off. Amelie knew about Flirty Girls Anonymous, yet she didn't know what the job entailed, and right now wasn't the time to find out.

"I don't want Jace's money. He's a nice guy," Tori said, not telling Aja she'd known Jace for years now. "I have a trust fund coming my way as soon as I graduate college with a perfect *A*. I've worked so hard for that shit."

"Yeah, my friend has worked her ass off. I'm proud of you, Tori," Amelie said.

"Thank you, although you may have messed things up for me, Little Messy Ass."

"I'm sorry, but desperate times call for desperate measures," Amelie said while smiling.

"Anyway, I like Jace, but the sex is becoming a bit of a bore."

"What? So, you're saying Jace's fine ass ain't packing? I've heard so many stories about that man, stories that are very different from what you're expressing," Aja said, getting all up in Tori's business.

"I'm not saying that. I'm just saying he doesn't know how to use what he's packing. His past is none of my business. From what I've personally experienced, those stories you've heard can't be true."

"Well, Amelie, don't worry. I'm sexy, and I know how to use *everything* I'm packing." Aja winked her eye.

"Yuck," Tori muttered. "I don't mind you guys flirting, or even fucking, but right now, I just cannot."

"Girl, bye. You're getting you some dick, and although it may be some wack dick, don't stop *our* fun," Amelie said, rolling her eyes. "Tori, why can't we fuck or talk about fucking?" Amelie asked. She stared at Aja as she spoke.

"Anyway, I don't care what y'all do, but let's just change the subject for now. So, take one of those guys over there." Tori pointed in the direction of two handsome men who sat at a table directly across from them. "They're fine and all, but imagine feeling him, giving him your time, making yourself all the way available to be fucked, and they don't curve you. All the women want him, some may have even had him, but when you finally get the dick, it ain't worth the time you waited."

"See, that's why I don't like men. Everything about their ass is deceiving. That shit would definitely drive me crazy," Amelie said.

"That's kinda where I am as far as Jace and I. He's a woman's dream, a sweetheart, and he likes me a lot. Get this, Amelie. He wants to meet the Givens." Tori slapped her forehead with the palm of her hand.

"Shit, *I'm* still waiting to meet him. Let us meet before you take him around your parents. Let me fill him in first."

Aja looked at Tori, confused, not understanding what the issue was. To her, Jace was the perfect man.

"I see how you're looking at me, Aja. Trust me. Jace may think he wants to meet my parents, but hell, *I* barely know they ass. My mother is a fucking bitch and a control freak, and my father . . . He just sits there and allows her to do the shit. I just need my money from them, and if I decide to continue what Jace and I have, then I'll consider introducing him. I might even disappear after that. Who knows?"

"I hear you. I was adopted, and my adopted parents were great people. God rest their souls," Aja said. "I'm waiting to meet my birth parents one day before God rests their souls too. I just need to know why they didn't want me."

Aja's mood changed instantly after mentioning her parents. So Tori changed the subject.

"So, back to those fine men over there. I think I'ma get the tall, bald one's phone number. His feet look pretty big. I know he has a mean stroke. I can tell by how he's sitting there, legs wide open. His lap can't handle all that dick sitting on top of it."

"And this is why your ass is in the predicament you're in now, judging a dick by its illusion," Amelie said. "Yes, he *is* sexy. If I had to guess, I would say he's about six foot five. His chocolate skin is to die for, and that bald head—damn, he puts me in the mind of Tyrese Gibson."

"Exactly. As deceiving as you may think his looks are, I can guarantee you that man can tear up some pussy," Tori said. "Jace is a pretty boy. I won't say he's bad in bed. If lovemaking interested me, then I would love the way Jace makes love to me. But I need something rough. I wanna be choked, slapped, and fucked. You know, some kinky shit."

"Girl, you need to be fucking with the type of men *I* fuck with then," Aja said.

"Nah, no thanks. I'll pass," Tori said while laughing.

"Well, you might be right, Tori. You know, I don't know. I don't even suck or fuck dick," Amelie stated.

Tori stood. "I'll let y'all know how it was in a couple of weeks."

"Girl, are you serious?" Aja asked.

"Dead ass."

"Tori, don't take your ass over there. He's going to fuck up your life, friend." Amelie grabbed Tori's arm pleadingly.

"Not if I don't fuck up his life first." Tori smiled, walked away from the table, and over toward the man she wanted. She had to prove her theory right. She wanted to get fucked, and fucked is what she would get.

She walked over to the bar and took a seat next to him. She intertwined her fingers together on top of the bar, smiled, and waited her turn to be served, looking over at the two men every so often. Her mind told her to talk to him, but in her heart, she knew she shouldn't. However, thinking with her pussy instead of her mind, she decided to feed her desire.

The bartender approached Tori.

"What can I get for you today?" she asked, wiping down the countertop.

"Can I have two double shots of tequila, please."

The Tyrese look-alike turned to look at me. He had taken the bait. When I saw him from afar, he was no doubt good looking, but now that I was sitting here face-to-face with him, he was *definitely* getting the pussy.

"Now, what's a beautiful lady like yourself doing with two double shots of liquor?"

"Well, I'm going to drink one, and the other one is for you." The bartender gave her, her shots, and she passed one over to him. "Here you go."

"I appreciate the offer, but I don't really fuck with Patrón, li'l lady."

He was so fine, and the way his words smoothly fell from between his lips had her dripping. She wanted to get to know him sexually, and she figured the liquor would be the perfect gesture. She was at a loss of words when he turned down her drink. But instead of sulking in her feelings, she took both shots and downed them as the two men laughed.

"Damn, love, you need a friend? You just threw those shots back like you need a hug or something."

"Nah, I don't need a hug; maybe a friend but not a hug."

Tori waved the bartender back over and ordered another double shot. Just like the other shots, she downed that bitch too. She felt the eyes of Devontae, the man she would come to know, on her the entire time.

"Damn, you need to slow down, love . . . Some creepy-ass man might try to take you up out of here and take advantage of you."

"Well, it's a good thing I sat next to you. You can protect me."

"Aye, put her shots on my tab," he yelled to the bartender while pointing at Tori.

"And give me another one," she slurred.

Devontae chuckled.

"So, since I'ma be buying you drinks, the least you can do is give me your name."

"It's Tori," she said, drinking her shot and setting down her glass.

"Nice to meet you, Tori . . . Von."

He stuck out his hand, and she shook it. She melted at how rough the palm of his hand and fingers were. He had to be a hardworking man, and she was here for it. The way his body was set up, she had a feeling he was laying a whole lot of dick. His body smelled so delicious, and his skin was perfect. She sat at the bar with him and his friend for hours, mesmerized and horny as hell. Tori thought about pulling him into the bathroom, but she didn't want to seem desperate. She had to play the role and maintain her composure. She was so into what she and Von had going on that she didn't even notice Amelie and Aja leaving. After drinking so many shots, she became a little incoherent, but that didn't stop anything. Her hands had grown a mind of their own, and Tori became a little touchy-feely. She found herself clinging on to Devontae's arm and laughing at everything he said. Every so often, she would rub his chest and then his leg.

"Whoa, whoa, whoa . . . Are you OK?" He grabbed her hand from his thigh and held it.

"Yes, I'm fine, Von. I'm just tryin'a see what Von Von is packing."

"Word?"

"Yes, I know we're not going to continue sitting, acting like this conversation is interesting. I'm sure you would rather be somewhere else, entangled with me."

"Can you close my tab?" he yelled out.

Devontae paid and stood. Tori was so ready for this shit, so she stood up too. She watched as he signed his name on his receipt. Afterward, he excused himself to the washroom. He told her he would meet her outside . . . and that was the beginning of a long, painful, dangerous, and complicated love affair.

Chapter Twelve

It felt as if the entire city were placed under a love spell. First, Tori found herself in a relationship, and then Amelie and Aja found themselves lustfully falling for each other. When they flirted back at the restaurant, Amelie knew Aja would be her new boo once they got through their rough first interaction. Even if Aja didn't like women for real, Amelie had plans to turn her out all the way. Aja was the next best thing to Tori. The two women looked so much alike and seemed to carry themselves the same way. Aja was willing to give Amelie some much-needed attention. They both entertained each other's advances and knew they would soon take things past flirting.

After Tori abruptly ended their little brunch, she gave the waitress her card number and told her the two ladies' bill was on her. Amelie and Aja stayed behind awhile longer, getting to know each other. They talked, ordered more liquor, and got super tipsy. They sat talking for over an hour while taking shots of the restaurant's house tequila.

Sooner than later, the ladies got closer, sitting side by side, and taking in each other's essence.

It was like the tequila had a dose of ecstasy in it. The longer they sat talking, the more explicit their conversation became, so they decided to take things back to Amelie's place.

Amelie drove from L.A. to Compton in an unusual state. Aja couldn't keep her hands off her. It was a wonder how they safely made it to their destination because Amelie couldn't fight the feeling to come over and over again. She drove the entire way with her eyes wandering uncontrollably. Aja put her knees into the seat. Leaning over, she kissed and licked Amelie's ear. Aja wanted her, and she wanted Aja bad.

"Oh my God, you're gonna make me crash," Amelie said, feeling her eyes rolling back and her pussy beginning to throb.

"Keep your eyes on the road. If we die, you won't get to taste me," Aja whispered in her ear.

Aja snaked her hand down Amelie's body and stuck it inside her pants. She used her index and middle finger to relieve Amelie of the puddle that was threatening to release. The excitement of this entire situation had Amelie ready to put her car in park and take it there with Aja in the middle of the street.

"Oooh, shit, we're gonna die today," Amelie moaned. She gripped the steering wheel tightly as Aja rapidly moved her fingers in and out of her, forcing Amelie's head back into the seat headrest. Then Aja grabbed Amelie's pussy as if it were a bowling ball.

"Take it. I know you can," Aja whispered. "Get us home," she encouraged. The car swerved to the left. It's a good thing they were the only two occupying the road at the moment because that would've for sure been an accident. "Straighten the wheel up." Aja gripped the other side of the steering wheel with her free hand, helping Amelie drive.

"Aja, damn, girl, you are doing too much right now."

"I'm not. I want you to come. That feistiness in you lets me know you haven't been fucked in a while." Aja now added a third finger while simultaneously playing with Amelie's clit with her thumb.

"Oh my, oh my, oh my God," Amelie moaned.

She panted heavily, and suddenly her foot hit the brakes. The car instantly jerked as it came to an abrupt stop. Amelie came all over Aja's hand. She gripped the passenger seat as she took in deep breaths and pushed out relief. Amelie looked over at Aja and bit down on her bottom lip. Her pussy muscles pulsated around Aja's fingers.

Aja took her hand from Amelie's pants and licked every single drop of cream from her fingers. Then she grabbed Amelie's face and kissed her, sharing with Amelie her own secretion, giving her a taste of her own pussy. Aja kept Amelie on the tip of her tongue as she shoved it into her mouth.

"Mmm, you taste so fucking good," Aja said seductively.

"I know," Amelie agreed cockily.

The two women were so caught up in a state of lust they didn't realize traffic had begun to build. They watched each other's lips as they talked seductively. They felt as if they were the only two people who occupied this planet . . . like they were in a world of their own.

"You're so fucking feisty. I love that shit."

"I know. I told you that you hadn't seen shit yet. We're not done. It's your turn to feel pleasure," Amelie said, ready to give after receiving. Suddenly, the blare of a horn and a car swerving around theirs caused the two to come back down to earth.

"Stupid bitch," a guy shouted as he drove around Amelie's car. She looked over as the car sped away. Then she took a peek out her back window and noticed the line of vehicles. Aja laughed and buckled her seat belt.

"You about to get us murdered for real," Aja stated.

"Oops, my bad." Amelie laughed uncontrollably. She took her foot from the brake and slowly drove away.

***

A few days later, Aja and Amelie were still tangled in each other's web. They'd been wrapped up and too busy to partake in anything in the outside world. Amelie's phone rang off the hook for hours, but she ignored every call. Right now, she was too busy fucking with a girl she didn't know . . . and a girl she probably shouldn't have been with. Aja had Amelie hooked after she took her on a very adventurous ride.

Amelie walked into her room with a glass of ice water in her hand. She looked down at Aja's long, chocolate body as she lay stretched out across the bed, looking through her phone, awaiting Amelie's return. The women had just taken a long shower together, and now, Amelie was ready to get shit popping again. She found herself a little sprung because no other woman had ever taken her body to the heights Aja had. Amelie walked past Aja, smacked her left booty cheek, and watched as it jiggled.

"You like what you see?" Aja smiled. "Look but don't touch."

"What you mean 'don't touch'? I own every bit of you now," Amelie said.

"You mean *I* own every bit of *you?*" Aja asked.

"I guess you can say that." Amelie licked her lips.

"I am all yours, but I do all the ass smacking around here. I would much rather you touch something else." Aja now wore a teasing smile on her face.

"Come here. I have something for you to touch and taste." Aja looked at Amelie with bedroom eyes.

Amelie drank a sip of the water, allowing an ice cube to fall into her mouth. She held the ice between her front teeth and set the cup down. Climbing into bed, she positioned her naked body on top of Aja's. Aja held on and gripped Amelie's ass. She leaned down and allowed the water to drip down onto Aja's body from the ice cube. Amelie rode Aja slowly as if something were in between Aja's legs to ride. Nevertheless, the sensation of their secret parts being so close together made penetration unworthy.

After allowing the water to drip, Amelie slurped it up. She kissed every inch of Aja's upper body while she took her time still rotating her hips. Aja placed her hands on top of Amelie's head, helping her move her way south.

"Taste me," Aja said, and Amelie stopped what she was doing. She climbed between Aja's chocolate thighs and placed her lips onto Aja's southern lips. "I shaved it bald just for you," Aja announced as she played in Amelie's hair. "Damn," she exclaimed as soon as Amelie's cold lips touched her. They both took their time with each other. After a few minutes, they were laid up in each other's arms.

"I have to go to work tonight, so I'm going to head out in a little bit," Aja said. Amelie lay in silence with her eyes closed and her legs still wide open. "Did you hear me?" Aja tapped Amelie's leg.

"Yes, I heard you. I was just lying here thinking." She rolled over on her side and looked at Aja. "A few weeks ago, Tori and I spoke about a five-year plan. I don't really have one. I just live life. Tori wasn't really feeling my answer, though, which got me thinking a whole lot. I did so well in high school. I just never had much motivation around me to go beyond a high school education," she said.

"Well, that's normal. A lot of people don't think about their futures. They live in the now. Me, personally, I do have a five-year plan, and I see progress already. Things are happening way faster than I thought they would. None of this shit was planned, but sometimes, God puts you in a position to make shit happen without even trying. You should listen to Tori. She's a wise girl."

"I'm listening. I will return to school, but I'll start with a small community college. I want these ambitions everyone else seems to have. I want to be more appealing, not only for my looks, attitude, and body. I'm smart as well." Amelie pouted.

"So, answer me something. How long have you known Tori? I mean, I met her a couple of weeks ago, but we haven't really had time to get to know each other."

"I don't know . . . since high school. I was her first and only friend. She was so quiet back then, but I've gotten the opportunity to know her very well."

"Have you met her family?"

"Yeah. Her mother can be a tough cookie, but I know she means well. Tori is her only child, and I guess she just wants her to succeed," Amelie said, and Aja frowned.

"Only child, huh? *That's* what's up. I wish I had that, someone to show me they cared about me, even if it was only a little bit."

"Yeah, I understand. I know you said your adopted parents passed away. What happened to them?" Amelie asked.

"From what the police reports said, it was a tragic car accident. It said something to the effect of faulty brakes. That happened a couple of years back. Their car somehow lost control, and they fell off a cliff. I never even knew I was adopted until my eighteenth birthday. I got into a small altercation with my sister, and she blurted it out. It almost felt like she was rubbing it in my face. She knew who her biological parents were, and I didn't. Of course, I thought she was lying. I mean, how did she know this information, and I didn't? She was younger than me. I asked my parents if it were true. They admitted that it was and showed me my birth certificate. It honestly felt like a slap in the face, but I've been searching for my biological parents ever since. Enough about me, though."

"That's sad. How is your sister doing?"

"I don't know. After my parents' death, we got that money and went our own separate ways." Aja stood and began getting dressed. "Do you mind dropping me off at home? I have a long night ahead of me."

"Yeah, sure." Amelie stood, walked over to her closet, and grabbed her clothes. Then she walked to her bathroom, quickly cleaned herself up, and got dressed.

"Come here." Aja grabbed Amelie. "I'm going to miss you. I wish I didn't have to work today." Aja gripped Amelie's ass, kissed her forehead, and exited the home. The two women held hands the entire drive. Every once in a while, Aja would lift Amelie's hand to her mouth and kiss it.

Aja wasn't falling in love or in lust with Amelie. She just needed to make her feel special in case she needed her later. They pulled up in front of her apartment building thirty minutes later, and Aja stepped out of the car.

"I guess I'll see you soon?" she asked as Amelie walked up the sidewalk to hug her.

"Yes, most definitely. Call me when you get a chance," Amelie said, breaking their embrace.

Chapter Thirteen

After Tori and Devontae's little sexcapade, she knew she couldn't treat their situation as a one-night stand. She wasn't willing to one-and-done him. She needed him to stick around a bit longer. So she continued to entertain him. She would've been stupid not to. He had some great dick, and now she was interested in exploring more.

Her phone buzzed, snapping her from a daydream. It had been a few weeks since she'd seen Devontae physically, but they texted every day. So, when she looked over at her buzzing cell, she immediately answered with a huge smile.

"Hello."

"Hello . . . What's going on, li'l lady?" Devontae asked, and Tori chuckled.

"Nothing. What's going on with you, bighead?" She couldn't help but flirt with him.

"Bighead? That's my new nickname?" he asked, smirking.

"Yes, that name fits you very, very well."

"Oh shit. Now, which head are we referring to? The head in between my shoulders, or the head sitting on my lap?"

"Of course, the head in between your shoulders, silly."

"Yeah, a'ight. This ma'fucka on my lap feels way bigger than the other one. Shit feels like I'm toting around heavy machinery." Devontae and Tori both laughed.

"You are something else, bighead ass. What's going on, though?"

"Shit, I'm tryin'a see if you can fit me into your schedule tonight."

"I'll see what I can do, but I make no promises."

"Ouch. Did you really just answer that shit with a 'you'll see what you can do'? I was just fucking around and being nice when I asked for your time. Nah, li'l lady, now, I'm *demanding* that shit."

"Demanding? So, you're the boss of me?"

"Hell yeah. *Big* boss, fuck you mean."

"Oh, OK." Tori laughed. "I'm with it."

"I know, nigga. So be ready when I pull up."

"Yes, sir." Her voice was soft and seductive. "So, what's on your agenda for today?"

"I probably hit my cousin up, then go to the bar and have a few drinks. After that, I'ma be looking for something else to get into."

"Something else, or *someone* else to get into?" she asked earnestly.

"Same difference, love."

"I guess."

"So, I'ma come through and pick you up later tonight," he said.

"I'll let you know if I'm busy. Just hit my line when you're done with your cousin."

"Li'l lady, you ain't gon' let me know shit. Just be ready at nine."

She hung up the phone and called Jace to make sure he didn't have any plans for her later. She wanted Devontae so bad. His wanting to control her every move was sexy. He didn't have to ask if he could come to get her because for the dick, she was down to do whatever. She was with all the bullshit, and she didn't need Jace fucking up her night.

She put her phone to her ear while Jace's phone rang. A second or two later, he answered.

"Hey, bae," he said.

This nigga even answered the phone like a damn lame, she thought.

"Hey. You didn't have any plans for us today, right?"

"Not really. I'ma be busy with this studio session tonight."

"Cool, because I have so much work to do. It's gonna be a long fucking night of studying." She yawned.

"That's cool, baby. I'ma try to stop by after my session, just to see you for a minute."

"Make sure you call first," Tori said, stuttering. "Jus-just to make sure I'm still awake."

"A'ight. I'll do that." Jace cleared his throat.

"OK, talk to you later."

They disconnected the call, and she made herself comfortable in bed. Then she closed her eyes and fantasized about Devontae, imagining his perfect body in her mind. All she could envision was herself propped up against that wall. He had fucked her up against it the first time they had sex. Only that time, he didn't penetrate her. He had her legs thrown over his shoulders while he tongue kissed her pussy.

Moaning, she put her hand into her panties and slid her middle finger up and down her clit. She saw the top of Devontae's head clear as day, moving and rotating while he licked her entire yoni. Then her middle and index fingers slipped inside her pussy, and almost instantly, she applied pressure to her G-spot. She held her fingers in place sturdily, and with the palm of her hand, she massaged her clit.

Feeling an intense orgasm building, she opened her legs wide, giving herself more wiggle room to add another finger. Her body shook, her thighs stiffened, and her toes curled. She was on the way to pure ecstasy. In her mind, Devontae began to nibble and suck on her pussy lips. He opened his mouth wide and flicked his tongue on her pearl. She felt her pussy dripping. The water that ran from her vagina gave her all the lubricant she needed to work herself into an orgasm. Next, she pushed her fingers inside and tightened her walls. Diving her fingers in and out rapidly, she felt the grooves of her insides and massaged them. That one thing was all it took for her to come.

At about 7:30 that night, she began getting dressed. She took a long, hot, steamy bath with a splash of rose oil and a rose-scented bubble bath. She sat in the tub for at least an hour, making sure her body felt and smelled amazing.

As she soaked, a text from Devontae came through on her phone, and she almost jumped out of her skin. She sat up, grabbed her phone from the edge of the tub, and read his message.

I'll be pulling up in twenty minutes. So, be ready. OK.

She set her phone back down and proceeded to wash her body. She lathered her washcloth and took her time. She admired her body as she slowly ran her washcloth across her neck, breasts, thighs, and vagina. She closed her eyes as she thoroughly cleaned every spot she wanted Devontae to kiss.

After bathing, Tori unplugged the tub. She turned the shower on and rinsed off. Then stepping from the tub and drying off, she got dressed, fluffed out her hair, and applied lip gloss to her lips. As promised, a few minutes later, Devontae pulled up.

She stepped from the building, looking comfortable but sexy. She had on a pair of loosely fitted navy blue jogging pants rolled down a little past her waist, showing off the top of her thong. Her shirt was cropped, showing off the bottom of her breasts and her flat stomach. Of course, her shoes were Nike, and her hair was wild, in a huge, curly 'fro. She had her ho bag wrapped around her wrist and her damn common sense in her back pocket. Just call her "Reckless Renee" because Tori was definitely living trifling as hell. Walking up to the car, she smiled. Devontae was just too fine for words. He leaned up against the passenger door of what she assumed to be a brand-new BMW M5, with his arms folded. The closer she walked to him, the brighter her smile became.

"What's up, li'l lady?"

"Hey, Bighead," she beamed.

"You look good as hell. Bring yo' li'l chocolate ass here," he said, and Tori laughed.

He tugged at the top of her pants, pulling her to him and hugging her tightly. She melted into him. His entire body smelled so good.

"You had enough to drink? Your ass is a little aggressive."

"Nah, a nigga sober as hell, but I got some Crown in the car."

Devontae released Tori and opened the back passenger door. Then he took her bag from her arm and placed it inside. Grabbing her waist and pulling her back to him, Devontae moved her hair to the side and kissed her neck.

"Do you know how to drive a stick?" His voice was seductive.

"Now, what type of question is that? That's my favorite way to ride," Tori said, and Devontae smirked.

He handed her his keys and asked her to drive. She quickly obliged. She didn't have a problem chauffeuring him around, especially since they were riding in style.

"Shit, now I gotta put you to the test. I'ma see if you really know what you're doing."

"A'ight, a'ight. Don't try me now. I'ma beast with these driving skills."

"Yeah? We'll see, and I hope you can back them words up."

Her level of comfort with Devontae was just so automatic. It felt as if she had known him her entire life. She knew what he was talking about when he asked her to drive his stick, and she was ready to show and prove.

Tori walked around to the driver's side and opened the door. Climbing inside, she made herself comfortable. She closed the door, put on her seat belt, and put her foot on the brake, forcing the engine to come alive. Devontae climbed in on the passenger side and instantly began pouring them both cups of Crown Royal. Before she could even pull away from the curb, he handed her a cup. Wasting no time, she put the cup to her lips and drank it all down.

"I think you gon' need another cup because what I have in store for you, li'l lady, you gon' need all the liquor courage you can get."

"What the fuck, Devontae? I'm now with all that kinky shit?"

Devontae laughed, and Tori sucked her teeth. Still, he poured another cup of liquor.

"Just trust me. You're gonna love it," he said.

She put the car in drive, pulled away from the curb, and turned up the radio. Then she picked up her cup and decided just to take a few sips.

"Nah nah nah, li'l lady. Don't sip that shit. Throw that ma'fucka back."

"This shit is nasty. Where's the chaser? You gon' have me throwing up and shit."

"It ain't no chaser, now drank up."

"What the hell are you trying to do to me?"

"Everything you want me to do to you. So, throw that shit back and don't give me no lip."

"Bossy much."

"Don't say I didn't warn you, love," Devontae said. He certainly did warn her, but as always, she didn't listen. She took another sip and set down her cup. "Do you remember how to get to my crib?"

"Sort of."

"A'ight. Well, get us there."

He put his cup into the cup holder and proceeded to pull her pants down, but she stopped him.

"Lift up a little."

"For what, Devontae? What are you doing?"

"Man, don't ask me no questions. Now, lift yo' ass up." She did as she was told, taking her foot off the gas and lifting her body slightly. Luckily, she had on jogging pants. The way her pants slid down so effortlessly, Tori knew Devontae had to be a professional at this.

"So, you're gonna make me drive to your home without any pants on?" she asked. "The neighborhoods are gonna be looking at my ass all crazy and shit."

"So, let them look. I'm about to eat yo' pussy all the way there," he announced. "Then I'ma fuck the shit out of you when I get you home." She sighed deeply. She looked over at him and blushed. Not being used to doing anything like this, she was left speechless.

God, please don't let Jace find out, she thought. She was in a relationship with Jace, and he was a woman's dream. Yet here she was with a bad boy, a man from whom she should've steered clear.

"Open your legs," he ordered as he put his cup to his lips, gulping his Crown Royal.

"Devontae," she said, "I'm scared."

"Of what?" he asked.

"I'm sitting here naked, and you honestly expect me to drive us to your home safe while you're going down on me?"

"Nah, I don't expect us to get there safe. We ain't no little kids, so I'm not about to go down on you. I'm about to eat your pussy . . . Now, shut up." He set his cup down and turned the radio up as "On Me" by Lil Baby began to play on the radio.

"Come and put that pussy on me, don't be runnin' from me. If I like it, I spend money on it," Devontae rapped, grabbing Tori's thigh. As promised, he put his head between her thighs and his lips to hers.

"The number you have reached, 2-1-3-5-5-5-3-1-2-3, is not available. Please hang up and dial again," Aja heard the phone operator say for the fifth time that night. She quickly ended the call and threw her phone on her bed.

At this point, she was beyond irritated. She'd been calling Jace's number repeatedly for days, and just like any other time, he sent her calls to voicemail. Aja had left over fifty voice messages, probably filling his mailbox. She was a fucked-up individual, constantly feeling unwanted. Aja went through life trying to make others just as miserable as she was. She'd always been the underdog her entire life, and she found herself always coming last.

This time was no exception. Aja had finally met a piece of the puzzle she'd been trying to put together for years now, and it all was coincidental. She never knew that one day she would meet her fraternal twin sister. The crazy part of it all is Tori knew absolutely nothing about her. They seemed to have many things in common, as well as the same taste in men, considering the fact Aja had the chance to get a huge piece of Jace in the past.

The time she'd spent with Jace had her thinking by now they would be happy and almost married. The record deal Jace was offered was not by mistake. Aja and Big Percy had a personal relationship. He was her sugar daddy. However, Jace was her boo on the side. The two had so much planned for their future. Aja took it upon herself and dropped Jace's demo off in Big Percy's incoming mail. She was determined to win at least once in her life. However, when things with her and Jace began to seem too good to be true, they quickly dwindled. Jace decided he wasn't ready for a relationship. He had no concrete reason besides that he was young and still wanted to live a playa's life. Jace was on his way to the top, and Aja just wasn't who he wanted to bring to the top with him.

Big Percy's sugar daddy money began to lessen. He was trying to find a way to break all ties with her. Aja was a sneaky, conniving, toxic person. She had every reason to be who she was. After being fucked over all her life, she snapped and decided to show everyone her crazy side. She stalked Jace for months on campus, threatening any woman who came within two feet of him. She went as far as threatening to kill the next bitch she saw with him until he got her expelled and banned from the school. That was over a year ago, and Aja somehow still found a way to lurk.

Tori was just a soon-to-be casualty. Aja was out for blood, and she didn't give a damn who she hurt. She wanted Omeiha and Larry. If it weren't for them, her life would be perfect—or so she thought. In her mind, she knew that she would know who she is as a person, and she would have a family to call her own if they were in it. What was so special about Tori? The shit was beyond her. Why did Omeiha and Larry keep Tori and dispose of her? Aja didn't know, but she felt herself getting closer to finding out. And if Jace tried to stand in the way, he could get it too.

Aja looked down at her business phone and licked her lips. She smiled and stood to her feet. It was time to make a little money. This little telephone operator gig came on time because she needed the money. This quick little $200 would be greatly appreciated. Aja clicked the talk option, and right away, she spoke. Her soft voice flowed through the telephone receiver.

"I've been waiting on your phone call all day, sexy. My body and my slit are dripping wet here, waiting on you. I need you to get me right. I know she can't wait any longer. Honestly, daddy, I had to take care and please myself because you didn't call when you said you would. Now, it's your turn to play in my puddle," Aja said seductively into the phone.

"I'm sorry about that, baby. The wife has been riding me pretty hard lately. I think she knows about us," the unknown caller said.

"Mmm, that shit just turns me on, baby. Your wife just doesn't know the things you do to me, the way you make my body feel," Aja said seductively while moaning. She bit down on her bottom lip, giving him the illusion of her being in a euphoric state.

"That shit turns you on, huh?" he asked.

"Yes," she responded. "Your neck, it tastes like fruit, babe. You know how much I love that shit."

"Don't get off the subject. So, my wife catching us together somewhere out in public while fucking turns you on?"

"Ooooh yes, baby," she moaned into the phone. "What do you think she knows about us?" she asked rhetorically, releasing a sexy breath. "Does she know I get your dick wet every night?"

"Maybe."

"Maybe? Well, does she know I suck you off every single night?" She made a slurping noise as she spoke slowly with a subtle voice. In her job industry, illusions were everything. She had to paint the picture.

"Hell yeah."

"Hell yeah? Well, does she know I sit my phat juicy ass on your face every single fucking morning?"

"Fuck yeah, she knows you're my breakfast, lunch, and dinner."

"Does she know I can handle your dick? I can guarantee she doesn't ride you reverse cowgirl style the way *I* do."

"She knows you can take so much pipe, and she knows I've been giving you every inch of the pipe she loves so much." He was now moaning as he spoke softly into the phone. He wanted her in the worst way. The images in his mind had him beating the fuck out of his wood.

"Bend over, baby, and take this pipe," he said.

"How far down do you want me to bend, daddy?" she asked. "I'm touching my toes. I'm ready for you to get in this pussy."

"Damn, baby, you have such a filthy mouth. I have something for that later. Come here." He stuck his hand deeper into his pants, now fondling his balls, imagining himself in the same room as Aja with her bent over. He saw his hand grabbing her hair tightly. He imagined her hair being coarse, brown with a touch of blond and thick. The caller saw himself rotating his hips in circles while moving in and out of Aja.

"Oh my God, I fucking hate your wife," she moaned, sounding as if she were full of his penis. Aja was putting on an outstanding performance, and she did it every time he called her line. "She allowed me to get some good dick, but I have to give it back. I can't keep it," she whined.

"It's all yours, baby," he said.

"It's not mine, baby, but I plan to be the runner-up in this race. Don't stop. Your fat cock feels so good." Aja sat on the phone, still fake moaning as she talked to him. She looked at her nails and grabbed her fingernail file from her desk drawer. "Baby, fuck me harder. I want to come all over your big-ass cock." She laid it on thick.

"Fuck yeah, come all over this big dick," he exclaimed, panting. "Is this dick too big for you?"

"Yes, daddy."

"Do you want me to stop?"

"No, daddy."

"Are you going to let me come in that phat pussy?"

"Yes."

"Let me know when you're ready for me, baby. I'm ready to explode," he said. Of course, that was always Aja's cue to moan as loud and fast as possible.

"Baby, ooooh, I'm coming," she said, rolling her eyes.

Aja stood with her nail file still in hand and stretched. Soon after, she heard his loud, erratic moans. He followed her lead, letting out loud grunts. He came, and he came hard.

"How was it? Did I get you right, sir?"

"Damn, baby, that shit was so good. You got me more than right. I think I'm starting to fall in love."

"Boy," Aja said with a laugh, "you are crazy. What are you falling in love with? My voice?" she asked and then answered. Their fifteen-minute phone call was almost over, and after getting this mystery man right, their conversation quickly changed to a normal one.

"I'm falling in love with you. We just have the best sexual chemistry. It's weird how you make me come without intercourse. I've never experienced this type of lovemaking before, and I want to explore whatever we have one-on-one."

"You have two minutes left. To end this call, simply hang up," the automated voice announced.

"Baby, this is my job. We could never do this on a one-on-one basis. We have to keep this professional. However, I do enjoy your company. I appreciate you calling me every day."

"Yeah, professional. I have to remember that." He paused and sat in silence, then took the phone from his ear and chuckled.

"What's so funny?"

"You have one minute. Please hang up and call again."

"Nothing, baby. Thank you for tonight. I appreciate it." He sighed. "Now I can go home and cuddle up next to the misses."

"After I fucked you good, you're going home to your wife? Typical, but no problem, babes." Her voice offered a chuckle. "Well, tomorrow, same time, same place?" she asked.

Before he had a chance to answer her question, the phone disconnected.

Chapter Fourteen

Tori sat on the side of Jace in his brand-new E-Class Mercedes-Benz. He watched the road intently as he drove 80 mph on the expressway. She couldn't believe she was on her way to meet his family, and she couldn't believe out of all the things she'd been through as a child, she would be sitting here next to a man who should've never been her man. It's like the universe pulled the two together, and no matter how much she tried to fight it, Jace just wasn't giving up.

"What are you thinking about?" Tori asked. She stared at him and smiled, wondering if he was just as nervous as she.

"Shit, I'm just ready for you to meet my moms and my pops," he said subtly, still deep in thought with his eyes focused on the traffic.

"Are you sure?" she asked.

"You know what? I'm lying. Something *is* on my mind."

"OK, tell me."

"I won't say it. I'll just play it for you." Jace picked up his phone from his lap. He drove through traffic, scrolling through his phone searching for the song he titled "A Lifetime." It was a song dedicated to Tori. Also, it was one of the songs he planned to let one of the artists on 290 record label sing. Finally locating the song, he spoke. "This the first song I'ma be working with a new artist on at the label," he said, pressing *play*.

The beat so beautifully serenaded the vehicle, and the lyrics filled the entire car, making Tori feel all mushy inside. Her eyes instantly misted. The song was a cute little vibe, and the lyrics sounded personal. She could tell the words had come from his heart, so how could she not love him? These words were clearly written with her in mind. He put their entire future into this song. As guilt surrounded Tori's heart, she let one tear drop.

"You like it?" he asked.

"I love it," she said. She gripped his hand and squeezed it softly. This love shit was just not for her. Tori didn't know how to love because she didn't grow up that way. Pornography and mastur-bation raised her, and there was no love in either.

"I had a hard time figuring out where I knew you from. When I first saw you again, I knew you looked familiar, but I just couldn't place it." Jace pulled up in front of his parents' house and parked his car. He turned to look at Tori, and she put her face in her hands, embarrassed. Then she smiled.

"So, you *did* remember me, and you still approached me? Wow."

"When I approached you, at that point, I was still trying to figure it out. But when I came to your dorm room, I was for sure you were the Tori Givens who tutored me back in the sixth grade. I also knew you were the same Tori Givens that ran away crying back in the eighth grade. That was the last time I saw you."

"Yeah, I know. I asked my mother to transfer me."

"Look at me." Jace grabbed Tori's face. "Us seeing each other again confirmed so much shit. To be honest with you, at first, I was just on some smash-and-dash shit," he said honestly, and Tori pushed his chest. "For real. If I can't be honest with you, we don't need to be together."

"Well, I appreciate your honesty," Tori said. At that moment, she wished she could be just as honest. *I hate the way you fuck me. Well, the way you make love to me. I don't enjoy that shit at all. I don't know how to love, and it's hard for me to let you in. I want to love you, but I just don't know how,* Tori thought to herself. She felt her heart palpitating rapidly as these thoughts took over her mind. There was so much she wanted to confess to, but instead, she bit the bullet and kept her mouth closed. Then she smiled at him.

"Let's get on in here so you can meet Mr. and Mrs. Doss, your future in-laws."

Jace climbed from the car and walked around to Tori's side. He opened her door, and she swung her legs out. Her outfit for the night was a blue, high-waisted, pleated skirt with a white ruffled silk shirt. When her four-inch, knee-high, black heels hit the concrete, Jace grabbed her hand and helped her to her feet. He kissed her hand, not wanting to smear her beautifully painted nude pink lipstick. Her makeup was flawless, and just like any other day, her hair was in a kinky, curly Afro that hung down to her shoulders.

"You look so perfect," he said.

"I am getting so hot." Tori fanned herself as she walked side by side with Jace. She wanted to make sure her makeup stayed cool. The sweat she felt in her armpits and around her nose was evident. For so many reasons, Tori felt transparent. She was so afraid to meet Jace's family. He placed his arm around her waist.

"Calm down, baby. They're going to love you. I've already told them all about you and our history."

"You told them what?" Tori stopped in her tracks. "They're going to think I'm some type of stalker, and things weren't coincidental. We need to leave. I can't meet your parents."

"Bring yo' ass on, man. Everything is OK. I don't care what they think. You're my woman." Tori blew out a breath of apprehension, and Jace chuckled. He looked at her seriously, not really knowing how to convince her. "If I didn't know you were Tori from Hollenbeck, I definitely would've figured it out right now."

At that moment, Tori felt as if she needed to masturbate. The jitters she had were just too much. She thought about going back to the car and getting herself right. Tori always made sure to bring her bullet vibrator wherever she went, just in case of situations like this. The thought was so vivid that she saw herself leaning back in the car with her eyes closed and her legs wide open. She even heard the hum of the purple vibrator in her mind as she moved it in and out. Afterward, she saw herself meeting Jace back inside his parents' home.

"I am not the same Tori from Hollenbeck; trust me," she said, smiling.

"I know you're not. Don't take what I just said to heart. Let's go inside, and if you still feel uncomfortable after an hour, we can leave," Jace pleaded. He walked into Tori's space and lifted her chin. "You goin' in with me?"

Tori sighed. She wanted to say no so badly, but she knew she couldn't. Jace had already told his entire family about her, and she didn't want him to look like a fool if she didn't show up with him.

"Yes, I'm going in with you." She smiled.

"OK, let's go." He grabbed Tori's hand, and they made their way to the door. Jace went ahead and turned the doorknob to let himself in. Tori followed closely behind, hand and fingers still intertwined with his. "Ayyye!" Jace yelled out as the two walked through the foyer and toward the family room. As he held Tori's hand, she looked like the perfect piece of chocolate on the side of him. Her slim body and dark skin glowed.

"Where is everybody?" Tori asked Jace.

"Shit, ain't no telling. Let's check one more place." The two walked toward the dining room, and as soon as Jace flicked the lights on, they were both in shock.

"Surprise!" everyone shouted. "Congratulations!" they all screamed.

"Congratulations?" Tori asked. She was confused. Nothing that she knew of had happened to receive any congratulatory greetings.

"I didn't get the chance to tell you yet, but I just signed my record deal this morning. This shit is official, baby. Like a referee with a whistle."

"Oh my God." Tori hugged Jace. "Congratulations, babe."

"Thank you, man. This has been a long time coming." Jace released Tori and made his way around the room, hugging everyone from his mother to his father, his grandmother, then a few close cousins, uncles, and aunts.

Tori stood off to the side, watching Jace as he made his rounds. She stood shyly with her fingers together, smiling with her head down. She didn't know what to do or how to act. She hated being surrounded by people she didn't know. Tori was never an outgoing girl, and this situation made her highly uncomfortable. It was all overwhelming, she and Jace being the center of attention. She didn't know if she should pull her cell out and pretend to smile and laugh at a text, scroll through old pictures pretending she was doing something important, or just stand there and continue looking lost.

"Tori," Jace yelled, and she looked up. "Come here," he said.

Tori was instantly brought back from her thoughts. She smiled at the closeness and interaction she observed between mother, father, and son as Jace stood conversing with both of his parents. Tori made her way over, now wearing a half smile on her face. She waved her hand at both Mr. and Mrs. Doss. When she got within arm's reach, Jace pulled her to him, hugging her around her waist. "Moms and Pops, this is Tori."

"Hi, nice to meet you." Tori shook hands with both of Jace's parents.

"You are so pretty, Tori," Mrs. Doss said.

"So are you, Mrs. Doss. Beautiful home too," Tori said, looking around.

"Thank you, hon, but call me Mila. And this is my husband, Jace Sr. I'm so happy to meet you finally. This boy talks my ear off about you all the time."

Tori looked at Jace and smiled.

"Yeah, Tori and I go way back. This is the same girl who tutored me in sixth grade. If it wasn't for her, I probably would still be my ass in the sixth grade." They all laughed.

"You would've eventually passed." Tori snickered. "You just needed to focus a little, that's all."

"Yeah, I know, and you did the damn thang by making sure I was focused. I appreciate that shit more than you know."

Tori smiled modestly. She didn't do Jace's homework or take his tests for him, so she couldn't take *all* the credit.

"Believe me, if you hadn't helped this boy out, his ass would still be in the sixth grade," Jace Sr. said.

"I'm tryin'a tell her, Pops. Her man ain't as smart as she thinks he is," Jace said as he stood behind Tori, holding her. He wrapped his arms tightly around her waist and kissed her neck.

"Slow down, son. Give her some space," Mila said while laughing. She reached over and pushed Jace's shoulder softly. "Do you mind if I steal her for a little while?" she asked.

"Yeah, son. Let her go on with your mama and hang out with the women. I got something to show you. I hope you brought your hooping shit because a party ain't a fucking party without hitting a few baskets," Jace Sr. said aloud.

Tori observed him. Jace Senior's voice was loud and country. He looked exactly like his son: beautiful eyes and a short, faded haircut with waves on top of waves. But, of course, his older age was apparent.

"A'ight," Jace said. He kissed Tori on her cheek and spoke softly into her ear. "You OK? Do you need me to stay here with you?" Before Tori could speak up, Mila spoke up for her.

"Boy, go away. We don't bite, Tori. I just want to introduce you to Jace's grandmother and aunts," Mila announced.

"Yeah, I'm fine. I would love to meet the rest of your family," Tori said nervously, but she quickly shook off the jitters. She felt her purse and tucked it tightly.

"All right, I'll see you in about an hour. Keep your phone in your hand," Jace said.

"Boy, go and play basketball. You don't need to keep tabs on her," Mila scolded.

"C'mon, son. You know how your mother is," Jace Sr. said.

Damn, Mila runs the show just like Omeiha, but her and Jace's relationship is so beautiful. I wish my mother and I were close, Tori thought. "Do you mind showing me to the bathroom? I have to tinkle," Tori announced.

"Yeah, sure. There's one right this way, next to the family room." The two ladies walked down the hallway, and Mila showed Tori where the lavatory was. "When you're done, meet me in here." Mila pointed in the direction of the family room. "Also, is there a particular liquor you drink?"

"No, no thanks. I'm not much of a drinker."

"Nonsense. At least have a glass of wine. I heard all the young 21-year-olds are drinking that cheap wine . . . What is it called?" Mila said while snapping her fingers. Tori looked at Mila with curious brows. She was a little offended, but she kept her mouth shut. "Moscato. These young kids heard about it in a song and went crazy. Surprisingly, I found a bottle on the shelf."

"Surprisingly, I've never had any, but sure, I'll take a glass," Tori said.

"I have one with a 10 percent alcohol volume. It's a celebration . . . What the hell? Let's get tipsy."

"OK," Tori responded while shrugging her shoulders.

"Your drink will be waiting on you."

"Thank you, Mila."

Tori walked into the bathroom and locked the door. She felt like a crack addict as she feverishly searched for her drug of choice—her vibrator. Sex was a good addiction, but this itch, this nagging pain of yearning, hit her in the wrong setting. She pretended to use the bathroom as she went back and forth with herself. After two minutes, she flushed the toilet and turned on the faucet. Tori empty all the contents from her purse onto the sink in search of her beautiful purple baby. Pushing past her phone, nude lipstick, and a package of gum, Tori's eyes wandered to her love stick.

When it was finally within her grasp, she continued to allow the water to pour into the sink while she pulled off her underwear and propped one heeled foot onto the toilet. Then she pushed her bullet deep inside, and her head fell back. It was like an instant high as relief swarmed her. Tori's heart pace sped up as her adrenaline began to rush. She sucked her bottom lip into her mouth, putting the vibrator on its highest setting. She felt the intensity. Moving her hips back and forth while simultaneously forcing her small woman pleaser in and out, a moan fell from her lips.

"Oh my," she whispered, eyes rolling back and panting softly. Tori moved her hand swifter. She was so wet and slippery. Her pussy made a squishing noise every time she ground her wetness onto the vibrator. "I can't believe I'm doing this," she said, but she didn't regret it. She *needed* this. She was about to climax and then go out into the family room as if nothing had just happened. "I'm almost there."

She paced herself; Tori was ready to explode. It always only took her a couple of minutes to relieve herself, and this time was no exception. She leaned her head down as her blood rushed upward, and her ears began to ring. Tori gulped in the air, feeling her body becoming weak. Soon enough, she released clear fluids.

"Aaaahhhh!" Tori screamed out loud. Relief took over her nerves. Now she was ready to be social. She pulled the vibrator from her vagina and put on her underwear again.

Boom, boom, boom.

Tori jumped while holding her chest.

"Is everything OK?" Mila asked. The entire family room heard Tori's scream and grew concerned.

"Yes, I'm OK. I'm on the phone," she lied.

"All right. Well, your wine is waiting on you, but take your time."

"I'll be out shortly," Tori said and laughed inwardly. She was almost caught with her pants down.

Tori finished getting dressed, cleaned up after herself, and left the bathroom a brand-new woman.

Chapter Fifteen

After Tori got acquainted with Jace's parents, the entire family dispersed. The women went into the family room, and the men went to the backyard to play basketball. She couldn't help but relieve herself of all the tension that controlled her mood. Yes, she was shy, but this was Jace's family. After so many years of being alone, she never thought a man would invite her to meet his family. It seemed as soon as she had sex, her pheromones were off the charts, and every nigga wanted a taste. Well, maybe not *every* man. But when it came to getting what she wanted as far as sex, Tori wasn't afraid to approach the situation.

She sat in the family room with the rest of the women, slowly sipping her cheap Moscato. Instantly, she felt the effects of the 10 percent alcohol volume. She laughed and smiled, watching as Jace's mother, grandmother, and aunts made her feel right at home. Mila introduced Tori to her mother, Maggie, but all the grandkids called her G-ma. She then introduced Tori to her three sisters. Monica was the oldest, Devita was the second to the youngest, Tia, the youngest sister, and Mila was the second to the oldest.

They all sat around having a good old roasting session, something Jace's family often did whenever they were together. Today was no exception. Tori sat quietly, though. She wasn't a part of this family, just a spectator. She sat with her phone in her hand as Jace told her to, looking back and forth between her phone and the women.

Jace: What you doing?

Mocha: Drinking this cheap Moscato as your mother called it and watching Mrs. Doss and her sisters crack on each other.

Jace: Oh shit, you let my mama talk you into getting drunk?

Mocha: Well, I couldn't say no. She insisted. I really like your family, Jace. I wish I had something close like this. Your grandmother is so quiet.

Jace: Now you have it. You're really a part of the family now. My mother and aunts about to ease your ass in on the jokes. G-ma, she just sits back and lets her daughters give her a couple of good laughs. She's a sweetheart.

Mocha: No, thank you, the jokes they're telling will make me cry. They're telling these harsh, relentless jokes. They're funny, though, and yes, your grandmother is just sitting back, chillin'.

Jace: Aye, I'll be in, in a minute. I'm about to kill JS in basketball real quick.

Mocha: lol, OK.

Things like this . . . a family, people to belong to, a mother to call on whenever she's in
need . . . made Tori want to love Jace. His family was just too perfect. They welcomed her. They
didn't make her feel disease-ridden like she wasn't
good enough to be a part of their close-knit family.

"So, how long have you been dating my nephew?
I heard all the girls on campus love them some
Jace. How did you get chosen out of so many?"
Jace's auntie Tia asked. She was the youngest of
the four sisters. She and Jace were only two years
apart.

Tori looked up from her phone and placed it
face down on the table. Her eyebrows raised in
confusion. She didn't know if this was a genuine
question or if Tia was being facetious. Now, it was
interrogation time.

"Jace and I have been dating maybe a couple of
months, but we've known each other since grade
school," Tori said. "I hadn't seen him since eighth
grade, and suddenly, we saw each other our last
year of college. Imagine that." She sipped the
last drop of her wine.

After that one-on-one session in the bathroom
and this cheap-ass wine, Tori was prepared for
whatever.

"I can tell my grandson really likes you. What's
your name, baby?" G-ma said.

"It's Tori," she said with a fake smile.

"You gotta excuse my mother. Jace told us your name more than a thousand times. She's just very forgetful," Mila said.

"It's fine," Tori replied.

"I remember you, Tori," Tia said. "You were really quiet in school. You were in the sixth grade when I graduated from Hollenbeck. I always envied your pretty chocolate skin."

Tori cracked a smile. She couldn't picture anyone being envious of her.

"I've grown into my looks, but back then . . . bay-be, I felt like my skin color was a curse."

"Whhhaaattt? No, baby girl. You are so pretty, and I love how tall you are. You put me in the mind of Naomi Campbell," Monica said as she winked her eye. "Nephew knows he has good taste in women. He's never brought any around, but I've seen him in pictures with plenty of hot mamas. White ones, brown ones, chocolate ones, Puerto Rican ones, exotic ones, tall ones, short ones, skinny ones, thick ones." Monica painted the picture. "Nephew must be slapping hoes with the dick."

Tori didn't respond. She just raised her glass, signaling she needed more wine.

"OK, Monica, she gets the damn picture," Mila said. "You making my son seem like a damn playboy, and he's far from that."

"Don't start no mess, Monica. My grandson is an angel. He can't help that all the women want him. They ain't shit to him, baby. Just a bunch of tramps and whores," G-ma said.

"Well, shit—Excuse my language, Ma, but Jace sure thinks there's something beautiful about you, Tori. You're the first girl we've ever met," Devita said. "So, pay Monica's messy ass no mind."

Tori still had her glass up in midair, waiting for her beverage to be refreshed.

"Girl, get your own damn wine. You're family now. And instead of that cheap shit, crack open that $200 bottle of Cabernet Sauvignon. It's not sweet, but it sure has a kick to it," Mila said.

Tori stood and did as she was told. She grabbed the bottle of wine, popped out the cork, and watched as smoke filtered from inside the bottle. After pouring herself a glass, she sat back in the hot seat.

"Take a sip and tell me what you think," Mila said.

Tori first smelled the wine, taking in the aromas of dark berries and a hint of oak spice. Her eyes involuntarily closed, and she knew she would enjoy it. She twirled the wine around in her glass as she anticipated the taste. Then she put the glass to her lips and took a sip. At that moment, she felt like a wine connoisseur. It felt like sex, orgasmic almost, as the wine flowed smoothly down her throat. She'd pressed mute on the entire room and indulged in this wine. There was a world of difference between a cheap bottle of Moscato and an expensive bottle of Cabernet Sauvignon that could touch one's mind, body, and soul. That was all the explanation Mila needed.

"Girl, look at her," Tia said, tapping Mila on the leg. "She looks like she's about to come at any moment now."

Tori's lip balled up into her mouth, and her eyes closed. This wine had her so horny. She never knew that a bottle of liquor could make you feel so frisky.

"Tori, are you OK?" Mila asked.

Tori opened her eyes and looked at the women that sat before her.

"Umm," Tori cleared her throat. "Yes, I'm OK. Do you know what time Jace will be finished with basketball?" she asked.

"No, girl. But it looked like that wine took you into another world. You sure you good?" Tia said.

"Yeah, I'm great."

"OK, let's stop beating around the damn bush," Monica said. "We brought you in here to get in your head."

"Monica, shut the hell up," Mila said.

"For real, y'all up in here pretending and stuff."

Tia and Devita sat back and watched as Monica took off. She was the oldest, and she always had to be so damn bossy. Jace was her nephew and like a son to her. Monica had no kids of her own, so she would pretend to be Mila for the moment and get all in Tori's ass.

"What is it y'all want to know?"

"Me, personally, I don't want to know anything. My nephew is happy, and that's all that matters to me," Tia said honestly.

"Fuck all that. So, I'm sure you know he just signed a major record deal, right?" Monica said, and Tori nodded. "Cool. So is that the *only* reason you're with him?"

"I just found out today, actually, just now when we got here, that he signed a recording contract. Jace pursued me, and I've liked him since we were in kindergarten."

"So, you fucked hi—" Monica said but was quickly cut off by G-ma.

"Now, what the hell did I tell you, Monica? Why would them fucking be any of your goddamn business?" G-ma asked heatedly.

"Mama," Devita exclaimed.

"If any of this was important, don't you think his mother would be asking these questions?"

"I'm just asking what Mila *wants* to ask but doesn't have the nerve to do like I do."

"Honestly, none of what you're asking is important to me. I just want you to make my son happy and not mess over his heart. He has a huge heart, baby. He will give anyone his last. So, if being with him is not what you want, please, let him go."

"I plan to make him happy," Tori said, and that was all she could say. She never was a person to express her feelings, but Jace's family made her feel welcomed. Well, everyone except Auntie Monica, that is.

"Yeah, all right. I tried, but y'all just had to jump on the defense. Little girl, if you hurt my nephew, I'ma hurt you," Monica said. "You still pretty, though."

Things in Jace's life couldn't have been any better. He was preparing to graduate college with two songs he coproduced climbing the charts, a newfound love in an old acquaintance, and $5 million sitting handsomely in his bank account. He couldn't ask for more. This love a woman, one-woman thing, was new to him, but he planned to take things one day at a time. He couldn't promise Tori a lifetime of faithfulness and happiness because he was only human. That was just impossible to promise. Especially considering the journey he was getting ready to embark on.

The weirdest part of it all was how quickly he fell for her and how easily he gave up all the "tramps and whores," as G-ma called them. From the day he asked Tori to be his, he deleted every woman from his phone and life. His block game was strong, and his curve game was even stronger. After all was said and done, Tori, and only Tori, became the woman on his arm around campus. The more things changed, the more they seemed to stay the same. Just like in middle school, Tori and even Jace heard the whispering. However, this time, these whispers were from haters.

Tori had snagged the man every woman wanted. Jace didn't mind giving the entire world something to talk about. Tori was beautiful in his eyes. She complemented him. Her mocha-colored skin and smarts elevated his toffee complexion and handsome features. She definitely was not the same Tori he remembered all those years ago. Jace was determined to become a better man. God had blessed him with so much, and he knew that he and Tori coming back together just couldn't be coincidental.

Jace stood wearing a pair of basketball shorts, was shirtless, and wore a pair of Air Jordans on his feet. Playing basketball was his second passion. If producing ever fell through, the game of hoops would be next up in line. He stood in front of Jace Sr., calculating his next move. He was already handing Jace Sr.'s ass to him. However, he was ready to shut the entire game down. He stood ready to cross him over and shake him up.

Jace dribbled the ball from side to side. He got low, swinging the basketball between his legs, ready to break both of his father's ankles. He swiftly swung around Jace Sr. and ran down the backyard court to the three-point line. Jace Sr. was too slow for him. Jace took the ball up and went for the shot. The ball flowed through the air, and every man knew this was the winning shot. It swooshed inside the rim, hitting nothing but net. All the men who occupied the court went crazy.

"Damn, unc!" and "Damn, cuz!" were the only things the men could say. Jace had schooled his father quickly, and he had no problems doing it.

"You too slow for cuz," Jace's favorite cousin Devontae said teasingly.

"This li'l nigga cheated," Jace Sr. said as he put his hands to his knees and bent over, out of breath.

"I see you still ain't fucking with me, Pops. I was gon' let you win, but that shit wouldn't have been right," Jace said while laughing.

"Come on, let's play again," Jace Sr. requested. He was still trying to catch his breath as he stood and walked over to his son, but Jace was ready to get back to Tori. He figured Mila and the girls had her long enough. He knew his Auntie Monica was probably in the house terrorizing poor ole Tori.

"Nah, man, you lost. I need to get back in here to Tori. I know her ass about drunk now, messing around with Ma."

"I was about to fuck up your whole understanding, son," Jace Sr. said. "But shit, hell yeah, go get that girl. You know how your mother and aunts are."

"Shit, she already texted me talking about Ma gave her some wine."

The two men stood in the middle of the court, conversing. They could've easily been mistaken for twins from a distance. Jace was the younger version, a replica of Jace Sr.

"Aye, Jace, we gon' ahead and head out," said a couple of Jace's cousins. They walked to the middle of the court, where the two men stood and shook hands with them both.

"A'ight. I'ma holla at you," Jace and Jace Sr. said, dismissing the men.

Everyone left except for Jace's cousin Devontae. After the game, the three men went back into the house. Jace Sr. poured them all a shot of liquor and a glass of champagne to toast to Jace's success.

"Yo, cuz, I'm proud of you. I knew this shit was gon' happen for you, man. I was just waiting on that shit. You better fuck 'em up with the hits, bro," Devontae said.

"Thank you. I already got a slew of hits just waiting to be touched by the right voices. Man, I'm about to enter this R&B shit on a whole other level; trust me."

The men clinked their champagne flutes together and threw back their shots. Then they chased the hard liquor down with the bubbly.

"You got this shit, son . . . Let me hear a sample of that hot shit," Jace Sr. said.

"A'ight. Let's take this party into the entertainment room," Jace requested.

The men agreed and grabbed the liquor bottle along with their champagne and shot glasses. They made their way through the large home and huge hallway. They walked past the dining room, and Jace's eyes met with Tori's as she lifted her orgasmic wine to her lips. He peeped his head inside the room.

"Aye, can I borrow Mocha for a minute?" he asked. Tori smiled seductively and bit down on her bottom lip.

"Boy, who the hell is Mocha?" Monica asked.

"Oh, that's just a little nickname Jacey gave me," Tori answered and stood up, glass still in hand. She walked over to Jace, and he put his arm around her shoulder. Monica's lips scrunched up, and Mila laughed.

"Cute nickname," Mila said.

"I'm about to sing a couple of my new songs in the entertainment room. Come check me out," Jace said over his shoulder as he and Tori walked from the room.

Jace took a seat in front of the piano, hot and sweaty, still in his basketball clothes. Everyone stood around and watched as he played with the keys. He played a melody and rocked from side to side, bobbing his head, catching the notes.

"Come here, Mocha." He beckoned her, and she walked over to him, taking a seat right beside him. He continued to press his fingers to the keys with his left hand, and with his right, he wrapped his arm around Tori's waist.

"I wrote this song for a female artist, and I wrote this shit with you in mind," he said.

Tori smiled shyly. She looked up at Jace's family as they all stood around, even G-ma, awaiting Jace's deep baritone. Suddenly, Tori stared at the person who caught her eye. He stared back at her seductively, and she instantly became nervous. She was so hot and bothered. Tori bit her inner cheek and put the glass of wine to her lips, diverting her attention because her vagina began to water. She thought about all the things this man could do to her while this very song played.

Romance was the last thing on Tori's mind, so Jace would never be able to get her off to this song. Instead, she pictured this sexy, chocolate, bald, Tyrese duplicate named Devontae in between her legs, lip fucking her while Jace's voice entertained them both. Just as she stated at the Mexican restaurant, Devontae looked like a nigga that was hung low and went hard in the bedroom. Devontae smiled at her and raised his glass. Jace nodded his head, thinking the gesture was toward him. *He is playing entirely too much. Jace is going to beat our ass. Shit, I think I just came. He is so freaking sexy. Damn, Devontae is for sure playing a dangerous game, but I like that dangerous shit,* Tori thought.

Rocking her entire body, Jace grabbed Tori tightly. He leaned over and kissed her jaw. She snuggled closer to him as her sights zeroed in on Monica, who stood staring a hole through Tori's entire face. Tori's heart began to beat so rapidly, remembering the threat from earlier. She didn't want to hurt Jace. She just wanted to be fucked. She wanted Jace to get her body to a climax without forcing it. And in return, she wanted to make him happy. But where did *her* happiness fit in? She figured maybe if she told Jace what bothered her sexually, he would be willing to fix it, but she didn't want to make him feel emasculated. He knew what he was doing in the bedroom. Tori was just a different type of woman.

The day she met Devontae in the restaurant, she fucked him. Well, *he* fucked *her,* and he fucked her *good*. They later exchanged phone numbers but had yet to meet up again for another sex session. How was she supposed to know the Tyrese look-alike was Jace's cousin? Tori looked down into her glass. She had a feeling she was caught red-handed.

Jace opened his mouth and began singing. The music came out effortlessly. Tori leaned up against him as he sang his heart out. His body moved and tightened every time he hit a note.

"I'll get you in the mood and give you something hood. What we got ain't for everyone to understand, so place your heart in my grasp, your life in my hands. Baby, give me what you got. I want to push my way inside your love land. Make you feel like you're the one (the one), my only one (my only one). You're my moon, and I'm your sun. Tonight, I will give you all that I got. Don't fight it. Yeah, baby, give me that. Tonight, you gotta give me something to cherish. Just give me a little more leverage. Tonight, I will give you all that I have. For you, I'm willing to take it there. You're givin' me a taste; I've given you a taste."

Chapter Sixteen

Jace didn't lie when he said the instruments did something to him. There was something about feeling the strings of a guitar, the keys on a keyboard, and the sticks he used to beat a drum that brought all his senses to the forefront. The keys on the piano he played subtly felt good underneath his fingertips, and he couldn't wait to lay Tori across the top of it. The same way he made love to the song and penetrated Tori's ears, Jace wanted to do that exact same thing to her body.

Jace gave his family a sample of what was to come. Although his name wouldn't be in the flashing lights, everyone would know his stamp of approval was all over that shit. Jacey on the Beat was about to be in full effect, so he had to set the tempo right to give his immediate fam something to look forward to. After his small performance, he stood, and his father made a toast. The excitement of finally being able to pursue something he was passionate about had Jace in awe. This entire situation had his family ready to pick out their red-carpet outfits.

"In honor of my son, I want to say congratulations again. You got your career going and a fine-ass lady on your side. Oh, and those songs . . . Man, you gon' kill the industry with it." Jace Sr. held his glass up.

"Thank you, man. I really appreciate that. I just want to say this has always been a passion of mine. I'm just happy to have so much support. Mama, G-ma, aunties, Pops, and how could I forget my man, Devontae? Y'all been in my corner, rocking with it all since day one. My family is definitely the shit," Jace said.

The entire time the family talked, Tori and Devontae made eye contact. Tori pretended to sip on her wine while Devontae didn't cover up the fact that he wanted her. He stared at her with squinted eyes. Even after Jace mentioned his name, Devontae couldn't keep his eyes off her. Everyone was so involved in Jace's little speech that they didn't pay any attention to Devontae and Tori's interaction. The two stared intently, seemingly infatuated with each other.

"I love you, son," Mila said as she walked over and hugged Jace.

"I love you too," he said. Then he turned to Tori, breaking her from her stare down with Devontae as he hugged her. "Thank you for coming back into my life at the right time. Straight up, this here just proves we were meant to be from day one. Or cupid's li'l short ass is playing games with our lives.

I know we're still in college, but I promise you, it's only up from this point on. I want you to move out of your dorm room and in with me." Jace pulled a set of keys from his pocket. He dangled them, and Tori held out her hand. "I know we've only been together for a little while now, but I've known you my entire life, and I want to get to know you better. Us moving in together is what's best. We haven't been able to spend as much time as I would've hoped for because I'm so busy. But at the end of the night, I know who I'm coming home to."

"That's a damn shame," Monica said. Everyone looked at her, trying to understand her sudden outburst.

"Monica, shut the hell up. Congratulations, grandbaby," G-ma said. Jace walked over to G-ma and hugged her.

He wrapped his arm around her shoulder and looked at Tori as she looked at the keys to his parents' guesthouse. Jace knew that $5 million wouldn't get him far in California. He would wait until he became a more prominent producer before investing in Tori's dream home. So, he gave her the next best thing. A beautiful, egg-shell-painted, spacious, four-bedroom guesthouse with grey-specked, granite-tiled floors, floor-to-ceiling windows throughout, 2.5 bathrooms, a spacious kitchen, and a small but comfortable living room.

"Now, you know, Tori, you're his number three love because first, it's G-ma, then Mila, and after that, it's you. So, don't be upset with your position," Tia said.

"That's not true, baby. You're his number one. I'm happy for you two. Make my baby boy happy," Mila said.

The family all drank a glass of champagne. Jace still stood with his arm around his favorite lady. He kissed her cheek as Mila walked over to his other side, and he wrapped his other arm around her shoulder. Tori still sat on the bench, looking straight ahead at Jace, his mother, and his grandmother. She felt all eyes on her, but she focused on her man. The wine was a lifesaver. The more she felt out of place, the more she sipped from her glass.

"We gotta get ready to leave. Ma, are you ready?" Monica asked.

"Yeah, baby. OK, grandbaby, enjoy the rest of your night." G-ma kissed Jace's cheek, and he released her.

Everyone prepared to leave. The only people staying behind for a while longer were Jace and Tori. Mila and Jace Sr. walked the rest of the family out, then headed to their bedroom.

"Good night, Jacey and Mocha," Mila yelled out. Tori and Jace both laughed and returned the good nights.

When they heard the bedroom door close, the young couple continued their evening. Jace took his rightful place beside Tori. They were finally alone, and Jace planned to take full advantage. He turned his body to Tori's and opened his legs. Pulling her body to his and between his legs, he wrapped her up in his embrace as she sluggishly leaned her head on his shoulder. Jace felt her up, grabbed her ass, and squeezed her cheeks tightly. He didn't want to talk. He wanted to play with her body the same way he'd just fondled the piano keys.

Tori was so intoxicated and horny from the effects of the wine that she didn't mind it. In the back of her mind, all she could think of were the erotic stands and positions they could create in this room full of entertaining things. On top of this piano was her number one focus. He needed to show her if he wanted her to move in with him.

Jace put his left leg on top of Tori's legs and kissed her lips. He knew his parents wouldn't bother them for the rest of the night, so he planned to take his time. They had so much to celebrate, and Jace wouldn't hold anything back. He needed her, and he wanted her. Tori was about to be his brand-new instrument. He was ready to beat her insides like a set of car speakers with the subwoofers turned up to the max.

"I'm tryin'a see something real quick," Jace said.

"Yeah? What's that?" Tori asked.

He removed his leg from Tori's and stood. He climbed from the bench, walked over to the wall, and dimmed the lights. Tori looked up as the room became a little darker.

"OK, it's one of those types of shows?" Tori asked.

Jace walked back over to her and grabbed her hand. He helped her to her feet and picked her up, gripping her thighs right underneath her ass.

"Aaaahhhh!" Tori screamed. The unexpected gesture caught her off guard. "Put me down, Jace," she said, laughing.

"Put you down?" Jace asked as he looked up at her. "Nah. If I put you down, you ain't getting back up for the rest of the night," he warned.

Tori used her hands to pull her skirt down over her exposed behind, and Jace used his strength to wrap her legs around his waist.

"Maybe that's what I want," she stated.

Jace laughed and put Tori down on top of the piano. He looked at her with a smile still on his face and reached underneath her skirt. Tori's stomach hollowed. She was instantly turned on. Jace stood between her legs as he prepped her for a night to remember. They both watched each other as he pulled off her panties. Then he reached behind himself and put Tori's underwear in his back pocket.

Tori leaned back on her hands. She was ready, and she prayed to God that this time, Jace did her body the way she needed him to. She used her hands to lift her bottom while Jace pulled her skirt up over her waist. Tori's chocolate thighs still glowed, even in the dimly lit room. It took everything in Jace not to lick her from head to toe.

He ran his hands up Tori's body and down her legs. Reaching her knees, he parted them. Then he took a seat on the bench and scooted as close as possible to her vagina. Her pussy was pretty and perfect. Jace put his lips to Tori's intimacy and pecked her softly. Her body instantly shuddered from the feel of his lips. Jace lifted her legs and placed them on his shoulders. He put his fingers to the keys, and the piano hummed. Pulling at Tori's clit with his lips, he played a soft and slow melody with the flat keys. He finessed her entire soul. He showed her just how experienced he was in all areas. Tori was laid out in front of him with her legs wide open, and he took in every bit of her essence with his nose and lips. To the melody of "Drip Demeanor" by Missy Elliot in acoustic form, Jace ate Tori's entire candy land. He made love to Tori without missing a note. He sipped on her mocha drip and used his tongue to go in and out of her fun dip. Tori moaned aloud, and Jace went harder with every moan. Tongue kissing her down, splitting her lips in two, Jace slurped on her, allowing her juices to drip from his chin.

"Jacey," Tori moaned. She gave him complete control. From the way he ate her, she knew the dick would be even better. Jace went even louder with his fingers now up against the sharp keys.

Tori rotated her hips and pushed her sex into Jace's face. His mouth salivated. He feasted on her, and as she moaned, she felt as if she were losing her mind. Suddenly, Tori thought she was hallucinating as her head fell to the side, and she saw Devontae standing in the doorway, staring at Tori and Jace, looking Tori directly in her eyes. Seeing Tori in such a pleasurable state had him slightly jealous. If only that were him between her legs, making her drip the way Jace was. Devontae watched Jace indulge deeply in Tori's middle with a scowl across his face. Devontae saw everything from afar. He stood with one hand to his manhood and his other hand wrapped around a glass of liquor. Slowly, he raised the glass to his lips.

Tori moaned, looking at him, arching her back. She bit down on her bottom lip and watched Devontae sexily. Her legs hung around Jace's shoulders, and her heels scratched slightly at his back.

"Jace," Tori said.

She winked her eye at Devontae, teasing him. Tori grabbed Jace's head, bringing him in even more. Tori lay there and put on a sexy-ass show for Devontae. Her moans were daring, and her body was tempting. At that moment, Tori wanted *both* men to have her . . . to spread her open and drill into her. Tori could tell by how Devontae stared at her that he wanted her too. So, she puckered her lips and blew a kiss at him. Deviously, Devontae smiled at Tori, running his fingers across his chin. He drank the rest of his liquor. He positively had something for her but in due time. Devontae placed two fingers to his lips, kissing them before walking away.

At this point, Jace was playing the piano so loud he didn't realize Devontae had been watching them. He stood to his feet with Tori's legs still on his shoulders and fingers glued to the piano. Then taking one hand and wiping Tori's juices from his face, he sat her up. The song's climax came to an end, and that should've brought Tori to a climax as well.

"Come on. Let me take you home," Jace said, still wiping off his face.

"Take me home? You're not going to fuck me?" Tori asked. She needed more.

Tori pulled Jace to her by his shirt. He took her panties from his back pocket and fisted them as he leaned into her.

"I'm ready to go to your dorm room and get all your shit. We have forever to fuck."

"Jace." Tori poked her lip out. "I know your dick is on hard." She reached for his belt buckle.

"You have no idea of how much self-control I have."

"Fuck your self-control, Jace. I want some dick," she whined, pulling down his pants. They hit the floor.

"Tori," Jace said. He stepped back a little, almost tripping over the bench. Then he pulled his pants back up and grabbed Tori's hand, attempting to help her down from the piano.

"Let me go." She snatched away. She'd caught an attitude. She just knew Jace was about to tear up her entire body after the great head he'd just given her.

Jace did what he was told. He released Tori's hand, handed her panties to her, and she threw them back at him.

"What's up, Tori?"

"You not fucking me is what's up." Tori climbed down from the piano and walked toward him.

"So, you didn't hear shit I just told you?" he asked and grabbed her around her waist.

"Yes, I heard you, Jace. How could you just do that to me, though?" Tori said.

"I didn't do shit but offer you me. We can fuck every single day if that's what you want. We don't even have to take things any further."

"So, you're saying you don't want to be with me because I asked you to fuck me?"

"Hell naw, I'm not saying that. I'm just leaving the decision up to you." He grabbed her face.

Tori looked at him. Her expression was serious.

"Jace, don't make me beg," Tori said. "Just a little bit, Jace. That's all I want."

"I'm tryin'a move you in my crib, and all you want to talk about is fucking," he said. "A'ight, I got you. . . . I never wanted to treat you like one of my little hoes, but if that's what you want, I got you."

He aggressively grabbed Tori around her neck and pushed her to the wall. Then he looked at her in her eyes as she stared at him.

"You want me to fuck you?" he asked as he turned her toward the wall. He pulled his pants down. "I *don't* want to fuck you, Tori."

Tori was silent the entire time Jace aggressively moved her body. She was excited with his take-charge demeanor, and she couldn't wait until he got his pants down completely. Tori put her hands up against the wall and opened her legs wide.

Jace grabbed her hair as he bent her over. He rubbed his erect manhood up against Tori's wetness before forcefully entering her. Jace grunted as he pushed himself all the way in.

"Oh my God, Jace," Tori said, tears instantly dripping down her face. The force Jace used while he moved in and out of her had her stomach in knots. The shit was painful, and although Tori would never admit it, what she wanted so badly, she really couldn't handle.

"Is *this* what you wanted?" Jace held her around her stomach, making sure she had nowhere to run. "You wanted *this?*" He pumped furiously. His entire face was scrunched up. Anger took over, and his mood became very hostile.

"Yes, I wanted this," Tori managed to cry out. "You're hurting me, Jace." Her eyes rolled back, and her head leaned down.

Jace violently bounced Tori back and forth on his pole. He attacked her insides, killing it without too much regret because this was what she wanted. The heavy breathing that came from Tori had Jace in a trance of its own. This was his element, but this wasn't something he wanted to give Tori. He wanted to be a soft nigga for her, an R&B type of nigga. He wanted to be an all-around good guy in her eyes. But Tori was a naughty girl, and this type of intimacy is what her body yearned for.

Jace kept one arm wrapped around Tori's stomach to keep her steady, and his other hand tamed her back. He pushed her all the way down. Fuck an arch. He needed to see if she could bend. He needed to know how flexible she was. Tori was a freak, and he wanted to break her in two, making her understand exactly what she asked for. His feelings for her were shoved to the back of his mind as he pushed deep inside of her and pulled back aggressively.

"Aaahhh, Jace . . . stop." Tori hit her hand to the wall, tapping out, but nah, Jace wasn't finished with her. He pulled her up by the back of her neck and pushed her body up against the wall. Placing one hand back around her neck, Tori held on to his hand. Then Jace grabbed her other hand and intertwined his fingers with hers, pressing their hands against the wall. He kissed her cheek and felt Tori's tears on his lips. Finally, he smirked.

"Look at you. You can't even handle this shit," Jace said, whispering into her ear as she breathed heavily. He pulled out of her and turned her around. Jace wiped the tears from Tori's face and picked her up.

She wrapped her legs and arms around him like a big baby, ready to cry on daddy's shoulder about the boy who had been mean to her. He pinned her up against the wall and took his time penetrating her. This time, his movements were slower. He kissed her passionately, apologizing for how he'd just punished her.

"I'm sorry. I don't want to make you cry," he said as he slowly made love to Tori, trying to soothe the spot he'd just bruised.

Tori enjoyed pain. Him fucking her was what she asked for. Her tears came from pleasurable pain. She didn't want to be treated like a ho, but if she had to play that role to get fucked, she was willing. Of course, she didn't expect him to go so hard. But with Jace, there was no in-between. He either gave you his soft side or his hard-core side. The rumors Aja claimed to have heard about Jace were true, and the harsh side is what had all the women sprung.

"I won't do that shit to you again. I promise."

Tori lay her head on Jace's shoulder, enjoying the ride. She'd just realized that everything he gave her was something she really couldn't handle. She couldn't handle Jace treating her like one of his hoes. She needed the part of Jace that she so comfortably took advantage of.

Tori and Jace's night wasn't perfect, but it wasn't something to break up over. She knew that Jace wouldn't understand her as a woman, so she would never try to explain. For whatever reason, all she knew was that love was equivalent to pain, just as feelings were to being in control. Tori had given up all control awhile back when she decided to be in a relationship with him. It didn't matter how she felt. She knew she didn't want to grow old alone, and she felt it in her heart that they didn't reconnect for nothing. There was a reason behind it. There's a reason for everything in life, and Tori knew that to be a fact.

After a night of getting fucked by Jace, she re- alized that was not something she wanted from him. She felt like one of his whores or sluts when all Jace really wanted to show her was how to be his queen. However, Tori didn't know how to be a queen. Ever since being broken in sexually, all Tori thought about was dick. Jace's dick, Devontae's dick, Davis's dick, her purple vibrator . . . dick, dick, dick. Thoughts of penises occupied her mind. It had only been a couple of months since she'd lost her virginity, and already, she'd given herself away to so many forbidden men.

Tori sat on the bench with her elbow leaned against her leg, and her fist pushed into her jaw. She stared at the wall in a daze about how things in her life had changed so quickly. She thought about that girl who used to be all about her schoolwork. The girl whose mind stayed on mathematics and pursuing the subject as a profession. Nowadays, she couldn't wait to complete school, collect her money, and live lovely off the Givens's dime. She now had a man in her corner who was willing to take care of her and give her dick whenever she wanted it. She might have to take that ho title every so often, but she was willing.

Her phone chimed. She looked down at it, and seeing an email from Professor Davis on her screen, she was curious to know what he wanted.

Professor Davis: Good evening. How has my favorite student been?

Tori: Professor Davis . . . I'm great. How are you?

Professor Davis: I'm good. I saw that you were online, so I thought I would shoot you a quick message.

Tori: I was not online, but nice try . . . That was a cute way to start up a conversation. How may I help you?

Professor Davis: Lol, you caught me. Can I call you?

Tori: No, we're fine emailing each other.

Professor Davis: Do you have a man? And have you thought about that date?

Tori: With all due respect, Professor, I don't think that is any of your business, and as we discussed before, going out on a date is out of the question.

Professor Davis: Well, can I at least come see you?

Tori didn't respond. She just shook her head and closed her email.

"You ready to go?" Jace asked as he walked into the room. Tori jumped and looked up at him with her hand to her chest.

"You scared the shit outta me. I'm ready." She stood and walked over to him. He grabbed her hand, and they walked through the house, bypassing every room as they made their way toward the kitchen.

"My mouth is dry as hell," Jace said. He led Tori into the kitchen, and she jumped again when she saw Devontae sitting at the kitchen island, drinking a glass of dark liquor.

"Damn, shorty almost jumped outta her skin," Devontae said. He shook hands with Jace as Jace made his way to the refrigerator. He opened it and took out two bottles of Sprite. With his back still turned, he spoke.

"Did I introduce you to—"

"Tori. Yeah, you said her name in that li'l speech you made. What's up, beautiful?" Devontae said, cutting off Jace.

"Hey," Tori responded. She bit her inner cheek and squinted her eyes at Devontae.

"What's up, baby?" she mouthed.

"Aye, cuz, let me holla at you for a minute," Devontae said to Jace. "Don't worry, Tori, I won't keep your man for too long." He smiled.

"A'ight . . ."

Jace closed the fridge and walked back to Tori.

"Are you ready?" he asked.

"Yes," Tori responded. She placed her hand inside Jace's as Devontae stood from his seat and smirked. The trio made their way from the house to Jace's car. He held Tori's door open for her, making sure she was safely tucked inside. Then he closed Tori's door and knelt to the window.

"I won't be long. Give me about five minutes," he said and stood. He and Devontae walked to the trunk of the car in silence. Jace leaned back and crossed his arms across his chest. "What's going on?" he asked.

"Shit, man, I been chillin'. Now I see why you been MIA. She is a good look, cuz."

"Nah, she ain't had me missing. I been working on a lot of shit with my music, tryin'a get the ball rolling with this record label, meeting up with lawyers, and shit. Mocha's ass just been a real fucking breath of fresh air," he said.

Devontae smirked and nodded his head in understanding. The first day he met Tori, she was a breath of fresh air to him too. Especially after she expressed how much of a freak she was. Devontae had to take her up on that offer, but she never told him she had a man. In all honesty, even if she did tell him she was involved with someone else, he would've still smashed. Tori was a temptation, and Devontae would never turn down a good time. However, that would've been one party he would've said no to if he'd known she belonged to Jace, especially if she meant something to him.

"So, she's like the rest of 'em?" Devontae asked, ready to spill all the beans.

"Nah, cuz. I got a big-ass soft spot in my heart for shorty. She's most definitely different."

"Cool. That's what's up. Whatever happened with the other *different* one?" Devontae asked. Right away, Jace knew who he was talking about.

"Who? Taja's crazy ass? I had to let that shit go, fam. I ain't seen her in a while. Hopefully, everything's cool with her," Jace said.

"Shit, I think I saw her a couple of weeks ago at El Compadre, but I'm not sure. Shorty looked like her but more mature."

"Shit, you know what? Somebody been blowing my phone up for the past couple of days, leaving me all types of voice messages and shit. Now that you mention her, it all makes sense, but I ain't worried about her ass. What's been going on with you?"

"Nothing, man. Just watch out because shorty in the car look just like that other chick. Shit could be a setup."

"Nah, me and Tori go way back. I've been knowing her my whole life," Jace said.

"A'ight, my boy," Devontae said, and the men shook hands. "Be careful with this one, bro."

While the men stood outside talking, Tori decided to give her friend Amelie a call. She sat with the phone up to her ear. The phone rang once, and Amelie quickly answered.

"Hey, boo," Amelie said excitedly.

"What'cha doing?" Tori asked in a playful tone.

"Girl, nothing. Sitting here talking to my new boo since your ass has been missing."

"Hey, Tori," Aja yelled out.

"Is that Aja?" Tori asked. "Why are you two together?"

"It's a long story, but what's going on?"

"Mmm . . . nothing. I just came from meeting my man Jace's family."

"His family?" Aja asked. "Mmm . . . I thought he didn't have any close relatives in Cali." She frowned.

"How would you know anything about Jace and his family?" Tori asked. She was curious to know. The way Aja sounded through the phone, one would've thought she and Jace had a personal relationship.

"Oh, girl, you know he's like an open book. He's talked to a couple of people I know."

"Mmmm, I suppose," Tori said. "But yeah, he is such a sweetheart, and his family is everything. I swear, how close he and his family are—" Tori said, but Amelie cut her off.

"Oh, so, this is a for real, for real relationship. He took you to meet his family and shit," Amelie said. Tori heard Amelie's voice louder and clearer now, so she knew the call was no longer on speakerphone.

"Yes, I met his parents, grandmother, aunts, uncles, and cousins. Their entire family is so close.

That's a family I want to marry and birth children into," Tori said.

"Wait, boo. Why are we talking about kids and marriage right now? Are we pregnant? Or did he propose?"

"What?" Aja blurted out, only hearing Amelie's side of the conversation.

"No, no, none of that. I'm just saying. I love his family, and they welcomed me with opened arms." Tori paused and looked out the rearview mirror, making sure the coast was still clear. "But this is why I *really* called you." She paused again for dramatic effect. "Are you ready?"

"Tori, stop playing and *tell* me," Amelie ordered.

"Why the fuck that nigga, the Tyrese look-alike from the restaurant, is his cousin?"

"Whhhaaattt?" Amelie said. "Girl . . . Are you serious?"

"What? What happened?" Aja asked. Tori heard Amelie shushing Aja through the phone. Tori frowned in confusion but continued the conversation.

"Yes, I'm dead serious. They're standing outside the car talking right now. I can't believe this shit, but that's not it."

"Damn, there's more?" Amelie asked. "This is some juicy gossip. I just wish you weren't in the middle of it."

"The Tyrese look-alike name is Devontae, and this crazy-ass boy stood in the doorway watching while Jace and I had sex. Amelie, I hope he doesn't tell Jace about us. Girl, from the way Jace just did me tonight, I think I'm in fucking love," Tori said.

"Well, you better break up that little conversation." Amelie laughed. "He's probably telling on your ass right now."

"I don't know, Amelie. I think he would've said something when he first saw me if he was going to tell. I am so scared right now."

"Well, if I were you, I wouldn't stick around to find out. You better blow that horn or something, boo," Amelie said.

"Girl, I'm about to summon his ass to the car now." Tori laughed. "Also, make sure your ass is at my graduation. I guess, if you want to, you can bring Aja. Since I haven't seen either of you ladies in a couple of weeks, I'ma need for us to catch up."

"OK, boo, you know I'ma be there with bells on. Take care of that little situation, and we'll talk later."

The ladies ended their call just in time. As soon as Tori set her phone down, she saw Jace and Devontae shake hands. Then Jace walked around to the driver's side and got in while Devontae walked to his car. Jace started the ignition, kissed Tori's cheek, leaned his seat back, and drove off.

Chapter Seventeen

One week later . . .

Tori stood with her back up against the front door, watching both of her men move her boxes into the house. It seemed like she had been standing in the same position for at least thirty minutes. Both guys were in a pair of basketball shorts and bare-chested, so, of course, she was in heaven. Her eyes had a mind of their own as they gawked at both Jace and Devontae. Her arms were across her chest, and a slight smirk graced her lips as she stood there staring in admiration. As Jace attempted to walk past her, she decided to make Devontae a little jealous. Placing her hand on Jace's cheek, she pulled him to her and kissed his lips.

"Thank you, babe," she said.

"You know I got you, Mocha."

Jace stepped inside and walked past her as Devontae stepped through the threshold behind him. Tori looked at him with seductive eyes while biting down on the corner of her bottom lip. She wanted him. Hell, she wanted him *and* Jace at the same damn time. She looked to her left to make sure Jace was no longer in sight, and as Devontae walked past her, she ran her hand down his print. He laughed, and so did she. She was playing with fire.

"Thank you, cousin," Tori said, winking.

"No problem, love."

Tori watched Devontae as he walked away. Involuntarily, she licked her lips. At this point, she was *definitely* getting beside herself. Then sighing heavily, she heard Jace yell that they were done bringing everything in. She closed the front door and walked toward the back of the house where Jace and Devontae were standing in the kitchen, talking.

Look at both of my men playing nice; she smiled, feeling like a proud mama.

"Thank you for coming through for me. I appreciate it."

The men shook hands as Devontae playfully smacked his lips.

"Come on, man. You know you don't have to thank me."

"This shit was short notice, and you came through like I knew you would. So, I do have to thank you."

"Nigga, I ain't do this for you."

"Yeah, a'ight, nigga."

Tori smiled inwardly at Devontae's remark, and although Jace thought he was playing, she knew he wasn't.

"I did this for my new favorite cousin." He smiled at Tori and walked over to her. He hugged her as she hugged him back, smiling, as Devontae discreetly ran his hand across her ass.

"That's fucked up, bro. We been in this shit too long for you to be switching up on me like that." They all laughed as Devontae released Tori. The two men said their goodbyes, then Devontae left. Now, Jace and Tori were finally alone.

"Come here," Jace said.

She walked over to him, and he took her into his arms. He looked into her eyes, and she instantly shied away. Putting her face into his chest, she kissed him softly. The way he looked at her made her feel meek, as if he thought or knew something. She couldn't take him looking at her that way.

Jace put his all into every single thing he was passionate about, including a relationship with Tori. Although things between the two began to move so rapidly, he didn't plan to slow anything down. He offered her the keys to his crib, and she accepted. Jace knew he wanted a wife, children . . . the whole nine. He was a man full of ambition and determination. He knew Tori wouldn't turn him down. Them being together was something that was written in the book of Jace Doss and Tori Givens long before either of the two existed.

Jace knew within the next five years, his career would be excelling over and beyond the sky's limits. What would life be without someone to share his success with? Before, when he thought of a five-year plan, it didn't include Tori. However, it did include a lifetime full of happiness. Jace saw so much happiness with Tori. Fulfillment was written all over her. Her being his was something he wasn't willing to sacrifice. Tori was the one, and Jace knew it. He knew she wasn't with him for what he could provide. She was graduating college with a degree in mathematics. She had everything a man could ask for, and that was her own . . . her own mind, her own desires, and her own future. Tori had her head on straight, and she knew where her life was headed. That shit made Jace even more attracted and infatuated with her.

Her determination was so fucking sexy in every way, and Jace made sure to show her how much he appreciated her. Now, he planned to give her more than she could ever desire. Jace loved the fact that Tori had all these things going on for herself, but no wife of his was going to lift a finger and work.

So, her degree would just have to be something to fall back on if needed. A week earlier, Jace knew for sure that Tori was where he wanted her to be, especially after seeing how his family accepted her with open arms. Tori always seemed to be very shy, but she clicked with his family for some reason. So, with the stamp of approval from Mila and G-ma, Jace was ready to give Tori his all.

The only thing that held him back from becoming wholly invested was that he hadn't met the Givens, and he was still confused about why. So today, he decided to get a little understanding. He'd just moved Tori into his space, his personal space. Everything that once belonged to only him was now theirs. So now, it was time to meet his wifey's side of the family.

Today, he wasn't going to beat around the bush. He would be straightforward because he knew, given the opportunity, Tori would find a reason why now *wasn't* the right time. Tori was a very hard person to read. She kept so many secrets. Everything about her was like a mystery.

"So, when will we let your family know you moved out of the dorm?" he asked her. She slowly approached him as he set the last box of her things on the floor. Their home was something he thought Tori would be excited to let the entire world know about. Yes, it was a part of Jace's family home, but it was still theirs.

"Jacey . . . Can I at least get moved all the way in first?" She walked up to him as he leaned against the wall and put her arm around his waist. "I mean, I'm grown. They don't need to know everything I'm doing. Plus, you're going to see them tomorrow at the graduation. We can tell them then."

Jace leaned down and kissed Tori on the top of her head. He wanted to know why this was a secret. Tori was a grown-ass woman, but she was afraid to tell her peoples she'd found love and a new home.

"A'ight, cool. I can't wait to meet them. I've been trying to figure out why you never really talk about them."

"Honestly, I don't really have anything positive to say about them. They birthed me, gave me nourishment for about the first five years of my life, and after that, I was on my own. They have a business, so they neglected me to run it. I raised myself," Tori said honestly. "I wish you didn't want to meet them. However, I *will* put you out of your fake misery and introduce you."

"Damn, that's sad. If it bothers you that I want to meet them, I don't have to."

"Yeah, you do need to meet them. I need you to understand why I am the person I am. I know everything about me is so fucked up, Jace. All I ever wanted to do was make them happy. This school shit used to be a passion until I felt forced to do it. There's so much you don't know, but I will give you the Givens," she said seriously.

"You're not a fucked-up person. I understand more than you think. I appreciate and feel so honored that you're allowing me to meet your family. Hopefully, they will accept me being in your life," Jace said, and Tori smirked.

"They don't even accept me," she murmured quietly.

"Look." Jace grabbed Tori's face. She looked up at him, and he saw the hurt in her eyes.

"When we have our babies, we will give them all the attention they can handle," he promised.

Tori put on a half smile and leaned her head up against his chest.

"Yeah, I want my family to be so close, Jace, like you and your family. When I give birth to my babies, I will be all up in their business. My kids are going to love me."

"Yeah, baby, they are. Thank you for sharing this. I know it was hard for you to do, but I'm sure you feel better after getting all that shit out," he said.

"Yeah, I feel a little more confident."

"That's good to hear, but look, I have to get ready to meet up with Big Percy and a new artist he wants me to work with."

"Woman or man?" Tori asked. She pulled away from his chest and looked into his eyes.

"It's a female artist," he answered honestly.

"Well, Mr. Doss, please keep this work arrangement strictly business," Tori said, remembering the man Jace used to be and thinking about her own cheating ways.

"I'm not worried about no other woman. Trust me, Mocha, business will always come before pleasure," he promised.

"You know I love it when you call me Mocha. That's one thing my parents blessed me with," Tori said, and they both laughed. She recited the words he had so cornily used on her in the past.

"Funny." Jace stood, wrapping Tori up in his embrace from behind. The two walked to their bedroom, and it felt so good to belong finally. Jace gave Tori a peck on her cheek, and then he quickly changed into something more appropriate for a business meeting. Tori lay across the bed with her cell phone in her hand, looking back and forth between her device and Jace as he moved around the room, getting his gear together.

"How long will you be?" she asked. Jace knew this would be an all-day meeting, and although he hated to leave Tori alone on their first night living together, he had to. He hugged her one last time.

"I'll be back as soon as possible." Although "as soon as possible" wasn't a good enough answer for Tori, she let it be. What could she do? She certainly didn't want to come in between Jace and his money.

An hour later, Jace was pulling up to Big Percy's office. He parked his car and walked toward the building, thinking about the weird-ass calls he'd been receiving for some time now. Jace had yet to listen to any of the voice messages because they weren't important to him. Plus, the shit kept slipping his mind. With so much swarming around his brain, like graduation, Tori, and the music he had up his sleeve for a female artist, Jace had no time for foolishness, so that bullshit would have to wait its turn. He walked in and signed his name on the log at the front desk.

"What's up, beautiful?" Jace said. He low-key flirted with the pretty, exotic-looking receptionist, making her smile from ear to ear, showing off every single tooth in her mouth, including the beautiful gap separating her two front teeth. Jace turned on the charm, making sure he still had the game he subtly tucked away. "Is Big Percy available?" he asked.

"Yes, he is. He's been waiting for you to arrive, Jace," the receptionist said, grinning hard as hell.

"Yeah? Damn, I like the way you just said my name. Say that shit again." Jace leaned over the desk, now face-to-face with little miss receptionist.

"I'll say your name all night long if you let me." She grabbed his hand and opened it.

"Call me sometime." She began writing her number on his palm.

"Man, what the hell you out here doing to my daughter?" Big Percy said. He'd been watching

Jace and his daughter's entire interaction from a monitor mounted on his office wall.

Jace closed his hand and stood.

"This your daughter?" Jace asked. "I didn't mean no disrespect, Big Percy," he said, walking over to greet the man he'd come to see. Their hands locked, and a firm handshake followed.

"Yeah, that's my baby girl over there," Percy said. "I don't play games over that one, so keep this shit business, or shit will become personal."

Jace smirked as his eyes squinted. "Yo, I didn't mean no disrespect. I understand that's your baby girl, and I can keep shit professional. No need for the threats," he said.

He wasn't a soft-ass nigga, but he knew when to stay in his lane. Nothing about Percy scared him. Jace grew up with a family of goons, and with one phone call, the entire office of 290 record label would be flooded with shooters. However, Jace wasn't trying to go down that route over pussy that didn't belong to him.

"As long as we have an understanding," Percy said.

"Shit is clear," Jace responded, standing tall and not backing down. The men broke their embrace, and Big Percy led Jace to his office.

"This is shorty you're going to be working with. Destiny, this is the infamous Jacey on the Beat."

Destiny stood from her seat, and Jace took a quick glimpse of her entire body.

If he had to guess, Destiny was about five-six, and her body looked like the perfect sculpture. Her measurements had to be 36-24-36. Her caramel complexion was cute, but her green eyes were very sexy. Destiny had the perfect button nose and medium-sized lips. Jace couldn't help but stare. She was so fucking attractive and intriguing. If it were pussy Jace was chasing, Destiny would've been a quick and easy fuck. However, a bag to secure seemed more captivating.

"What's up, Destiny?" Jace said in a mellow tone. He flashed his sexy grin, and she returned the gesture.

Destiny reached her hand out for a handshake and licked her pretty lips. Jace grabbed her hand and shook it while he looked into her eyes, almost instantly becoming hypnotized. The old Jace was starting to rear his ugly head.

"How are you, Jace? I'm so excited to work with you. Percy has told me so many great things about you," Destiny said excitedly.

"Yeah?" Jace asked, still holding her hand.

"Yes," she responded.

"I knew this shit was going to work. I see the sparks flying between y'all already. I'ma fucking genius. Chemistry is everything. I know y'all vibe is going to be dope, and I can't wait to hear the shit y'all come up with," Big Percy said, patting himself on the back. "Shall we get started?" he asked. He was ready to see what Jace could do to reinvent Destiny's music career.

"Hell yeah, I got some shit for you to sing right now. This song will show me the type of artist I'm working with. Destiny, do you have an email? I need to send you the lyrics," Jace said.

Destiny quickly read her email address off to him, excited about whatever he was getting ready to drop on her. Jace was a dope producer. She heard his two songs on the radio, and whatever that shit was he sprinkled on those songs, she wanted the same shit sprinkled on her music. Jace pulled the lyrics up in his phone and sent them to her.

"I want you to go over these words and then tell me what you think," he said.

"OK, but you do know I can write a little bit too?" Destiny said.

The trio walked from Big Percy's office to the studio.

"Cool. We can bounce a couple of ideas off each other later, but look over those lyrics for now," Jace ordered.

Destiny smiled. Jace bossed up on her so fast. His craft was something he couldn't help but be serious about, and if his name was going to be associated with something, it had to be hot.

Walking into the studio, Jace quickly took a seat in front of the massive recording and monitoring equipment. He began connecting his cell phone to the studio's computer. He made himself comfortable while Big Percy excused himself. The speakers boomed, and the sound of Jace's brand-new beat he'd created days earlier played loud, but the melody was so soft. He nodded his head as the guitars, piano, and bass began to play.

He felt right at home. This was his oasis, and he was ready to create a masterpiece. Destiny certainly had the sex appeal to attract an audience. Now, it was time to see if she had the voice. She took a seat on the chair next to Jace and listened to the vibe of the beat. The two bobbed their heads to the slow tempo as Jace began to sing the lyrics, giving Destiny the flow of how the song should be sung.

"You get me in the mood and give me something hood . . ." Jace paused for a second, allowing the 808 to boom a little. *"You can be a good boy, but tonight, I need a hood boy with a grown-man appeal. What we got ain't for everyone to understand, so I place my heart in your grasp, my life in your hands."* He took another breath in between the lyrics. *"Baby, give me what you got when you push your way inside my love land. Make me feel like I'm the one (the one), your only one (your only one.) You're my moon, and I'm your sun."*

Destiny listened intently as she smiled at him. To Jace, that was a clear indication she was feeling his song. He cut the instrumental and turned to her.

"What you think?"

"Oh my God, Jace! I'm ready. Just put me in the booth and let me bring this entire song to life," she urged, screaming excitedly as she hugged him. "I'm sorry, but I am *so* excited. You're *not* going to be disappointed."

"Is that right?" Jace smiled. "Tell me something, Destiny. What part of this song do you like the most?"

"I like the entire song, especially since it's something I can relate to. Recently, I went through a breakup with a guy I gave my all to. At the time, I didn't give a fuck if he was only giving me part of him. He was a hood nigga, but at the same time, his sex and love felt so . . . What's the word I'm looking for?" Destiny said as she stared Jace in his eyes.

"I don't know," he responded.

"When he and I were alone, everything between us just felt so special. In my presence, he was a good boy, but in the streets, he was a hood boy. I love that gangsta shit. But you, Jace, you are so different. You're very intriguing," she said.

She moved closer to him, biting down on the side of her lip, anticipating a reaction from him.

He wanted to give Destiny exactly what she was looking for, but in the back of his mind is where Tori lay. Jace wiped at his face and scooted his chair back.

"A'ight. Get in the booth. Let me see what you got," Jace said, rubbing his hands together. He played off the entire awkward moment. This was only the beginning of a story of music and notes. Jace planned to turn Destiny's singing career into something beautiful. "All that emotion and shit you had for dude, put that into this song."

"OK." Destiny stood.

As promised, she sang Jace's song with all of her, bringing each and every lyric to life.

Chapter Eighteen

Tori decided to spend her entire day unpacking, catching up on old Love & Hip Hop episodes, cleaning, cooking, and making herself right at home. Jace had left her alone with nothing to do, so she had to find little simple things to occupy her time. First, she settled on Jace's grey suede sectional couch in a pair of baggy grey joggers and an oversized white T-shirt. She slid her feet into a pair of slippers and pinned her hair to the back of her head in a bun. With a tub of vanilla bean ice cream, Tori wrapped herself up with a beige fur throw and grabbed the TV remote.

She quickly made her way to VH1 on-demand and settled with *Love & Hip Hop: Atlanta,* season 5, episode 1. Now, it was time to binge-watch. She sat back and watched as the entire cast made an ass of themselves. This was something Tori and Amelie did together in the past. They would wait until the entire season was over before they cuddled up close together and binge-watched a whole Saturday. But today was a new day, and

Tori was living a different life with a man, her man. Her five-year plan was beginning to come together perfectly. It would've been against one of those cheating rules to snuggle up with her best friend at this moment and watch television.

Tori sat watching and predicting the entire episode. This show always gave her some good laughs, especially that damn Yung Joc. It wasn't long until this fine-ass man with long pigtails stepped onto the screen. Scrapp DeLeon was his name, and Tori said his name aloud.

"Damn, Scrapp, who is that?" Tori said. She picked up her phone and called Amelie. Tori let it ring out until the voicemail picked up. "Amelie, call me back, girl. I'm watching the new season of *Love & Hip Hop,* and I need to know who this Scrapp DeLeon person is. Not little Scrappy, but Scrapp DeLeon. Call me back ASAP," Tori said and hung up.

She put the TV on pause and decided to do a little unpacking. Tori knew she couldn't finish this episode without some understanding. Amelie needed to call her back as soon as possible. She climbed from the couch and put down her empty ice cream tub. Then she walked into her bedroom and began her long journey of unpacking. She went through box after box, pulling out clothes, shoes, and accessories. She didn't know she had so much shit stored away.

"What the hell are these?" Tori said, holding up some K-Swiss tennis shoes. She laughed to herself, remembering her old-fashioned sense, or lack thereof. "I probably thought I was the shit in these." Tori humored herself. She tossed the shoes to the side and dug deeper into the box. She smirked and pulled her hand from inside. When Tori found her old pair of glasses, she cleaned the dust from them and put them to her eyes. The old days came to her rapidly, and the memories were things she wished she could forget.

Blackie, black, black. Tori heard the names, and she envisioned those days. They were so vivid in her mind. She quickly took off the glasses and broke them in half. Tori screamed as her strength did so much damage to her old glasses. Although she'd never broke mentally from her past, she couldn't say the same things about her old bifocals. Tori threw all her old bullshit to the side and reached back into the box.

"Man, you've gotten me through some very, very tough times." She pulled out her very first porno. It was in VHS form, so she had no way to watch it. She dusted the tape off and read the title. "*Once Upon a Valentine: Mr. Chocolate Edition,*" Tori said. "Mr. Chocolate got the job done *every* time." Putting the tape aside, she continued digging.

She soon grew bored, but everything in these boxes was something she hadn't seen since she had put it into storage four years ago. When she left her parents' home, she had no plans ever to return. Instead, Tori planned to collect her dough after college and keep it moving. Finally, the final box came into view, and Tori smiled. She was almost at the finish line. Tori flipped the flap to an old, torn, brown box and stared at an old picture album.

"I'ma need a bottle of Mila's special wine to look at this shit," she said and pushed it aside.

Tori just wasn't ready to go down an old, depressing memory lane. Nothing in this album was anything good, and memories from back in her childhood felt like a setup for failure. She decided now was a good time to go ahead and get something to cook. Tori gathered her purse and car keys. She walked from the guesthouse to her car and took the short drive to the local supermarket.

She took her time looking through each aisle for the perfect meal to cook her man. Tonight was something special. Jace had given her more than enough, and now it was her turn to offer him something. It wasn't much, only a meal. But from what Tori heard, the way to a man's entire heart and soul was through delectable food. She wanted to give Jace a piece of her South African heritage, so she planned to cook him a dish that her mother prepared for her every Sunday as a child. Tori shopped around for the ingredients to cook Bobotie, yellow rice, and plantains.

Quickly picking out everything she needed, she made her way to the register. She stood in line and looked at her watch repeatedly. It seemed as if the line was everlasting and never moving. She was becoming restless as she waited her turn in line. *Why is this line moving so slow?* she questioned herself. She stood on her tippy toes, trying to scope out and count how many people were in front of her.

"Tori!" She heard her name loud and clear, but she hesitated before turning around.

"Aye, Tori." Tori heard her name again. She rolled her eyes and looked at her watch.

What the fuck? she thought to herself. She sighed and turned around. When she spotted Professor Davis, her heart dropped.

"Excuse me," Davis said, making his way through the crowd of customers.

"Oh my God," Tori said, putting her hand to her forehead and quickly turning around.

She felt his hand touch her shoulder and took a deep breath. Tori quickly snatched it away. She didn't want to cause a scene, but she thought she had made herself clear to Davis. She didn't expect to see him again until graduation, and during that time, she knew he wouldn't dare approach her.

"How are you, Miss Givens? Long time, no see," Davis said.

"Didn't I tell you to leave me the fuck alone?" Tori asked in an almost soft whisper.

"Yeah, you did, but since I made your grade look perfect, I figured you would take me up on that date." He put his arm around her waist.

"Don't fucking touch me," she said, moving from his grasp. Davis scoffed.

"Are you serious right now, baby?" he asked, grabbing her again.

The entire line of people stood quietly while Davis tried to force himself on Tori. Shit like this seemed to be the norm in this part of town because no one budged or came to her rescue. It was clearly an uncomfortable situation as their conversation got louder and more aggressive.

"This will be my last time telling you this, Davis. Leave me the hell alone." Tori walked forward out of his grasp.

"Come on, Tori. Don't be like that," he pressed. He wrapped his arm around her waist and pressed his dick against her ass.

Quickly turning around, Tori threatened, "If you *ever* touch me again, I *will* kill you."

She yanked away and ran outside to her car. She got in and locked her doors. Tori started the ignition and took off, doing fifty miles per hour out of the grocery store's parking lot. She watched in her rearview as Davis's big-ass body came wobbling from in between the store's automatic double doors.

Tori didn't feel safe, so she continued driving as if she were the only person occupying the road. Fast and reckless, Tori couldn't take any chances. Davis was on his stalking shit, and she wasn't trying to be a victim. Tori was trying to get back to the safety of her residence, unscathed. She drove down Grand Avenue and, without thinking, made a sharp right. She was now doing thirty miles per hour.

"Fuck!" Tori screamed as soon as she realized a police car had been following her the entire time. The car was unmarked, making it impossible to spot. She hit the steering wheel as the lights from the car began to flash, and the sirens blared.

Tears instantly ran down her face. With all the violence and police brutality surrounding the entire world, she was now scared for her life, but she had to think quickly. She led the police to the next street ahead and pulled over. She wiped her tears and sat quietly, thinking the entire time. Her next move had to be her best move. If this officer had been following her long enough, she was about to get more than a few traffic violations. Tori looked out her side mirror and watched as the officer sat in his car speaking on his walkie-talkie. She took advantage of the time. She fixed her breasts in her shirt, making sure her titties were perky and visible. Then she rummaged through her purse, looking for something to make her lips pop. When she finally located her lip gloss, she applied a thin coat of the gloss and puckered her lips. Fuck crying and fuck a ticket. Tori knew why she was being pulled over, but she couldn't risk her mother finding out about her getting a speeding ticket. Tori pushed her big, poofy hair behind her ears and removed her seat belt. She saw a man in uniform quickly approaching her car, so Tori knew she had a way to fix it if things went left. She watched him, and she knew *exactly* who he was.

"Good evening, ma'am. Do you know why I pulled you over?" he asked.

"Uhm, I'm not sure," Tori responded. She looked at him seductively, flashed a smile, and perked up her breasts again.

"No sudden movements, ma'am," he warned.

"I'm sorry," Tori apologized.

"I pulled you over because you've been doing eighty for about ten minutes now. You ran a couple of stop signs, and then you turned this corner driving like you own the road. Is everything OK?" he asked.

"Yes, everything is OK. I was just in a hurry." Tori batted her eyes.

"All right. A hurry . . . I see. Well, in the meantime, here's a ticket for speeding." The officer began to write.

"Well, wouldn't you need my license and registration to write me a ticket?" she asked.

"No, I don't need a license or registration. I know who you are."

"I highly doubt you do. If you're going to write me a ticket, ask me for my identification," Tori said seductively.

"Ma'am, are you getting smart with me?"

"No, but how will you give me a ticket without my basic information?"

"I ran your plates. I know just who you are. Omeiha Givens, right?" he asked.

"Officer, Officer, I don't look shit like Omeiha. That bitch could never compare. Here, since you can't do your fucking job right." She tossed the officer her license.

"Ma'am, can you step out of the vehicle?" he asked.

"May I ask why? I'm trying to help you do your fucking job, right?"

The officer grabbed for his gun while reaching for Tori's door handle.

"Get out of the car," he requested, swinging the door open and pulling Tori out by her arm. He slammed the door shut and pushed her up against the car. The officer turned Tori's back toward him and placed her arms behind her back.

"You a tough one, huh? What you want?" he asked. "You wanna throw me some pussy to pay off this little debt?"

"Officer." Tori chuckled. "Nah, I wanna throw you some pussy just because. And if that helps this little ticket disappear, that's a win-win."

The officer felt Tori up, pretending to be looking for something in particular. However, he was feeling for everything Tori's body had to offer. He wondered if she was worth the trouble. The officer moved his fingers from her ass to her inner thighs, pussy, her stomach, and in between her breasts. Tori smiled and put her bottom lip in between her teeth. Her head fell forward. The feeling of him roughly fondling her body had her soaking wet. Tori was ready to fuck him right there, traffic stop or not. She was eager to pay her small debt to society.

"I can't make this ticket go away. It's already written, but how about an exchange?"

"What type of exchange?" she moaned.

He kissed the side of her neck and walked away, leaving Tori in suspense. He got into his patrol car, and just as quickly as he pulled her over, he was gone. Tori watched as he drove away. Everything seemed so weird, and the fact that she'd just been ambushed by her old creepy-ass professor was pushed to the back of her mind. At this point, Mr. Officer had her ready to fuck. Sex was calling, and she needed to answer. It was like a fucking drug. It always seemed to take her mind off the bad things.

She left the scene and decided to buy Chinese food for dinner, thanks to Professor Davis.

An hour later, after purchasing Chinese carry-out, Tori was back home. She went into the Doss's home first and borrowed a bottle of Mila's Cabernet Sauvignon. She left a promise-to-pay note behind, then made her way back to her living quarters and continued her unpacking extravaganza. There was nothing extravagant about the task at hand, but if she didn't do it, who would? Tori sat on the floor in the middle of Jace's and her bedroom with her legs crossed Indian style, going through the old pictures from her childhood. Although there were very few pictures, Tori still approached the task with caution.

She stumbled upon a picture from the fifth grade and smiled. She thought back to when things seemed as if they would never get better. The first person her eyes fell on was a brown-skinned boy with the cutest brown eyes that seemed to stare directly back at her. Underneath his picture, it read *Jace Doss*. Tori took her thumb and ran it across Jace's baby face. Even back then, she adored him. He was flawless. Everything about him was perfect. Jace had always been a part of the beautiful society. He had no issues fitting in with the people Tori silently but desperately wanted to belong to. Jace just had such a beautiful, kindred soul. Tori appreciated that about him. Their only issue was him fulfilling her sexual needs.

Her eyes traveled west from Jace's picture and landed on her own. Underneath, it read *Tori Givens*. Written underneath her name in a black Sharpie, she read aloud, "*Blackie, black, black.*" Tori looked at her picture, and instantly, her lips scrunched up in disgust. She absolutely hated who she used to be, how she used to look, and how much of a weak individual she once was. But looking back, appreciation swarmed her heart. If it weren't for the things she went through in the past, her future might have been even worse.

Emotions plagued Tori as she finally placed the wineglass underneath her nose, taking in its unique aroma. She put the wineglass to her lips and took a sip. Her eyes closed, and her hand traveled down her leg. Just as before, this wine had her feeling herself—literally. Tori unfolded her legs and opened them wide. She leaned back and, without thinking, drank the entire glass down. There was something about this drink that made her hormones rage.

Tori placed flat hands against the floor as the empty glass tipped over. Her head fell back while her finger grew a mind of its own. Tori's hand wandered its way into her baggy grey joggers and panties. Her fingers were ready to take control. She took hold of her clit, grasping it in between her fingertips. Then she slowly rolled and manipulated her small bud attempting to make herself ocean wet. Her toes pointed and dug into the floor as her mouth fell open, and a pleasurable cry escaped her lips.

"Hell yeah, keep doing that shit."

Tori was startled by his voice. She jumped and quickly removed her hand from her pants. Her eyes opened . . . And she looked at him. He stared at her with a big-ass smile across his face. Then standing in the doorway, he leaned up against the wall, holding his service weapon with one hand, and his other hand laid smugly on top. Devontae watched Tori make love to herself.

"Devontae, what are you doing here?"

"That's *Officer* Devontae to you, Tori," he announced as he walked over to her. "I see you started the party without me."

Tori looked up at him as he stood between her still wide-opened legs.

"Devontae, you shouldn't be here. What if Jace comes home early?" she asked as Devontae helped her to her feet.

"Fuck that soft-ass nigga. Let him come in here on some bullshit, and I'ma pop his ass," he said honestly.

"No, you're not," Tori countered. "You're trespassing in his home and trying to fuck his girl."

"I'm not *trying* to do shit. I'm *about* to fuck you. I'm a *real* nigga, so that pussy-eating piano shit ain't what I do, but I got you in that area too. How else are you going to pay off that debt?"

Devontae pulled Tori by her pants, and she didn't protest. He walked her to the bed and began undressing her. Tori was feeling every moment of what they were about to share. This entire thing was so risky, but Tori was willing to live on the edge. She was a dangerous individual. Emotions and feelings meant absolutely nothing to her because, in the past, she was forced not to have any. Tori decided she wouldn't fight anything. She wanted to go with the flow, so she returned the favor. She began stripping Devontae from his uniform, slowly and sensually. When they both were naked, he lay on the bed. He planted his feet to the floor and motioned Tori to kneel in front of him.

"I've never done this before," she said.

"That's cool. I'ma guide you," he rebutted.

There was no running from Devontae. Whatever Tori didn't know how to do, he was willing to teach her. Devontae was going to be her personal dick trainer. So, Tori did as she was told. She got on her knees and grabbed hold of Devontae's erection.

"Open your mouth," he said. Tori opened wide. "Put your teeth behind your lips and wrap them sexy ma'fuckas around me." Devontae and his filthy mouth gave Tori the rundown on Dick Sucking 101. "Use your hands too. Play with this big ma'fucka."

Tori followed suit. She did exactly what he said. Devontae gave her the basics, and after he felt she was comfortable enough, he allowed her to take control. She sucked, slobbered, choked, slurped, and imbibed every drop of Officer Devontae. He took hold of her hair and wrapped it around his hand, guiding her head up and down on him, choking her with his length and bringing tears from her eyes. Tori loved that kinky shit. She was ready to die for the dick. Dying from strangulation wasn't too bad of an idea considering the situation.

"Shit," Devontae said as he brought Tori's head back. "You're a pro already, baby." Tori breathed heavily as she caught a little wind into her lungs. "Get up," he ordered. He wasn't done with her just yet.

Usually, Tori craved being in control, but she listened to Devontae's commands. There was something about him. He possessed a whole lot of big dick energy. Devontae grabbed her thighs and guided her to his body. He threw caution to the wind and went in her without any protection. Tori climbed on top of him and took her time. She eased her purring kitty down onto his rock-hard tool. She fisted her hair as her eyes rolled back. Tori had yet to ride Devontae, but the feeling of him being inside of her was driving her completely insane. He placed rough, aggressive hands to her waist as he held on tightly. Tori got on her feet while still squatting on top of Devontae's length. She went up, and his girth instantly pulled her back down. They both sighed aloud. The feeling was so orgasmic, but neither was ready to come.

"This the shit that's gon' have a nigga sprung," Devontae said.

He smacked her ass so hard, placing his nails into each cheek. Devontae gave Tori that rough shit she longed for.

She bounced on him hard and fast. The aggression of her body movements was sending them both over the edge. Up and down, in and out, Tori was breaking Devontae off very proper. She felt her climax coming, and so did Devontae, but he wasn't ready to come. He hadn't fucked Tori the way he knew she needed it, so he released her and coached her to get on all fours.

Then Devontae climbed behind her and quickly climbed inside of her. He stabbed her insides with his inches, and his nails found their way back into her behind. Devontae fucked Tori. He went in and out of her fast and recklessly. The sound of skin smacking echoed throughout the entire room. Devontae was so deep inside Tori that she felt him in her soul. If only she'd found Devontae before she decided to give her all to Jace. This was the type of love she wanted. Emotionless and harsh with a side of great dick. She wanted and *needed* this shit every single night. Tori didn't want to continue putting on a fake-ass performance just to get fucked properly when it came to Jace. Devontae smacked Tori's ass so hard with all his might every time he dove in. This was the price she had to pay for speeding and teasing him with that little piano performance.

"You can keep fucking Jace's soft ass, but this shit right here is mine. I *own* this pussy," he said.

"Yes, you own this," Tori said honestly. The words fell from her lips lustfully as her body moved to Devontae's rapid grooves.

"My name is all over this pussy. You hear me?" Devontae leaned into Tori and wrapped his hand around her neck. He leaned down on her back while still pounding into her.

"Devontae," Tori said as tears gathered in her eyes and rolled down her face.

Her wind was cut short, and her body felt limp. She came, and so did he. Tori's body dropped to the bed.

"Lights out," Tori heard Devontae say before everything went black.

***

Tori woke up four hours later after feeling Jace climb into bed behind her. Her body was still naked, but all signs of sex were wiped away. Her body smelled like soap. Devontae allowed her to be at peace. He didn't want her in that way. He didn't want to come in between what she and Jace had, but fucking her was something he planned to do whenever and however he wanted to. He cleaned her body while she slept, and afterward, he left quietly.

Jace wrapped his arm around Tori and held her close to him. They cuddled and brought their entire day to an end. This was right up Jace's alley. A woman. Tori was someone he had plans to come home to every single night. She was his. No other woman could ever measure up to her. He closed his eyes and placed Tori's right breast into his palm. Tomorrow was a brand-new day, and a new obstacle was waiting to be crossed. Jace was ready to meet Tori's parents.

Aja

"All work, no play, baby," were the first words I heard when I picked up my vibrating cell.

My baby Von didn't even allow me to say hello because he knew he'd caught me at an unusual time. It was 2:30 a.m., and he knew that was my usual hibernation time. However, I was willing to wake up and get straight to business for him. Devontae spoke in code as he talked to me. I knew he needed to make sure our plans were still on schedule. I stretched my legs and groggily spoke into the phone.

"This isn't professional. This shit is all the way personal," I responded.

I looked at my phone and read his name. Of course, I already knew who was on the phone, but I had to make sure. "Von?" I inquired.

"Yeah, baby, it's me." His baritone was so deep and sexy. I love him. After Jace and I split, Devontae took me in as his own. I feel the love, and he's willing to go along with my plans of robbing and murdering my biological parents.

"How are things going with you and best friend?" he asked. I felt as if I could be all the way honest with him.

"I haven't gotten the opportunity to lay everything out on the table yet. I've been fucking her the way you taught me. I've been trying to make her fall for me. That way, when I put this shit in her mind, she'll be with it," I said. "She still doesn't know about Tori and me. I've been trying to ease that part on her."

"Fuck that easing shit. She either gon' get with the program or click." Devontae made a clicking sound into the phone, and I knew what words would follow. "Her ass can catch a couple of hot ones too."

"She's gon' be down for it. From what she told me, my parents aren't good people at all, and they are sitting on millions," I said. "Amelie has been opening up slowly. Tori is supposed to be getting her cut of the money later today after she graduates. Maybe I should just kill her ass and take her cut along with my cut," I rambled, thinking hard as hell. Devontae was so quiet that I forgot I was on the phone with him. I had so many people talking to me at once in my head, and while they spoke, I talked, saying whatever made the most sense to me.

"Nah, we ain't gon' touch Tori. I got something else planned for her. We gon' let her ass breathe, but those parents of y'alls, yeah. We got them."

What he said brought me back from the voices. They all shut up at once, and I agreed.

"OK, baby. I'll let you know how everything goes later. This will be my first time meeting my parents, and I can't wait. Their asses are going to look like two fucked-up deer in headlights."

"A'ight, baby. Talk to you later," he said.

I hung up and set my phone down. Then I closed my eyes. My mind was so fucked up. I thought about the Givens and the ways I would torture them. In my mind, they had to pay for my misfortunes, and they would pay with their lives.

When I was younger, I was diagnosed with schizophrenia. I blame Omeiha and Larry. They abandoned me and left me with two strangers. I always wondered why I looked so different from my mother and father, but I could never voice anything because they kept me doped up. My foster parents used to give me these meds, and I never knew what they were for. They calmed me, and they calmed the voices, but since finding out all these fucking secrets, I decided to stop taking that shit. I don't *want* to be calm. I needed the voices to guide me. They've been doing their job, and they hadn't steered me wrong yet.

From the first day I met Tori, I knew God had my back. He introduced us just in time. I had been watching her for years. I knew everything about her. From her insecurities to the fact that she didn't have any friends. Even the fact that my parents had her set up with a beautiful trust fund. I paid attention to her whereabouts and the fact that she sat her lame ass on that same damn patch of grass every single fucking day. She was an easy target, but I still had trouble getting to her. Tori and I entered college at the same time. For years, I wanted to say something to her, but I didn't want to scare her away. During my junior year, I met Jace and Devontae. Jace and I had a really quick relationship, but somehow, I allowed myself to fall in love. That shit was not planned at all. After being kicked out of UCLA, I still needed a way to be around Tori, praying that we'd become friends one day so she could introduce me to her family. I wanted to surprise them with my presence.

Lo and behold, Tori began dating my man. That gave me all the reasons to do what I had plans on doing—which was fucking up her entire world. Finding out she didn't love Jace the way I loved him gave me the motive to expose her ho ass. Guess what? Without a doubt, I got something for that ass. Amelie . . . She just became a pawn in it all. Tori trusted her, and if I got Amelie to trust me, I would be able to get in where I fit in. Omeiha and Larry don't know what's in store for them. I know for a fact they won't even see me coming. If they never told Tori about me in the past, she has a rude awakening coming, as well.

I know, I know. I sound crazy as fuck, and guess what? I *am* crazy as fuck, but I am so fucking brilliant at the same time. My mother, father, and sister have something special coming . . . more sooner than later. Now, let me get a little bit of sleep. I have a graduation to attend soon.

Chapter Nineteen

Mirror, mirror on the wall, who's the beautifullest of them all? Tori and Jace stood side by side in their bathroom, getting prepared for their graduation. Tori thought about the words she used to say to herself as a kid, the words that always seemed to get her down. She was never able to get the mirror to respond to her. But this time around, she received a silent answer. *Biiitch, you are and that fine-ass man standing on the side of you.* Tori's mind gave her so much validation.

Today was a significant step toward everything their future had in store. Tori walked into college, unsure of her future. She was a sex addict who had never been touched before, and all she ever wanted was to belong. Her parents had complete control over her life from day one, and because they controlled her life, a man was the one thing they kept at bay. Fast-forward to the present. Tori was now walking out of college, a beautiful woman with a man on her arm and a degree in her grasp. Her future now seemed brighter,

and although the jitters of making proper introductions bothered her, she was ready for it all. It
was graduation day, and she'd made it through
everything without defying her parents. Things
between her and Jace didn't get serious until she
was sure she was graduating with a perfect GPA.

Tori smiled as she looked back and forth between herself and Jace. He looked so sexy, dressed
in a Burberry button-up shirt and Shibden Chinos
Burberry pants. Tori drooled over him. If they
weren't already running behind schedule, she
knew she would've copped a quick attitude so that
Jace could fuck her like one of his little hoes.

Tori blew a kiss at the mirror in the direction of
Jace as she applied coconut oil to her coiled hair.
Her lips glistened as always with her pretty nude
lip gloss.

"You look so handsome, babe," Tori said.

"You look good too," he responded.

"No, I don't. I'm not even dressed yet." Tori
opened her robe and flashed her nude strapless
bra and panty set at him.

"So, you still look good, baby."

He walked behind Tori and hugged her. Tori
placed her hand on the side of his face and leaned
her head to the side. Smiling, Jace took Tori in,
and his face fell into the crook of her neck as he
spoke softly to her.

"I never knew that one woman could change a man like me. You did that shit, Mocha. I love you," he said.

Tori stood flabbergasted. Aside from Amelie, she'd never heard the words "I love you" attached to her name, and she didn't know how to respond. She thought about how she would say it back. Before saying it, she thought about if she should come clean about Devontae, her sex addiction, and Professor Davis, or should she keep that shit to herself? Confusion took over Tori. She just didn't know what to say. She didn't know what love was, and all this emotional shit was just too much.

No, you don't love me, Jace. What the fuck is love anyway? Tori wanted to say, but she was stuck. Jace felt Tori's apprehension, so he looked up at the mirror and stared into her eyes. Tears flooded her face, and he wiped them away.

"I'm sorry, Jace. I'm so fucked up. I-I-I . . ." Tori stuttered. She stared back at him in the mirror and cried.

"I understand, baby. You're not used to this love thing. It's OK. When you're ready to say it, you will. Stop crying," he responded. He truly understood. Jace hugged Tori from behind, giving her zero space. He knew she had insecurities, and he knew bits and pieces about her past, but he didn't know that her inability to love or recognize love ran so deep.

"What do you even see in me?" she asked. "I'm not even worth the headache, Jace. My family will never accept you. They don't even accept me, but they are all I know."

"That's what this is about? Me meeting your parents? Whether or not they accept me, I'm not going anywhere, Tori," he said as he stared at her through the mirror.

She nodded her head and placed flat, sweaty palms on the sink. Tori stared down, and Jace quickly redirected her focus. "What's down there?" he asked. "Don't worry about nothing and stop holding your head down so much. I'm not worried about your family. I told you yesterday, I don't have to meet them," he said, and Tori sucked in a deep breath.

"OK, Jace."

Tori turned to look at him. She leaned up against the sink and placed her hands to the sides of his face. She stood on her toes, becoming the same height as him. Then she kissed him, wiping off every bit of her lip gloss. They stood in an embrace for what seemed like forever. Jace had to make sure his girl was OK. He was a man who had no problems putting his heart and emotions out there. That was a trait he'd gotten from his mother.

"Are you good?" he asked as she still clung to him.

"Yes, I feel a little better," she responded.

Jace released Tori and allowed her to continue getting dressed. Thirty minutes later, the two stepped from their home, hand in hand. Just like a gentleman, Jace walked Tori to the passenger side of his car and opened the door. He watched her climb inside wearing a beige two-piece pencil skirt and tube top set. Tori sported a pair of nude peep-toe heels. Her fingernails were painted a nude color, and so were her toes. Tori's entire ensemble was compliments of Jace. He made sure everything she needed for graduation was taken care of.

Tori made herself comfortable in Jace's car, and he closed the door behind her. He walked to the back door and opened it. Inside, he neatly laid his and Tori's gowns across the seats. Now, it was time to walk across the stage with his lady. Their future was so beautifully bright. No other journey in Jace's life meant so much to him. The fact that Tori broke down in front of him and showed him she trusted him with her feelings and emotions and seeing her cry made Jace's decision to give his all to her well worth it.

Their graduation was beautiful. With Jace receiving a bachelor's degree in music as his major and business administration as his minor, he was ready for whatever the world threw his way. He planned to work under Big Percy at 290 record label and then branch off a little, creating his own

lane with his own artists. When his name was
announced from the podium, the entire crowd
went wild. Everyone knew Jace, and they didn't
mind paying for a front-row seat to his graduation.
The applause made Jace feel like he was receiving
a Grammy Award. He walked on stage and smiled.
He was a natural. He stood striking a pose while a
thousand cameras flashed.

Mila was the loudest person in the whole place.
She was her only child's number one fan. She was
so proud of her baby boy and all his accomplish-
ments. Jace was on his way to a new start. It was
only up from here. Now that school was over, he
was ready to dedicate all his time to Destiny and
her artistry.

"That's my baby," Mila yelled out. "I love you,
son!" she screamed at the top of her lungs.

Jace shook hands with the officials on stage
and received his degree. He raised his accomplish-
ments high into the sky and smiled. The cameras
continued to flash as he put on a show. In the end,
everything he'd ever gone through in life was well
worth it because it led him here in front of thousands. It also led him to live out a lifelong dream.

Tori stood twenty people away from Jace. She
smiled and clapped, watching her man receive his
honors. She was ecstatic for him as she waited her
turn. Her stomach did somersaults. She was ready
to get this entire thing over with. She was ready to

accept her diploma, introduce Jace to her parents, collect her beautiful check . . . and keep it moving. She waited to hear her name. Tori wasn't sure what she was going to do with her degree. Before she and Jace began dating, her life was all planned out. After receiving her bachelor's, she was supposed to jump right into a graduate program. Now, she didn't know if that was something she wanted. The money her parents promised her was almost in her grasp. Her trust fund would be just enough to get her through the next four years. However, if invested correctly, she would be able to make it stretch a lot longer.

Tori looked into the crowd, trying to spot her parents. She knew they were there somewhere. To her, Omeiha and Larry, along with Amelie, were the only people rooting for her. Tori stood full of nerves as the announcer called the person who stood in front of her. She smiled and clapped her hands nervously because she knew she was up next. All attention was going to be on her. Every single pair of eyes would be watching her as she took that walk across the stage and into her future.

"Just close your eyes and run, Tori," she said to herself. She lived in her own head, and the entire conversation was discouraging. She never really had any positive things running through her mind.

"Graduating with a 4.0 GPA and a degree in mathematics. This year's summa cum laude, everyone, so put your hands together for Tori S. Givens."

Tori heard her name, but she didn't move. Instead, she took a deep breath and looked into the crowd. She saw Amelie run to the front with her camera phone out. The crowd's claps were so loud that it scared her, but seeing Amelie gave her a little confidence.

"That's my bestie!" Amelie screamed, giving Tori the nerve to run out on stage and receive her diploma. She smiled so hard and shook hands with every person on stage, taking her time to pose for a few pictures, some professional and some compliments of Amelie and Mila.

"You go, girl!" Mila shouted. She stood next to Amelie with her camera locked and loaded.

Tori's anxiety was high, but this moment was special. This was a huge accomplishment. She couldn't help but wonder where her parents were. She just knew they would be standing side by side with Amelie instead of Mila. Tori made her exit from the stage and to her designated seat. As she passed Jace, he grabbed her and placed his lips to hers. Tori held on to her cap as she kissed him passionately. The gesture was so sudden that Tori had to go along with it. She couldn't play it off, especially since she felt all eyes on them. She heard applause and her best friend's voice. Tori didn't see her parents around, so she didn't worry about how they found out about Jace. In her parents' eyes, they would've seen a sudden kiss from a stranger and Jace's show of affection in public as disrespect. Nah, she needed the opportunity to introduce Jace to Omeiha and Larry in an appropriate way.

When all was said and done, no one would come in between what was meant for Tori. She wanted her cake, and she would savor that shit— the money, the man, her degree, the kids, the love, the sex. Whatever Tori wanted, it would be hers, regardless of how she obtained it.

After Tori and Jace's beautiful embrace, she made her way to her seat. She spent the rest of the graduation ceremony with her hands clasped together, twiddling her thumbs. Tori was a nervous wreck, and she was ready to make her exit. The announcement was made for the final remarks, and Tori grew excited. She smiled and listened to the speaker because this day was almost over. She saw the light at the end of the tunnel, and now, it was time to get on with her life.

As soon as the final remarks were over, Tori and Jace walked outside. They both stood in the grass, taking pictures with their loved ones. Tori and Amelie took a couple of pictures, hugging and smiling. Amelie loved her some Tori. Tori meant the world to her, and it showed. Introductions were finally made, and Amelie understood what Tori saw in Jace. He was handsome and charming.

"Amelie, this is my beau, Jacey. Jacey, this is my best friend, Amelie," she said.

"Nice to meet you, Jace," Amelie said. She reached her hand out to shake Jace's, and he pulled her in for an embrace.

"We don't do handshakes around here," he said. "Nice to finally meet you, Amelie."

"Yes, finally. I'm not as crazy as you probably thought I was. Your very first impression probably wasn't the best," Amelie said. Tori stood back and watched as her best friend played nice with her man.

"It's cool, baby girl." Jace smiled. He flipped the camera around in his phone and held it up over his head. Then he turned his back to the ladies. "Come on, y'all. This a Kodak moment right here."

The trio posed and took a selfie.

"This is soooo cute," Tori said.

The two were still dressed in their cap and gowns as they posed and smiled. Soon after, Amelie announced she had to leave. She'd planned to meet up with Aja as soon as she left Tori's graduation ceremony.

"OK, boo, I have to go," Amelie said. She hugged and kissed Tori. "Hopefully, I will see you again, Jace."

"No doubt," he said.

Amelie walked away, and after a couple of minutes, Jace Sr. and Mila walked up. Just as Tori and Jace did with Amelie, they took so many pictures. This was a day full of memories, and these were memories they would be able to share with their future children.

"Are you kids ready for the real world?" Mila asked. She stood on the side of Jace Sr. with her arm around his waist, and he placed his arm around her shoulder.

"Yeah, I'm ready for everything. As a matter of fact, I have an appointment with an artist later on today," Jace said.

"Are you serious, Jace?" Tori's eyes squinted. "You're *really* working the night of our graduation?" she asked.

Jace was ready to get the project with Destiny done and over. He kind of figured Tori was going to be upset, but money was calling.

"Yeah, but it'll be later tonight," he said, hugging her.

"Well, we'll see you two at the house. Tori, are your parents coming?" Jace Sr. asked.

"I don't know." Tori sighed. She was irritated by Jace's impulsive decision to work on a special night they were supposed to spend together.

Mila and Jace Sr. walked away, and Jace inhaled. He slowly blew breath from his mouth and began taking off his gown. He saw a couple of his buddies standing and taking pictures, but he didn't want to leave Tori's side.

"So, who are you spending your time with tonight?" Tori asked sarcastically. She rolled her eyes, and Jace quickly grabbed her. He wrapped his arms around her and kissed her, taking her poked-out lip into his mouth. Tori promptly moved her head back. "Answer me, Jace."

"I have to lay a couple of tracks down with Destiny. After that, I'm coming back home to you," he said honestly.

Tori pulled away from him and folded her arms. She turned her back to him, and Jace grabbed her again.

"Spoiled ass," he said. Tori yanked away. She turned her back again, and Jace smiled. He walked up to her from behind and hugged her. "Don't be like that, Mocha. This shit is all business with Destiny." He spoke softly into her ear. Jace was being honest with Tori. He cared about her feelings too much to contribute to her insecurities.

"Tonight is supposed to be about *us,* Jace," Tori said, still pouting.

Jace's sweet talk wasn't doing anything to make her feel better. He kissed her cheek reassuringly. Before the conversation could go any further, the two were startled by someone clearing their throat. Tori turned her head to the left and saw Omeiha and Larry standing there, staring at her and Jace.

Tori quickly removed Jace's arms from around her and turned to face her parents.

"Mama, Papa," Tori said in surprise. "When did you guys get here?" she asked. She instantly stared down at the ground, afraid of what was to come.

Her mother's mug was strong. She didn't have to say much to control Tori's mood. Omeiha and Larry didn't say any words. They just looked at their daughter, unimpressed and disappointed. Jace looked over at Tori and saw how afraid and hesitant she was, so he spoke up.

"How are you doing, Mrs. Givens, Mr. Givens?" He stuck his hand out, awaiting Mrs. Givens's hand. However, Mrs. Givens looked at Jace in disgust. "Nice to meet you two." Jace spoke again.

Larry firmly shook hands with Jace, but Omeiha quickly yanked Larry's arm away.

"Larry, what are you doing? We don't know this person," she said in a thick accent.

"Tori," Omeiha yelled. Tori jumped and looked up at her mother. "Did your father and I teach you to be outside in public, doing ungodly things?" Omeiha asked. "Who is this man?"

"Thi-thi-this is Jace," Tori stuttered. "My friend."

Jace looked at her. She was clearly shaken up, looking like a scared child.

"Seems like more than just a 'friend,'" Larry said in a low tone.

"What did we tell you, Tori? How *dare* you defy us?" Omeiha asked.

"I didn't defy you, Mama. Can we please just talk about this in private?"

"No, we cannot. You clearly want the world to know your business, so let's air it all out, right here and right now," she said.

"What's the issue?" Jace asked, finally speaking up. He was trying to understand what was going on.

"The issue is *you*. How *dare* you disrespect our daughter like this in public. In my culture, we don't show public displays of sex."

"Ma'am, I would never disrespect Tori," Jace said calmly.

"You see this?" Omeiha pulled Tori's check from her purse. "We agreed you would focus on school and not date until you were completely done. This is only a bachelor's degree. You haven't started graduate school, and already you have this boy in your face." Omeiha took the check and ripped it into tiny pieces. "So, Amelie wasn't lying. *You* are the one who was lying, Tori."

Tori felt embarrassed. She was a grown-ass woman, but her family treated her like an unruly child. It seemed as if the only time her parents paid her any attention was when they were disciplining her. A little sexual attention didn't sound too bad at this moment. Tori was so stressed, and her heart was broken. This was her graduation day, and she should've been happy. Tori had found love, and her family should've just accepted him. She'd worked so hard in school and accomplished so much. Tori deserved that check, but what could she do? Her tears ran down her face. Tori didn't know why she was crying. Was it the money or hurt feelings?

"Mama!" Tori cried and reached her hands out as the pieces of paper rained down onto the ground.

Jace grabbed Tori and hugged her. He was so confused and lost behind everything. He couldn't just stand back and watch Tori's parents make an ass of her. He didn't want to be disrespectful either, so he kept his comments to himself and consoled Tori.

"Let's go, Larry." Omeiha took Larry's hand into hers. The two walked away, never looking back.

When they reached their vehicle, Larry unlocked the doors and ushered Omeiha to her side. The two never once exchanged words; everything was dead silent.

"Hey, Mother and Father." Aja's voice broke through the quietness. "I know you remember me, right?"

Omeiha and Larry turned to look at Aja. They both frowned as they stared into the eyes of their long-lost daughter. Of course, they knew who she was. Aja and Tori looked so much alike. Omeiha grabbed at her chest, her face flushed, and she instantly felt weak.

"From your reaction, yeah, you remember me."
Aja laughed.

"I'm sorry, ma'am, but we are *not* your parents,"
Larry said. He opened the passenger door and
helped Omeiha in.

Aja continued talking, trying to get her parents
to acknowledge her at least. . . to no avail. Larry
quickly walked around to the driver's side and
locked the doors once he climbed in.

"It's me, Taja," Aja screamed and banged on the
car window. Omeiha looked straight ahead, not
giving Aja the time of day. She didn't know how to
face her. What could she say to Aja? How would
Omeiha be able to explain to Aja their decision to
keep Tori over her? Back then, Omeiha and Larry
were so young. They couldn't afford to care for
two babies. Choosing to keep Tori over Aja wasn't
something they wanted to do, but they had no
choice. They thought they did what was best.

"Mama, talk to me," Aja screamed. She cried and
punched relentlessly at Omeiha's window. When
Larry finally got the car started, he sped away.
They both were just heartless people. Omeiha
and Larry left Aja again for the second time in
her life. But this time, they made sure to distance
themselves from *both* of their daughters.

Tori

It'd been almost a year since everything in my life changed. Some changes were for good, while others could've turned out better. Jace's and my relationship had been so strong lately. We've been living like a real married couple. After Omeiha and Larry turned their backs on me, the Doss family took me in as one of their own. Jace and I were already living together, and I had already established a relationship with his entire family, so it wasn't hard to fit in. However, my anxiety continued to get the best of me over the months. I had moments of sadness and melancholy, but Jace was so patient with me.

I wish I could report that my sex addiction has eased up a little, but it hadn't. I tried to get used to the whole lovemaking thing, but every time Jace and I were done, I would excuse myself to the bathroom and take care of the urges that continued to taunt me. One day, he caught me. Can you believe that shit? Jace caught me in the shower with my vibrator, fucking myself after he'd just made love to me. I heard the bathroom door creep open, and I knew I was busted. Although the shower was running, my moans and the pulsation from my vibrator were so fucking loud. I couldn't lie. I had to be all the way honest. Jace snatched the shower curtain back, and my heart pace sped up.

"What the fuck are you in here doing?" he asked. I slowly removed my toy. I was speechless. "What the fuck is *this?*" Jace snatched my baby from my hand and threw it across the bathroom.

"I'm sorry, Jace," I said, but I really wasn't. Why should I be sorry when it comes to my needs? The correct phrasing should've been "I'm sorry you caught me." His pride was clearly hurt, but instead of him starting a big-ass argument about it, we spent the entire night discussing everything about me.

He learned my needs and wants, even my insecurities. I had to fess up and tell him that his sex was mediocre. It didn't satisfy me. I told him this is what I did every time we had sex. Jace is a man, and I saw how much my words affected him, but this is what I had to do. I was surprised that my being honest with him wasn't a deal-breaker. So, Jace has been stepping up his game over the past months. He gave me in between lovemaking and being one of his little hoes. He started fucking me like he meant it. Clearly, however, what he was giving me still wasn't good enough. Although I retired my bullet, I continued being with Devontae. Jace worked so much, and I had plenty of free time on my hands. Whenever Devontae showed up at my doorstep, I invited him in with open arms.

Soon after I confessed to Jace about my vibrator, he proposed to me. He felt as though I were opening up to him. He didn't want to lose me, and I promised never to keep something so minor from him. However, I refused to confess my addiction to Devontae. That part was none of his business. In due time, I figured I would learn how to suppress it. I gave up the vibrator, and I was giving myself a few weeks before I would break things off with Devontae. I'd been feeling so sick lately, and I had a feeling I was pregnant, but I was scared to take a test. If I were, I would have no idea who I was pregnant by, so this was the perfect time to walk away. Plus, I had to prepare myself for Jace's and my wedding, which was set to take place on our first anniversary. Nothing too extravagant. I didn't need anything over the top. All I needed was Jace, my best friend, Amelie, and my in-laws to bless Jace's and my union.

Chapter Twenty

Everything Tori was planning for her future was bittersweet. Although her parents never really paid her much attention, she knew they loved her in their own way and wanted what was best for her. Them not giving her the money that was promised to her made her understand just that. However, Tori was a grown woman, and she should've been able to pick and choose her own future. She understood so much, but that didn't make Omeiha's actions right. Tori had to somehow disconnect from her inner self to understand where her parents were coming from. She realized how much she never really had control over her own life. They controlled everything about her from afar. Even though she hadn't spoken to them in months, Tori still wondered how Omeiha and Larry would feel knowing their only daughter was soon getting married. She needed their approval. Tori was weak in that way. This wedding wouldn't have their blessings, and weird enough, that notion bothered her.

Tori did everything she could to suppress her shortcomings, but she continued her sexual relationship with Devontae. For some reason, Devontae was like therapy for her. She needed him, and deep down inside, she began to love him. His attention was everything, especially his sexual attention. Devontae knew Tori's body inside and out, but he was Jace's cousin. Tori knew she and Devontae could never be. Whenever they were together, they lived in their own little fantasy world. People would never understand their relationship. Her addiction always seemed to get the best of her, and since meeting Devontae, he had always been the perfect fix.

After opening up to Jace about everything, Tori decided she would marry the man who made her feel human. Jace was the first man who made her feel something, even if it wasn't deep love. It was a feeling, and Tori had to give him props. She lay in bed alone, which was usual nowadays since Jace threw himself into his work. She was starting to relive her past, realizing the man who claimed to love her had chosen his job over being with her. In her dreams, Tori saw her future. She saw herself and Jace smiling while holding hands. She envisioned herself with a pudge in her belly as she stood before the judge at city hall, exchanging vows with her man. Tori dreamed, and she did it religiously. Mila told her G-ma had been having dreams about fish for weeks now, and that's when Tori took it upon herself to take a pregnancy test. After finding out for sure that she was, in fact, pregnant, Tori began to have this same exact dream every night. Pregnant stomach. Justice of the peace. And a man who stood so beautifully beside her. It was as if her mind were on repeat. This day was no exception.

Tori woke up and quickly placed her forearm to her eyes, using it as a shield to keep the sun away. She hadn't realized she'd fallen asleep until she woke up with the sun beaming down on her through her shades. Rolling over, so her back was facing the window, Tori grabbed her cell from underneath her pillow and looked down at it. She smiled knowingly after seeing a "Good morning. I love you" text from Jace.

Tori picked up her cell and sent Jace a heart emoji. It was weird how she didn't know how to express her love even in a text message. Then she clicked on her Facebook app and updated her newsfeed. When her picture was the first thing she saw, she became uneasy.

"What the fuck is this?" Tori said. She didn't have friends, and it wasn't her birthday, so why was her picture online? She clicked on the image and watched as everything populated. Tori's mind was blown when she realized that this article was about her, Jace, and Destiny.

Who is he really fucking? Tori read the caption and quickly grew infuriated. Destiny and Jace looked too cozy walking hand in hand into Studio 290.

It had been some time now since she and Jace could spend much time together because he was working so hard on completing Destiny's project. She should've known things were more than Jace led on. Destiny was someone she invited into her home. Tori accepted her, but in the back of her mind, she really didn't trust her. Considering the things Tori was doing with Jace's cousin, how could she ever fix herself to trust anyone? Whenever Destiny was around, there was nothing but respect. Tori never saw this coming. Destiny was like the perfect angel in the presence of Tori. *"Girl, Jace is my brother, and you are my sister,"* were the words Destiny always said to Tori, but this picture in this article looked nothing like a sister/brother relationship.

"Stupid bitch," Tori said aloud.

She quickly called Jace's number and listened while his phone rang several times. His phone finally answered. Tori heard Jace's voice laughing and joking around, but he never spoke directly into the phone. "Hello?" Tori said, but there was no response. She heard Destiny's voice, and her attitude became vicious. "Jace," she yelled. "I know you fucking hear me, so I will be up there shortly since I'm a joke to you and that bitch." Tori disconnected the call and dialed Amelie.

"Hello . . . Tori?" Amelie said.

"Yeah, are you busy?" Tori asked but didn't wait for a response. "I need you to ride somewhere with me."

"OK. How long will it be before you get here?" Amelie asked.

"I'll be there in an hour," Tori said and hung up the phone.

Amelie didn't ask any questions. She was down to ride whenever, and because her best friend sounded upset, she was riding wherever Tori needed her to.

Tori walked into the living room of Jace's parents' home and took a seat on the sofa next to her soon-to-be mother-in-law. She lay her head on Mila's shoulder and sobbed.

"What's wrong, Tori?" Mila asked. She ran her fingers through Tori's hair, trying to comfort her. Tori was reluctant to tell Mila what was bothering her because Jace was her son, and Tori figured Mila would never have her back. "Tell me what's wrong, honey." Mila stroked Tori's soft, fluffy hair.

Tori went to the article on her phone and raised her phone so that Mila could see why she was in tears.

"Who is he really fucking?" Mila read the headline and took the phone from Tori's hand.

"What is this? I knew there was something about that Destiny chick I didn't like. Oh my God, Tori, I am *so* sorry she's putting my son in this situation," Mila said.

Tori kept her head on Mila's shoulder. She, in a way, agreed with Mila. Jace being a lady's man was his past. Ever since falling in love with Tori, he'd become a changed man. Tori knew this shit had to be Destiny's fault.

"I can't just sit back and do nothing about this," Tori said in between sobs. "Plus, I'm carrying—" Tori stopped talking.

"You're carrying?" Mila asked.

"Yeah, Mila, I'm carrying so many other stressful things," Tori said.

"Well, did you call him?" Mila asked.

"Yes, he didn't answer, though. I'm going to the studio. I know he's there. Mila, if I catch him and her doing anything inappropriate, I'm leaving," Tori said.

"No, baby, you don't have to leave. It's because of Jace that you no longer have a support system. If anything, I want you to stay, and Jace can just come here," Mila said.

Tori sat up and hugged Mila. She appreciated everything Jace's family did for her. Tori knew she would always have a mother in Mila. Mila supported Tori even when she didn't have to. No one in Jace's family knew she was carrying the newest addition to the Doss kindred, so Mila's willingness to help was something beautiful and genuine.

"I'm gonna go. Pray for your son," Tori said.

"You don't need me to go with you?" Mila asked.

"No, I'm about to go get Amelie. I appreciate it, though." Tori stood from the couch. She left with her hair a curly mess and made her exit.

After meeting her parents, Aja decided to make things more official with Amelie. She realized that Amelie knew so much about Omeiha and Larry. Amelie was going to be her inside person. Aja was determined to obtain need-to-know information if that were the last thing she did.

With Devontae constantly in her ear about infiltrating the Givens's life, Aja knew she had to step up her game. So, she began dating Amelie exclusively. She fed Amelie thoughts about marriage and children. Everything that surrounded the two women was going great. Aja continued her job at Flirty Girls Anonymous, and Amelie decided to return to school. Their five-year plan was looking good. The closer they became, the more Aja knew she was only one step away from getting to her parents. She didn't understand why she had to pretend. Devontae was a police officer. She knew that he could obtain Omeiha and Larry's information if he wanted to. However, Aja didn't push the issue.

She did what she had to do, and if it came down to it, she was willing to get rid of Devontae as well.

"Baby, have you seen this article?" Aja said.

She climbed into bed next to Amelie and made herself comfortable, showing her an article on the infamous *Shade Room*'s social media page. In one picture, Tori waved at the photographer as she and Jace walked together down Rodeo Drive. Jace's arm was laid so protectively around Tori's shoulder, and her arm was around his waist. They both sported a pair of dark sunglasses while Tori entertained the paparazzi by puckering her lips together and blowing a kiss. The picture was beautiful. The two looked happy and in love.

One looking in would've assumed everything between the two was great, and in all actuality, things were perfect. However, it was just like the media to come in and break up a happy home. Amelie scrolled over, and in the other photo, Jace and Destiny were hand in hand as they made their way into Studio 290. Aja smirked. She wanted to laugh out loud. Miss Perfect Tori was getting a dose of who Jace really is. It seemed as of late, Tori had been losing just as much as she had. *Maybe it's a Givens curse,* Aja thought.

"Oh my God. Does Tori know about this shit?" Amelie asked. She reached for her phone, attempting to call Tori, but Aja quickly snatched it away.

"What are you doing?" Aja asked.

"What the fuck does it look like I'm doing? I'm calling Tori." Amelie snatched her phone back from Aja's hand.

"I wouldn't do that if I were you. Although you aren't into men, at the end of the day, you're still a woman. You know how emotional we are, and I know Tori will not take this type of information well. This shit has the potential to end a friendship."

"No, Tori isn't like that. Besides, I'm only the messenger. Plus, I'm going to be there to console her, no matter what."

"I'm sure Tori has seen this article, Amelie. We don't have the facts right now, so let's not assume anything. We have other shit to focus on."

"Whatever." Amelie waved her hand, scrolled to Tori's name, and before she could dial, her phone rang.

Tori sat on the other end of the phone, ready to ride down on Jace and his ho. Everything that happened between Tori and her parents was because of Jace, so how dare he play with her heart like this? The women disconnected the call, and within an hour, Tori was blowing her horn.

"I would go with you ladies, but I have a bunch of things to take care of today. Tell Tori I said hi," Aja said, giving Amelie a quick peck.

"It's OK. I'll call you when I'm on my way back home," Amelie said. Aja walked her to the door and waved at Tori as Amelie walked away.

***

"Are you OK?" Amelie said as soon as she took a seat in Tori's car. Tori's eyes were red and swollen. That was a clear indication she'd been crying for some time now.

"Yes, I'm fine, but I don't know if I'm going to be able to say the same thing about Jace and Destiny when I get done with them," Tori threatened.

When it came to feelings and emotions, Tori never really had any, so she wasn't sure what was bothering her the most. She had just found out she was pregnant weeks before finding out her fiancé was possibly creeping with someone he worked with, someone he promised to only have a "business relationship" with. A baby was something both she and Jace had spoken about in the past. Now that she was actually pregnant, she wasn't in the mood to celebrate it. For one, she didn't really know who she was pregnant by. Second, the pictures from the *Shade Room*'s news article seemed to overshadow her wonderful news. Tori quickly concluded that her entire life was bullshit. Happiness was not what she saw in her present or future.

"Come here." Amelie reached her arms out. "Give me a hug."

Tori hugged her friend and sighed. She felt overwhelmed. She needed a shoulder to cry on, and Amelie was just the person for it. Tori remembered her and Amelie's talks about a five-year plan and what Tori saw in her future. She thought she was working toward it. Now, she wished Amelie was a part of what she envisioned because she knew Amelie would've been very careful with her heart. Tori's buzzing phone quickly broke the women from their embrace. She looked down and smiled.

"I have to take this call," Tori said. She pressed the talk option and put the phone to her ear. "Hey, Von," she said, sounding full of sorrow.

"What's up, baby?" Devontae said. "Why you sound like that?"

"I'm on my way to Studio 290. I have to handle something real quick."

"Handle something real quick? You on some gangsta shit right now, huh? You can't say the shit you're on your way to handle over the phone?" He laughed. "What you on your way to handle?"

"Your cousin," Tori said.

"Awe, you must've seen that picture online. Just cool out, baby. Cuz ain't on shit." Devontae surprisingly defended Jace.

"Why are you defending him?" Tori said, and Devontae smirked.

"I'm not defending shit. I just know my cousin. He loves you; trust me. Now, ole girl, I don't know what *her* motives are," he said.

"I have to go, Devontae. My friend is in the car with me. I'll call you later." She hung up and pulled away from the curb.

The women drove to the studio, and Tori was a mess. It'd been awhile since she'd felt so low about herself. Amelie rubbed her shoulder and assured her Jace wouldn't intentionally hurt her. Ever since Tori had been with Jace, he always put her first. Recently, their time spent together had been nonexistent because Jace was a man who had to work to take care of his family.

When they reached the studio's parking lot, Tori quickly opened her door and vomited. Amelie climbed from the car and made her way around to Tori. She stood and rubbed her back.

"Are you OK?" Amelie asked.

"Yes," Tori said. She spat on the ground and almost began vomiting again.

"Girl, are you pregnant?" Amelie asked, face screwed up. "This that shit pregnant people do."

"Yes," Tori said honestly.

"Seriously? Oh my God. Tori, we don't need to go in there. I don't want you to stress the baby out. Does Jace know you're pregnant?"

"No, and I intend to keep it that way for now," Tori responded. She sat up. Her stomach was feeling much better after her moment of regurgitation. "Come on," she said, stepping from her car.

"Tori?" Amelie said apprehensively.

"You're either going in here with me, or you're not. Either way, I have to go talk to Jace."

Amelie decided to go. She wasn't about to let Tori confront Jace and Destiny alone, especially after finding out she was pregnant. What if Destiny wanted to act stupid and swing on her? Amelie had to be there to protect her best friend and her soon-to-be godchild.

"Hi, can I help you?" the exotic-looking receptionist said as soon as the two women walked into the studio. They both came on business. Tori wasn't for any small talk. She just wanted to be pointed in the direction of her fiancé.

"I'm here to see Jace. Where the hell is he?" Tori asked.

The receptionist smiled. She recognized Tori, and she knew this visit was about to be full of drama. Big Percy was currently out of the office, so whatever he didn't know wouldn't hurt him. Plus, she was about to have a front-row seat to this little performance.

"Oh, you're here to see Jace. Give me a second, and I'll walk you to the back," she said. She stood and walked from around her desk. The receptionist secured the front door and escorted the two women to the back. "I had to lock the door since I'm stepping away," she said, coming up with an excuse. Leading Tori and Amelie to the back, the receptionist made a little conversation. "It's good to meet you finally. Jace talks about you all the time," she lied.

"Oh, is that so?" Amelie asked sarcastically.

Tori remained silent as she got her thoughts together. She wasn't in the mood for chitchat. She needed to save her words for Jace and Destiny. The receptionist walked Tori and Amelie down a long hallway and motioned her hand toward the last door on the left.

"He's in there. Let me know if you need anything." She walked away, giving Tori, Amelie, Destiny, and Jace some privacy.

Tori and Amelie walked to the door and peeped in. Tori's stomach felt so empty as she watched Destiny massage Jace's shoulders. She'd never been the type to face her problems head-on, and just like any other time, at that moment, she wanted to run away and hide. She needed comfort and an escape from what was before her.

She couldn't fathom the thought of Jace doing her the same exact way she had been doing him. Jace sat in front of a piano with a sheet of paper in front of him. Tori's nostrils flared. She imagined Jace pleasing Destiny on top of this piano the same way he had done her in the past. When Jace grabbed Destiny's hand and smiled, tears graced Tori's face. She bit down on her bottom lip, stopping the cries that threatened to escape. Tori had to suffer through the pain of being a spectator to Jace's infidelity as Destiny walked to the side of him. She took a seat next to him and lay her head down on his shoulder. Their lips moved, but Tori couldn't hear anything being said. She was so heated. Tori looked at Amelie as Amelie looked back at her, ready to tear into Destiny's ass. Amelie wanted to protect the little emotions Tori had. Jace was the person Tori decided to share that part of herself with. Against everything Tori stood for, she gave her heart to Jace, and he stumped it into the ground.

"Let's go in," Amelie said. She was ready, and Tori decided she couldn't watch things go any further. Now she was ready to interrupt their cute little moment. Amelie kicked open the door aggressively as if she were LAPD, startling Jace and Destiny.

"Tori!" Destiny said, jumping to her feet. She was guilty, and she looked as if she'd just gotten caught doing something she probably shouldn't have.

"Tori, what are you doing here?" Jace asked as he stood to his feet and walked in her direction.

"No—what the fuck are *you* doing?" Tori demanded. Jace grabbed her and hugged her.

"Nah, let her go," Amelie said. She pulled Tori's arm, ripping her away from Jace's grasp. "You see, Tori, this is why I don't do niggas," she spat while standing in between Tori and Jace.

"Amelie, shut up," Tori said, but she allowed Amelie to hold her back. She was pregnant, and in all honesty, she had no business being in the midst of a stressful situation.

"I'm just saying," Amelie said.

"Tori, baby, can I talk to you, please?" Jace begged. "Away from everything and everybody."

Jace was trying his best to defuse this unnecessary situation. Destiny was just an artist he was working with, and although things between the two seemed a little "different," he wasn't doing anything inappropriate with her.

"Nope. You can talk to her right here," Amelie answered for Tori.

Tori looked into Jace's eyes as she stood silent. She had no words. The only thing that was on her mind was her pregnancy and Devontae.

Maybe this is the right time to hurt him, make him *feel the same way I do. Jace, I'm pregnant, and this is Devontae's baby*. She had every mind to say those hurtful words. However, she decided to choose her words wisely. "Why was she laid on your shoulder and massaging you?" Tori asked.

"Tori, I swear it's *not* what you think. Please, let me talk to you in the hallway."

"No, Jace. With everything I've been through, you sit here with this tramp, being disrespectful." Tori pointed in Destiny's direction, using the word G-ma taught her.

"Tramp?" Destiny asked. "Listen to your man, baby girl, before I *really* get disrespectful in this bitch." Destiny's pretty lips spoke, and Amelie turned in her direction.

"Get disrespectful and do *what*, bitch? Tori ain't gotta do shit. Bitch, I'ma get in your ass myself," Amelie warned.

Jace quickly intervened. He couldn't allow Tori nor her ghetto-ass friend to come in between business. He aggressively subdued Amelie and Tori, walking both women out into the hallway. The entire time, Amelie and Destiny argued back and forth.

"Please, Amelie, can you give Tori and me a few minutes alone?" he asked politely.

"Hell nah," Amelie responded. "Because if she come out here and try to fight Tori, I'ma kill both your ass," she threatened.

"Man, she ain't gon' do shit, not while I'm standing here," Jace responded.

"Amelie, it's fine. Just give us five minutes," Tori said softly. She looked down at the floor as tears began to flow.

"OK. I'll be right around the corner." Amelie walked away.

"Look at me." Jace grabbed Tori's face. "What's down there?" he asked.

Tori looked up at Jace. Her eyes were red and full of dismay. She was a selfish woman, and she had every right to be. She'd never had real love, and when she finally found it, someone else was threatening to steal it away. Tori loved pain, but this was a different type of pain. Her heart ached. Although she would never admit it, Tori loved the drama, but *this* drama she could've done without. Still, this was like a scene straight from her favorite reality show. The only thing she needed after this big-ass blowup was a happy ending.

"You really doing this shit at my job?"

"No. *You're* doing this shit at your job and all over fucking social media." Tori pulled her phone out and showed Jace the article.

"Man, fuck social media." He raised his voice.

Jace's anger took over. He snatched Tori's phone from her hand, and she instantly grew nervous. She tried taking back her phone. She was positive he was about to go through her cell and find out about her and Devontae's secret relationship. Instead, he threw the phone to the floor, breaking the entire screen. He backed Tori up against the wall and placed his hand gently around her neck.

"Me and that girl just work together. Why the fuck are you so insecure?" Jace hit Tori with a low blow. The shit she'd shared with him in confidence, he threw it right back in her face.

"*Why* am I insecure?" Her face frowned. She removed his hand from around her neck. Her feelings were hurt again, and she knew it had to be the hormones. "Because I'm fucking pre—" Tori stopped midsentence.

"Because you're *what?*" Jace asked as he stared through her. He backed up from her and spoke. "You're pregnant?" His eyes watered.

"Fuck this shit," Tori said. "Yes, Jace. I'm pregnant, and all of this is stressing me out." Jace didn't speak. He listened to Tori talk as tears rolled down his face. "Your mother said you can stay with her until I find my own place," Tori said.

She attempted to walk away, but Jace needed her in his grasp. He pulled her into him and hugged her.

"You're pregnant, Mocha?" he asked. He rubbed Tori's belly, put his head down onto her shoulder, and cried. And these were happy tears. Tori was his soon-to-be wife, and a baby was going to complete them. He couldn't let her walk away. "I respect your decision. I will leave and give you a little space."

"Jace, I have to go."

She unwrapped his arms from around her and walked away from him. She beat herself up. She wasn't ready to tell Jace she was pregnant until she got her dates correct. She knew there was a strong possibility she was pregnant by Devontae. How was she going to explain this shit? She knew she probably fucked up, but she prayed this little one growing inside her belly was Jace's.

Chapter Twenty-one

Jace stood in the hallway. He stared at Tori's phone that still lay on the ground and rubbed his waves downward. Then he inhaled deeply, and afterward, exhaled every bit of emotion he had pent up. Tori had just laid some heavy shit on him, and he didn't know how to feel. Yes, he was ready to become a father. He was ready to be a family man, and he did not see coparenting in their future. He feared the unknown because Tori had left him in suspense. She told him she was pregnant and walked away in tears. Jace wanted to run after her, but he still had a studio session with Destiny. This was business, not personal. He needed every dime to care for Tori and their growing seed. Even if it was fuck him and their relationship was done, he could never see her without.

Jace knew he'd fucked up. He allowed Destiny to flirt with him, and he allowed things to seem more than what they were. It was no secret that the two had a vibe, and they worked well together. However, Jace should've kept everything professional. Destiny shouldn't even know what his body feels like.

Jace picked up Tori's phone from the floor and put it in his pocket. His emotions were everywhere. Everything he'd always wanted was now coming together, and they were coming together quickly. He walked back into the studio and took his seat in front of the piano again. Jace put his face into his hands and sighed heavily. Destiny walked over to him and placed her hand on his back. She slid her hand to his shoulder, attempting to rub his tension away.

"Can you remove your hand?" Jace asked, moving her hand from his shoulder.

"I'm sorry. Did I offend anyone? Is everything OK?"

"Nah, and yes, everything is cool. Just get in the booth so we can finish these few songs," he said. His voice was tired and expressionless as he talked to her. He couldn't blame her for everything that'd just happened. He knew Destiny should've been halted before this very day. The news article Jace refused to look at had him tight. The media always had a way of coming in and destroying even the strongest bond. Jace remembered that very day, and he recalled thinking the world would perceive that image in a negative light, but he couldn't be bothered with what the world thought. However, now that Tori felt pain behind it, he needed to make it right. Tori never told Jace she loved him, but with her showing up at his place of employment, he knew her heart was affected in some type of way. This had to be love because she had no problems pulling up on him, ready to fight.

"Do you want me to call Tori and apologize? I mean, I didn't mean for any of this to happen."

"You can't call her." Jace pulled Tori's phone from his pocket. "Let's just keep this shit professional, Destiny."

"I'm gonna have to go over and see her. I'm truly sorry."

"It's fine, Destiny. She's pregnant, and she don't need the added stress. Just let the shit be."

"Oh . . . congrats." Destiny was in shock.

"Thanks," he said curtly.

"I don't mean to get in your business, but is she pregnant, pregnant, or is she, 'I just caught my man cheating, so I want to pretend I'm pregnant to make him stop cheating'?" she said. Jace looked up at her. He frowned and stood up.

"First of all, I've never cheated on Tori, and this the shit I'm talking about. Get in the booth and let's get this shit over with so I can get home to my fiancée," Jace ordered. He was done with Destiny's games.

"Fine," she said.

She walked into the booth, and she sang her heart out for the rest of the day. She went over

Jace's lyrics and made them her own. Jace watched her, and he had to give Destiny her props. She was so passionate and confident. That's when he realized why he allowed her advances. There was just something about her. She had it all. She was just as equally beautiful as Tori, but she possessed more than just a beautiful face. Destiny was secure within her own skin. Jace watched her sing with her eyes closed, and when she finally opened them, she stared at him seductively. He shook his head. Destiny's beautiful eyes were calling him.

"Destiny, can you step out of the booth for a minute." Jace spoke into the intercom.

Destiny placed her headphones down and walked through the doors, making her way over to Jace. She took a seat as he turned to look at her.

"Look, I'm sorry about earlier. This shit is just too much. She's pregnant and mad at me. Her ass even put me out of my own crib," Jace said. He put his hand on the back of his neck, feeling comfortable enough to confide in Destiny.

"I understand . . . just go home and apologize. If you need me to, I will also apologize. I like Tori. She's a nice girl."

"Yeah, I have to get her to see how much she means to me. But enough of me and my problems. I got a song I want you to record tonight. I sent you the lyrics. It's called 'Givin' You a Taste,' and I'ma hop on the track with you."

"Oh my God, really?" she said.

"Yeah, get yo' ass up. Let's gon' and knock this shit out."

They got in the booth, took turns, and killed the rest of Destiny's album. Finally, this project for Jace was complete. Now, he had to figure out how to make things good with Tori again. During the last and final song, Big Percy walked into the studio. Jace let him hear a few tracks, and Big Percy announced he was having a listening party for Destiny on Valentine's Day. Destiny came up with the perfect idea of Jace inviting Tori, and, of course, he agreed. The idea was genius. That was the perfect opportunity for Tori to see there wasn't anything "extra" going on between him and Destiny.

What are best friends for? That was not a question Tori ever had to ask herself when it came to Amelie. They may not talk daily, but she was always at her beck and call whenever Tori needed her. Amelie may have been many things, but disloyal was not one of them. Since the ninth grade, she always had Tori's back, and Tori wholeheartedly appreciated it.

"If you need me to, I can go home with you," Amelie offered. She saw how fucked up this entire situation had Tori, and all Amelie wanted to do was comfort her friend. Nothing sexual, but if Tori wanted that, she was willing to go there as well.

"I'll be OK. How have you and Aja been? Ever since she met you, she doesn't fuck with me at all," Tori said.

"She's been OK. She's been acting a little weird lately, but I guess she's cool. In all honesty, I've been thinking about moving on campus. I think I made the wrong move when I agreed to live with her. You know you learn about people's bad habits when you enter their space," Amelie said.

Tori drove through the city with her best girl at her side, and it felt like the old days. Where the time went, Tori and Amelie may never know. However, they both enjoyed this time they were spending together.

"I wish I could help you out, but you know I have my own little situation."

"Yeah, I know. It's fine. I'm a big girl, and I have to take care of my own business," Amelie responded.

They pulled in the front of Amelie and Aja's home, and Tori parked.

"Thank you for going with me. Girl, that was some crazy shit. I knew I would catch him doing something," Tori said.

"Can I be honest with you for a minute?" Amelie asked, and Tori nodded. "You didn't actually catch him doing anything. He didn't react to her advances the way you may have wanted him to, but I believe he's not messing around with her."

"I believe him too," Tori said. "My conscience has been so guilty. When I saw them together, all I could imagine was me and his cousin. The things I know I'm doing is all I could imagine Jace doing."

"You're still fucking him? Girl, you are playing with fire."

"I know. I tried to leave him alone, but Devontae's sex is like a drug. Amelie, you will *never* understand."

"You're right. I don't understand, but, baby girl, what if Jace finds out? You think *your* feelings are hurt? Men have a whole other type of ego and pride. He's going to kill you," Amelie said honestly.

"I know, I know."

"Well, you better *act* like you know. And who are you pregnant by? Girl, you're making Jace look like a damn fool."

"I don't know, Amelie, but I'm praying this baby is Jace's. I love him, and I just realized it today. That sounds so crazy." She laughed.

"You know what you have to do then."

"Yeah, that was already the plan. I'm going to break things off with Devontae. But before I do, I have to be with him one last time."

After dropping Amelie off at home, Tori decided she would go home as well. She had a lot to

think about. She never knew her life would become this. She didn't realize that everything the
Givens tried to instill in her was for the best. Now,
here she was . . . lost, pregnant, torn in between
two cousins, and pretty much homeless. Tori had
a degree to fall back on, but instead of looking for
employment after graduation, she decided to lean
on Jace and his family. At any time, Tori could be
put out on her ass with nothing or no one to run to.

She took the thirty-minute drive home and
altered her five-year plan a little. She wasn't crazy,
but she talked to herself. The drive from across
town was just enough time to give herself the best
advice. Tori entered the Dosses' home and was
greeted by Mila right away. Tori walked over to her,
and Mila embraced her.

"Is everything OK now?" Mila asked.

"Yes, everything is fine . . . even Jace. I decided to
ask him to give me a little space."

"Why? Did something happen?"

"Yeah, but I would rather him discuss that with
you."

"Fair enough," Mila said. "Well, you know I'm
here if you need anything."

"I know, and thank you," Tori said. "I do need
one thing right now, Mila."

"And what's that?"

"Do you mind if I take a bottle of your special
wine back to the guesthouse?"

"Go ahead, baby. Help yourself," Mila said, and Tori did just that.

She took a bottle of the red wine back home and placed it into the small wine cellar. Then she dragged herself into the guesthouse's hallway bathroom and stripped. First turning the shower on, Tori grabbed her toothbrush from its holder, ran it under the faucet, and squeezed a dab of toothpaste onto it. She placed the toothbrush into her mouth and stepped into the shower, figuring she would kill two birds with one stone.

Tori sang her ABCs twice while she brushed her teeth. Afterward, she rinsed her mouth with the shower water, then washed her body, taking her time cleaning her vagina. She started with her labia by opening her pussy lips and cleaning between them. Next, she moved her washcloth down to her vulva, sticking it inside and rotating the fabric until she felt she was clean enough. Tori had given up on masturbation, but she needed this. Her body needed a comfort zone.

Tori removed the washcloth from her hole and brought it up to her nose, sniffing it. Once assured that she still smelled satisfying below, she moved her washcloth to her clitoris. As soon as she touched her small bud, her body instantly shuttered. The sensation sent her body into instant gratification. In fact, her body yearned with desire. She dripped with temptation and wanting. The feeling of needing a moment of pleasure had her body coveting the anticipation. If Tori didn't know any better, she would have sworn her body had a mind of its own. The feeling her frame identified with sent a bolt of electricity shooting through her. Tori felt the tingle throughout her entire being, and the toothbrush she used only minutes before to clean her teeth, she now used to bring her body to an orgasm.

Opening her legs and placing her foot on top of the tub, Tori inserted her toothbrush into her canal. Her head fell back as she moved it in and out. The shower continued to pour down over her head, making her vision blurry. She moaned aloud. The toothbrush was scrubbing her walls just right. She pictured a sexy man, and that is when her imagination grew. She envisioned Devontae. She felt his strong hands lifting her onto his body. She felt his long, hard penis pounding her—fucking her brains out. Yes, Jace is who *should've* been on her mind, but the things she felt Devontae doing, rotating and bouncing her up and down, Jace could never compare.

Tori moaned uncontrollably. She bit down on her bottom lip as her juices began to run and drip down her leg. For her, masturbating was the next best thing to penetration. She never had an issue with bringing herself to a climax. All she needed was her imagination and concentration.

"Shit, Devontae." Tori smiled and removed her leg. She turned the shower off and stepped out, wrapping a dry towel around her body and walking to the kitchen.

Although she was now pregnant, Tori needed a taste of the red wine. So, she invaded her small wine fridge, popped the cork, and poured herself a glass of Cabernet Sauvignon. After a long day of tears and a few minutes of ecstasy, she took to the bottle of wine with ease. She brought the bottle and a wineglass back to her bedroom, where she quickly climbed into bed and got comfortable. However, she was restless. She didn't know what to do with herself, but she hoped this wine would do the trick. She picked up the remote and turned on the TV. Tori relieved herself of the towel and lay naked across the bed. Now, it was time to relax.

"OK. Now, let's find out who this Scrapp person is," Tori said as she went to On Demand and continued the episode from where she left off.

As soon as Mama Dee began talking, Tori picked up her glass of wine and took a sip. Almost instantly, she began to feel nauseated. Tori gagged and set down the glass. She placed her hand on her stomach and bellowed as the wine and her stomach acid rose within her. She caught her breath, and she felt like shit. This wine had put her gag reflex to the test. She wrapped her arms around her stomach, closed her eyes, and allowed the tears she held in to drip down her face.

"Now, ain't shit sexy about that." Devontae's voice pierced Tori's ears. She opened her eyes and looked at him. He walked over to her and took a seat on the bed. He placed his hand on her back and rubbed it softly. "It's a good thing I don't mind seeing this side of you."

"Devontae," Tori said while chuckling.

"What's wrong? You let that nigga drive you crazy? Now he got you in here crying and throwing up. You know I can't sit back and watch this shit," he said, still rubbing her back. Tori sat up and held her stomach, trying to keep her laughter in. Devontae always knew how to make her laugh, but her stomach was tied in knots.

"Devontae, cut it out. I'm stressed, but not for reasons you think," Tori said honestly.

"Yeah, I already know what's wrong. Your ass needs this fix, and I got you."

"No, I don't need 'a fix.' A fix is what got me into this situation."

"What situation?"

"I'm pregnant, Von."

"You're pregnant?" he asked rhetorically. "You know that's *my* baby, right?" he stated so matter-of-factly. "Now you can leave that square-ass nigga alone, and we can build our own family."

Tori sat flabbergasted; she had no words to speak. She was pregnant, and although she had doubts about who the father was, Devontae was

100 percent sure the baby was his. He stood and lifted Tori from the bed.

"Devontae!" she screamed aloud while hitting him on his chest. Her naked body melted into his strong arms as he held her and began tonguing her down. He kissed her lips, and she quickly protested. "At least let me brush my teeth."

"Nah, we ain't got time for that, baby. I'm in and outta this bitch like a thief in the night," he said. He put his lips and tongue to her neck and licked it as he made his way up to her earlobe.

"You are so freaky," Tori stated.

"Yeah, and you love that shit."

He softly laid Tori back down on the bed. Still dressed and all, he climbed on top of her and kissed her entire body. He knew she was stressed, and he needed to get rid of all her built-up frustrations. When he got to her stomach, he kissed it slowly and softly. He felt connected to what was growing inside of her. Tori gasped and held on to his ears. She couldn't believe she was finally getting all the attention she deserved and from a guy who, back in the day, would've never shown any interest in her. Devontae was just a man who wanted everything his pretty boy cousin had, and Tori, she was nothing more than a collateral beauty.

"What's up, Von Jr.," he said as he kissed and talked to Tori's belly. It wasn't just a feeling. Devontae knew for a fact that this little poppy seed baby was his.

"It's not a boy," Tori said as she rubbed Devontae's cheeks with her thumbs.

"I know what type of bullets I'm shooting outta my Tommy Gun, and my aim is official. Only soft niggas produce girls," he said while kissing Tori's stomach.

"Tori." Jace's voice instantly killed the entire mood. He yelled, and Tori pushed Devontae slightly.

"You have to go," she whispered frantically. "Devontae, get up," she said, now hitting him on his arm. She jumped up, grabbed the towel, wrapped it around her body, and rushed to the bedroom door.

"Tori," Jace yelled again.

"What? You scared of that nigga or something?" Devontae asked as Tori ignored him and scurried from the room.

She had to meet Jace at least in the hallway before he walked into the bedroom. That entire situation would definitely be an ugly one. As soon as Tori rounded the corner, she ran right into Jace. She bent over, feeling a sharp pain in her side, but she grabbed her stomach.

"Who were you in there talking to?" Jace asked. He helped Tori stand up and put his hand on the small of her back.

"Nobody. That was the TV," she lied.

"Has Devontae been over? I saw his car in the driveway."

"Nope," Tori said. She placed her arms around Jace's neck and kissed him.

"I thought you were mad at me," he said. He held Tori around her waist and locked his fingers together.

"I had time to think things over." She kissed his lips again.

"And?" Jace asked.

"And I'm willing to forgive you. But after you're done with her album, I don't want you near her ever again."

"Let's go in the room and talk about this," Jace said. He dug in his pocket and retrieved her cell phone. After he handed it to her, she smiled widely.

"You got it fixed? I don't want to talk about this in the room, baby. Let's take this to the kitchen," she said as she took Jace's hand. Excited, he followed her. He already knew what Tori wanted, and Jace was ready to deliver.

When they reached the kitchen, he lifted Tori onto the countertop. He took off his shirt and stood in front of her. He wanted to discuss things with Tori, but she wanted to use sex as a distraction, just like many other times. She needed Devontae out of the house, so she took Jace in the opposite direction of Devontae's exit.

"I want you to go to Destiny's Valentine's Day Listening Party with me. I know how you feel about her, but trust me, nothing is going on be-

tween us," Jace said as Tori listened. She only
listened without a rebuttal because she knew
Devontae was still in the house somewhere. "She
wants to apologize to you, and you deserve that."

"I guess I can go. I want to hear what the tramp
has to say," she replied. Jace stood in between
her legs, shirtless and ready to tear her apart. Her
mouth was so slick. He wanted to laugh at her
choice of words, but a sexy smile sufficed.

"Your mouth, Mocha. I gotta keep you away from
G-ma. Y'all gon' have my baby girl calling people
tramps." He laughed.

"Well, I call them how I see them. I can only stay
for a little while, though. This pregnancy is taking
over my energy."

"OK, baby."

Jace unwrapped the towel from around Tori,
and for the next twenty minutes, he pleased her.
First on the counter and then on top of a chair. He
sat back and allowed Tori to ride him. He watched
her and stared into her face as she moved her body
uncontrollably. The sex sounds they made were so
loud. The pregnancy intensified Tori's senses, and
the feeling of her pregnant sex wrapped around his
manhood felt unbelievably good.

All Tori could do was pray Devontae left by the
time they were finished. Jace made a loud grunting
noise as he came, and Tori cried out as she did
the same. Then she slowly stood from Jace and

watched as his ejaculation dripped down her leg. Tori was now exhausted and worn out, and so was Jace.

"Damn, I wish I could just lie here and go to sleep," he said.

"Come on, baby." Tori grabbed his hand and tried pulling him up. "Let's go to bed," she offered, and Jace stood.

The two got cleaned up, and afterward, they made themselves comfortable in bed. They snuggled up together and turned on old episodes of *Martin*. Tori was happy she didn't get caught. She knew that was a very close call.

Chapter Twenty-two

Knock, knock, knock.

Devontae placed his fist to the Givens's front door, knocking loud and relentlessly. This was the end of it all. He needed to get into their home without any suspicions.

Since day one of Devontae's and Aja's relationship, they had planned to rob the Givens blind, and Devontae prayed they gave up the money willingly. He and Aja went back and forth over how they would get into the home, and that is when Devontae came up with the perfect idea. He would put on his officer act to get in, and after that, anything went.

Tori's parents lived in seclusion. They had the money to not live amongst people, and they used it wisely. That was perfect for Devontae. He used their privilege against them. He had to catch the two off guard when they least expected it, like early in the morning, before the sun rose, and while the two were in the middle of a good night's rest. Or if they were like most people, someone was on their way to the bathroom about this time.

"Who is it?" Omeiha yelled.

Quickly, Devontae responded. "LAPD, ma'am. Can I speak with you for a moment?" He stood in the doorway awaiting an invitation, but instead, Larry's voice boomed.

"Speak to us about what? How may we help you?"

"It's about your daughter, Tori," he said, and the door swung open.

"What type of trouble that boy done got her into?" Omeiha asked. She knew that Tori was going to need her one day, and she waited for this very day. Now she was ready to say, "I told you so."

"If I can step in for a minute?" Devontae said. "You guys might want to take a seat."

Omeiha and Larry walked Devontae over to the sofa, and they all sat. Devontae laid his hat down on the coffee table and sat back comfortably.

"I don't know how to tell you this, but—" *Boom, boom, boom.* He was cut off by the next set of knocks at the door. "That's probably my partner," he said.

Omeiha stood and walked to the front door. She opened it and was immediately hit across the face with a pistol. She bent over, wincing in pain.

"Larry!" she screamed. Aja stepped in and pulled Omeiha up by her hair.

"Hi, Mother, dear," Aja said. She walked Omeiha back into the living room, where Devontae had Larry hemmed up against the wall with his pistol pointed in his face.

"You got the rope?" Devontae asked Aja.

"Yes." She tossed the rope over to him, and he hog-tied Larry.

"Who are you?" Larry asked as Devontae tied his legs and arms together. "What's the meaning of this?"

"You know who I am, Father," Aja stated. She held on to Omeiha tightly as she pointed her gun into her back. "I just want my cut of the money, and I want to know why I was thrown away like a piece of trash." Aja grasped Omeiha's hair and shoved her gun deeper into her back. "You decided to keep Tori but not me? Why did you give me your name and then give me away?" Aja demanded.

"Taja?" Omeiha said. Her eyes welled up with tears as she thought about why she had to give up her baby girl.

"Yes, it's me, Taja. Why, Mother?" Aja cried. "I deserved everything Tori had. You gave her my life, and now I suffer from it."

Aja walked Omeiha to a chair and sat her down. Then Devontae walked over and attempted to tie her up.

"No, leave her untied," Aja said. She pointed her gun at Omeiha and looked her in her eyes. "You have no idea of how you fucked up my life."

"I'm sorry, baby, I had no choice. Larry and I were broke, and we didn't have the means to care for two babies. Giving you up was a hard decision, but we had to do what was best for you," Omeiha explained.

"Bullshit. Why keep one if you couldn't keep both? You know what? I'm not even here for that. I just want my cut of the money, and then I'll leave you guys alone," Aja said.

"The cut of what money?" Omeiha asked. Aja quickly snatched her face, squeezing her jaws with all her might.

"Don't play stupid with me, Mother. My cut of the trust money. I need that, and you're going to give it to me."

"There is no money," Omeiha lied.

Devontae was tired of standing back and listening to Omeiha talk. He came on business. They were supposed to be in and out. He started to get anxious as the sun peeked through the blinds.

"This bitch wanna play games, huh?" Devontae pointed his gun at Larry. "Where's the money?" he yelled.

"Don't tell them shit," Larry said.

"Don't tell me shit?" Devontae repeated with a devious smile on his face. He cocked his gun and sent a bullet flying through Larry's head. Killing was nothing for him. He did that shit for a living. Omeiha screamed as Larry's body crumbled and blood began to saturate the floor. Devontae walked toward her. He knelt and grabbed her face.

"Please, don't hurt me," Omeiha said. She was full of tears and scared for her life.

"Now, bitch, I'm not fucking around. *Where's* the money? You got ten seconds, or I'ma do you so dirty." He stood and raised his gun.

"I have a few thousand in my bedroom safe and a couple million in a safety deposit box. The key to my safe box is in my bedroom. Please, don't hurt me," she cried again.

"Where?" Aja asked, and Omeiha read the information off to her. When they'd gotten everything they came for, Aja raised her gun. She looked her mother in the eyes one last time. Omeiha raised her hands to her mouth and prayed. "See you in hell," Aja said and emptied her entire clip into her mother's body.

"Damn, that shit was sexy as hell, Aja," Devontae said.

He walked to her and picked her up. Wrapping her legs around his waist, Devontae forced his lips onto hers. He kissed her roughly and felt himself getting extra hard. The fact that Aja wasn't afraid to tote a gun and surely wasn't afraid to use it had Devontae ready to give Aja the best dick she'd ever had.

"We need to get the shit and get out of here," Devontae said. He kissed her lips again.

"OK, Von," Aja whispered as she pecked his lips repeatedly.

They stood in the middle of the room lusting over Aja's handiwork, not realizing it was now morning and the sun shone through the curtains and shades. It was a good thing the Givens lived in seclusion. After a few minutes more passed, the two decided to hit the safe, and after the bank opened, Aja was to hit the safety deposit box. She and Devontae came out on top in this entire situation. The millions that were now within their grasp were absolutely something to celebrate over.

So, Aja spent the rest of her day on a small shopping spree. She went from store to store, dropping nothing but thousands on stupid shit. But she checked in with Amelie throughout the day, making sure she and Devontae were still in the clear. She was ready for a new chapter now that all the missing pieces to her life had finally come together.

This day came so quickly, and as night fell, Tori prepared herself for a night of laughs, conversations, and good music. Valentine's Day . . . a day for lovers. It's a day to show your significant other just how special they are. Although that should be an everyday thing, this day was explicitly reserved for love. Tori couldn't stand Destiny, but she had a point to prove. Plus, she couldn't front on the music Jace laced Destiny with. The shit was just amazing.

Days before, Tori decided to mend her differences with Jace. Of course, she had her reasons to feel the way she did, but in her heart, she knew that although Jace was once a playboy, he had since changed his playa ways. Tori agreed to spend her Valentine's Day at Destiny's little performance because she needed to hear her tired-ass apology, but afterward, she would give Destiny her ass to kiss. She had plans to tell Destiny exactly where she could shove her stupid-ass apology. Tori wasn't dumb by a long shot, and because game recognized game, she knew that if Jace showed Destiny just an inkling of attention, Destiny would most definitely fuck her man. She prepared herself to laugh uncontrollably in Destiny's face because she knew this apology was about to be fake as fuck. She saw through it all. Although she knew Destiny's apology would be a phony one, she just *had* to hear it.

"Damn, is that you, Mocha?" Jace said as he snuck up behind Tori and tapped her softly on her behind.

Since learning she was pregnant, her entire body began to fill out. Tori was slim where it mattered but thick in all the right places. She stood in the kitchen leaning over the counter with a glass of red wine at her side and her eyes attentively glued to her phone. Devontae's text had her full attention. Still, she couldn't help but giggle at Jace's soft love tap.

"You like what you see?" Tori said and stood up. She turned to Jace, and he wrapped his arm around her waist. He fixed his pistol on his hip, brought Tori's body closer to his, and rubbed her belly. Since becoming a little famous, Jace found himself toting his gun around everywhere, especially in certain environments.

"I love what I see. Plus, I see you rocking my name around your neck tonight."

"Yeah, I have to let everyone know who you belong to," she announced. Her entire life, Tori had never been the aggressive type. But just the thought of someone coming between her and her comfort zone had her ready to go to war.

"Everyone I work with knows I'm taken, and everyone I decide to work with in the future will know that shit as well," Jace assured her. He kissed her on her cheek and retrieved her glass of red wine from the counter. "You won't be needing this," he said. Jace drank it all and placed his index and middle finger to the side of his neck. He made a hissing noise, mimicking Martin Lawrence.

"You are so crazy." Tori laughed. She hit his chest and recited Tisha Campbell's infamous line, "You go, boy."

Jace laughed hard as hell, almost choking from the harsh wine still making its way down his throat. He coughed erratically and moved Tori's body away from his. He didn't want to get any of the wine on her sexy-ass outfit. She decided to get *extra* cute for this special occasion. Tori wanted to look sexy, and the fact that she was pregnant didn't stand in the way of anything. She needed *all* heads turned her way. Destiny's voice would be heard so beautifully, but Tori was going to *own* the entire place.

She wore red satin high-waisted shorts, a red satin belly top, and a red kimono with wide sleeves. She let the kimono hang from her left shoulder as her JD necklace sparkled and shone. The bold color complimented her skin. Tonight, she was stepping out looking like a hot, spicy mama. She believed Jace wasn't fucking around with Destiny, but Tori had to make sure Destiny knew he was still all hers. Tori decided to go with a blown-out, bone-straight, shoulder-length wrap with bangs. Her hair slightly covered her eyes, her lips were painted red, and the bottoms of her gold strappy heels were also red. She looked like a dark chocolate Asian with a bit of zing.

After Jace placed the glass back on the counter, he was ready to start his night, but he couldn't leave the house without first taking a few flicks. This was going to be a night to remember. Tori stood in front of Jace as she lifted her phone and began snapping so many selfies. They were so up close and personal.

Jace was dressed in all black, from his fitted turtleneck to his black slacks on down to his sneakers. His accessories were a white gold small rope chain and a matching bracelet. He also sported a red, single-breasted trench coat with gold buttons. Tori pulled on the collar of Jace's coat as she stuck her tongue out. She wanted to tease whoever was out there, ready to hate. Jace held her around her waist. His smile was so big and bright. Happiness and beatitude were written all over him. He felt blessed, and he had every reason to be.

On the other hand, Tori put on a brave act. Although she still needed space to clear her mind, she allowed Jace and even Devontae access to her heart. Tori knew she needed time to think about how she would break things off with Devontae, and she still needed time to figure out how far along she was. However, when Jace came home unexpectedly, she had no choice but to forgive him. She was caught off guard in a scary situation.

Forty minutes later, the two were pulling up in front of the small bar and parking. As always, Jace climbed from the driver's side of his vehicle and walked around to help his trophy, his fiancée, his one and only, Miss Mocha, from the car. Her long, chocolate legs peeped from in between the car door as Jace took her hand into his. Tori climbed out and saw all the flashing lights. This was another photo op, and today, Tori was all for it. She wasn't anxious, she wasn't shy, she didn't feel nervous, nor was she afraid to show just who she was in front of the cameras and paparazzi. Tori clung to Jace. She wrapped her arms around his neck and lifted one leg in front of him, allowing one thick thigh to show as her long kimono draped down. Jace put his hand on her waist and smiled. He was happy, and the smile he displayed was evident.

"You are showing out tonight," he whispered into her ear. Tori knew *precisely* what she was doing. Placing her red-polished fingers to Jace's chest, she laughed. It was the cutest photo. Tori cheesed widely as Jace's lips were to her ear.

"Tori, Jace, over here." The two heard their names being called in all directions. Jace was one of the hottest producers of his time, and everyone wanted him and the lady on his arm to bless their cameras.

After finishing giving the media a show, the two made their way inside the bar. Tori spotted Amelie and Aja right away, but she needed to get her apology out of the way first. So, she waved at the ladies, speaking to them quickly. She kept her other hand occupied with Jace's and walked a step behind him with her fingers locked with his. Jace led the way, and Tori followed him.

"I just saw Amelie and Aja, but I can talk to them later," Tori yelled over the music. She now walked side by side with Jace.

"Are you sure?" he asked, not realizing who Aja was. When he dated her, she went by the name Taja.

"Yes, I'm sure."

"A'ight. Well, let's go backstage for a minute."

The two of them moved through the crowd of people. As they maneuvered their way, Jace dapped up a couple of people from the industry. Tori was almost instantly starstruck by all the famous faces, but she maintained her composure. When they finally got backstage, Destiny smiled, seeing Jace as he peeped his head into her dressing room. She stared at him through the mirror while sitting in a pink silk robe with her legs crossed, getting her makeup applied.

"Jacey," Destiny said excitedly.

"Awe, damn, you still getting ready?" he asked. He moved his head back slightly, giving Destiny a little privacy. He didn't want things to become awkward quickly.

"Yes, I'm still getting dressed, but come in." She waved him in.

Jace opened the door and welcomed Tori into the room first. Destiny's attitude suddenly went from bubbly to peeved. She closed her eyes as she gathered her thoughts and emotions. Tori walked in looking like the perfect pinch of spice. Her red outfit was fitting for the occasion. The entire bar had a sexy little vibe with red lights and smoke floating around everywhere. In the past, Tori had never been so unkind and nasty, but there was no way she would play nice with Destiny. She walked over to the small sofa and took a seat. Tori sat quietly, awaiting Destiny's apology. She pulled her phone out and began scrolling through it. Tori had so much time to kill.

"I thought you would've been ready by now," Jace said. He looked back and forth between the two women as he made small talk with Destiny. He sensed the tension between the two ladies.

Sighing, Destiny spoke up. "Yeah, I should've been ready like twenty minutes ago, but beauty can't be rushed," she said sarcastically. Jace chuckled nervously while Tori laughed obnoxiously.

"Anywho, I heard we are expecting," Destiny said. "Congratulations, Tori."

"Jace, that *wasn't* for everyone to know. But thank you, Destiny. I appreciate it."

As the makeup artist put the finishing touches on Destiny's face, Jace stood next to her. The room was silent, and Tori took that opportunity to text Devontae. He texted her a couple of minutes earlier, and now that she was to herself, she decided to go ahead and respond. Tori clicked on her messages and went to Devontae's last text.

Von: What's up, baby?

Tori: Nothing, I'm here at this listening party.

Almost instantly, Devontae responded as if he were sitting and waiting for Tori to text him back.

Von: Oh yeah? Who you with?

Tori: Who do you think?

Von: Lol. You with that square-ass nigga, Jace.

Tori: Yes, I'm with Jace.

The two kept their correspondence as short as possible.

Von: When you gon' stop playing with that nigga's heart, man? You already know he is not who you want.

Tori: I'm not playing with his heart.

Von: Am I going to see you tonight?

Tori: Maybe.

Von: Maybe? Yeah, OK.

Tori smiled inwardly as she read Devontae's last response. She looked up at Jace and cleared her throat.

"You good, baby?" he asked, walking over to her.

"Yes, I'm fine. Just sitting here waiting on her apology." Tori rolled her eyes up toward Jace. He smirked, noticing her attitude. He didn't want to ruin the night, so he thought carefully before he spoke.

"Is she done yet?" Jace asked Destiny, referring to her MUA.

"Yes, and when she leaves the room, Tori, you and I can talk."

"Well, this conversation needs to hurry up. I have people outside waiting on me," Tori said heatedly.

Tori's phone buzzed, and she stared at an incoming text from Amelie.

"Calm down, baby. Come here," Jace said. He helped Tori up to her feet, attempting to step out of the room with her.

"No, Jace. I want to hear what she has to say. I mean, after all, I *am* like a sister, *right?*" Tori stated.

Destiny asked Jace and her makeup artist to give her and Tori a few moments alone. The makeup girl excused herself, but Jace was reluctant to do so.

"It's fine. We're just going to talk," Destiny said.

"Yeah, we're going to talk *as sisters*," Tori agreed with a look of annoyance on her face.

Jace decided to let the ladies have a moment to themselves. He stepped out and stood on the other side of the door guarding it, keeping his ear close enough to make sure there wasn't a catfight. Minutes went by, and everything seemed well, so Jace decided to join the crowd. Meanwhile, Tori and Destiny stood face-to-face, ready to exchange a few words. The words Destiny *really* wanted to say she kept to herself. She wasn't sorry. Jace was someone she wanted, and she had so many plans to have him. Destiny's apology was not genuine. However, she wanted to appease Jace.

"I just wanted to pull you aside and apologize about what happened the other night. What you think you may have seen was inaccurate."

"What I *saw* was *very accurate,* but I'ma let that shit slide. I know your type, Destiny. You're not fooling me. But since I know Jace doesn't want you, I've decided not to beat your ass. But let that be the *last* time you *ever* disrespect me. There won't be any passes next time," Tori said.

"Whatever, Tori. I don't look at Jace in that way," Destiny lied. "So, all that extra shit you're doing, you can save it. I have a performance tonight, so I will not fuck up my voice going back and forth with you."

"Of course, love. We're just having a *sisterly* conversation, *right?*" Tori smirked. "Well, I won't hold you up. I'll go ahead and get out of your hair. I'm getting a little tired." Tori rubbed her stomach. "Little Jace has had me so exhausted lately."

She rubbed her pregnancy in Destiny's face. Destiny frowned. She looked at Tori with malice in her heart and fire in her eyes.

"You have a great performance, *sis.*" Tori turned her back and left the room.

"Can y'all help me welcome to the stage the newest artist to 290 Records? Miss Destiny, get your cute li'l ass out here."

Everyone clapped as Destiny made her way to the stage in an all-red, strapless, floor-length dress. Tori stood up front with Jace and the rest of the 290 family, clapping and smiling. She was excited and ready to hear all of Jace's hard work. Jace stood behind Tori with his arm wrapped around her entire body. They swayed from side to side as Jace spoke softly into her ear while Destiny introduced her first song.

"Hey, y'all," Destiny said, and the crowd went insane. She was already a sensation, and she had yet to play any of her new music. "I am so happy to see everybody. I have a personal relationship with most everyone in this room, and I am so honored you guys took time out of your day for little ole me. I love you guys. I would first like to give thanks to God. He has put me on this path, this journey, and I am forever grateful for all he has blessed me with. I would like to give a special thanks to Big Percy and the entire 290 family." The spotlight fell on Percy. Destiny put her hands together and bowed her head. "And I want to give a very, *very* special thanks to the producer of my entire project, Mr. Jacey on the Beat Jace. Please come and join me on stage," Destiny said.

Destiny was just that petty. She knew Jace wouldn't be unprofessional and turn down her invitation. So, she smiled smugly at Tori as Jace unwrapped his arms and kissed her on her cheek.

The women had a silent argument for a couple of seconds, and with pursed lips, Tori made her way through the crowd to locate Amelie.

Jace joined Destiny on stage and placed his arm around her shoulder. She put her arm around his waist. Then she handed the mic over to him, and over the loudspeaker, Jace spoke.

"The first song titled 'Givin' You a Taste' was inspired by Destiny's and my first conversation. She told me about a couple of personal situations with a young man she's had dealings with, and I worked my magic. I put my pen to the pad and brought her vision to life," he said. "Y'all ready? A'ight, DJ, play that shit."

Tori stood next to Amelie and Aja as she watched the bullshit-ass relationship between Destiny and Jace. She listened to Jace talk and looked at Amelie.

"Are you OK, boo?" Amelie asked.

"Yeah, I'm fine. I really cannot stand her ass," Tori scoffed.

"Fuck her. Jace loves you," Amelie said.

"I've seen enough, Amelie." Tori was so heated. She knew that a stressful situation was not ideal since she was pregnant. She excused herself and went to the bathroom. She wanted to run away and hide in the last stall the same way she used to do in middle school, but she knew she couldn't. "Mirror, mirror on the wall, am I the prettiest of them all?" Tori said aloud.

Tori stared at her gorgeous hair and her beautiful skin. There was no doubt she'd come a long way. She was now the prettiest of them all. Winking her eye and smiling, Tori took her phone out and sent Devontae a text. When he didn't respond, she fixed herself up and walked out. As she left the lady's room, someone grabbed her from behind. A set of lips were placed to her neck and then her ear. The mystery person spoke softly into her ear, and she knew that her night was about to be an interesting one.

"Take my car and meet me at this address. Room number 3-1-2. I'll be waiting on you."

Tori did as she was told and left the bar without a word. She was on her way to a "private" event, and she didn't need any distractions. She took the car and went home first, quickly changed her clothes, then left. Room 3-1-2 was on the agenda for the rest of Tori's evening.

"What's up, Jace? How have you been?" Aja walked up behind Jace and put her arms around his waist. She leaned her head on his shoulder and took in his scent. He smelled so delicious. His body always smelled scrumptious, and Aja was ready to take a bite.

"Taja," Jace said, unwrapping her arms from around him. He turned to look at her. He didn't notice it before, but the more he looked at Taja, he realized how much she resembled his soon-to-be-wife. "You look really nice tonight."

"Thank you. Long time no see. I see you're fitting right in with Big Percy and the company. How has life been?"

"Yeah, 290 is my family, and life has been great. Thanks for asking." Jace kept his interactions with her at a minimum. "I gotta get back over here to my fiancée. It's been good seeing you," Jace said, coming up with a quick excuse.

Aja didn't know it, but Tori had already left. She allowed Jace to walk away, then made her way back over to Amelie.

"Are you ready to go?" Aja asked Amelie.

"If you are, we can head out," Amelie agreed. "But let me find Tori first. I need to let her know I'm leaving."

"Nah, I told her already. Let's just go. I have something I need to do," Aja said.

She was done with everything and everyone. Jace had given her his ass to kiss for the last time, and even though he was a gentleman about it, she hated rejection. Now that she had her riches and someone who sincerely gave a damn about her, Aja was ready for whatever was next in life. "This ain't business. This shit is all the way personal."

Chapter Twenty-Three

Girl, get facedown for a minute. Let me go down and change your mind. I wanna take you to your limit. I wanna go where you don't. Make a decision, baby. You got the fire that I'm looking for, baby. I wanna be your blessing. Get it over here now.

Tori stepped into the candlelit room wearing a long, black trench coat. Seductively, she sashayed past the man who'd greeted her at the door. Her long legs glistened underneath the glow of the beautifully lit candlesticks, and her breasts sat up perfectly, peeping through the top of her coat. The curves she possessed made her coat look glued to her skin like latex. Tori only sported a panty and bra set underneath the coat that was on its way to coming off her body within a matter of seconds. If this man that stood before her had anything to do with it, everything would be ripped off, piece by piece.

Come take a seat, put some' else on my tongue. You know I'm a freak. I'm a lick it while you come.

I'ma do some things, have you screaming, "Oh no."
I can fuck you right if you let go, baby, you know.

As Tank's "I Don't Think You're Ready" blared
through the tiny speaker in the hotel suite, Tori
heard the door slam behind her. She smiled and
swung her head around, turning to focus her
attention on him. She stared at his face and bare
chest. Then Tori set her sights on his muscular
stomach down to the white hotel towel that hung
loosely around his waist, calling her name. She
heard it loud and clear, and she was on her way to
put her body on his. Tori stared him up and down.
She had to investigate her prey before devouring it.

Almost instantly, her clothes were being forcefully removed from her body. She watched as he
tore away into the belt wrapped around her coat
and then her underwear. She knew she was in for
one hell of a night. He moved in closer, making
sure they were body to body.

"I can teach you lessons if that's what you want,"
his voice whispered into her ear as he held her
tightly around her waist. Devontae turned Tori
around and bent her over. He bit down on his bottom lip while Tori poked out every inch of her ass,
moving her hips, rolling her pussy on his length.
"You gon' contest it 'cause you think you grown,"
he said. Devontae pulled Tori up by her hair and
whispered in her ear. "You ain't grown, Tori." This
little role-playing shit was turning her on all the

way. There was a first time for everything, and if Devontae kept this up, he would have Tori sprung.

Tori's phone buzzed, and she knew it was her cell. No one was about to fuck up her evening, so she quickly silenced it and continued her night.

"I *am* grown," she said, smiling while closing her eyes. Devontae moved her hair to the side and brought her earlobe into his mouth, sucking on it. He used his tongue to lick her and planted French kisses from her ear down to her neck.

"Show me. Show me how grown you are," he whispered.

Tori turned back around so that she was facing him. She slowly unwrapped Devontae's towel from around his waist as he continued to assault her neck with his tongue and lips. He pulled her in by her ass, and Tori was in pure bliss. Everything he was doing to her just felt so right. For him, she was willing to give in. It didn't matter to her that she had a whole man at home, a man who loved her to death, and a man who would go to hell and back for her.

Tori was willing to reciprocate. She had just as much love for Jace. However, he couldn't fuck her the way she desired. Yes, he could make her come, but Tori had to force the feeling. She couldn't help but think maybe she dove in too quickly with Jace, and now, there was no turning back in either situation.

Devontae, on the other hand, was a hard-core nigga. He knew how to tame her and make her come with his kinky tactics. He was like a mind reader. Without Tori telling him, he fulfilled her needs.

Tori's phone chimed, indicating a voicemail, and almost instantly, it began vibrating again.

"It's probably important," Tori said. She picked up her phone and saw Amelie's name on her screen.

"It's not important," Devontae protested. He took her phone from her hand and answered. "She'll call you back," he said as he looked into Tori's eyes the entire time he talked.

Devontae hung up, turned Tori's phone off, and put it down. Tori was speechless. She stared into his eyes, loving everything about him.

"Now, let's get back to *us*."

Devontae continued slowly stripping Tori. The music changed to the next song. Jace and Destiny's new song played loudly. Tori had no qualms about fucking Jace's cousin to his voice. The vibe was sexy, and the song was so fucking provocative.

Can I fuck you in an unusual place? We don't need a bed. I want to throw you up against the wall; then I'll go down and get a little taste. Put it in my face, your body. I'll keep it laced. Can I put your legs around my shoulders? I want a piece of that cake. You can be my Rihanna, my little bad gal. Dirty whine on me, keep that pussy drowning me. I'ma eat that box like it's a free special delivery. Whatever you want, I got it. I'm a pussy pleaser, so, please, don't tease me.

Jace's voice sang, and Devontae could relate. He pushed Tori up against the wall and got on his knees. Then he put her legs on his shoulders, and her mouth fell open. She leaned her head back against the wall while Devontae took her pussy into his mouth. He didn't miss a beat. Devontae kept her steady. He held on to her ass as he stood to his feet.

Givin' you a taste of me, tell me what you want from me. Every little inch of me, I'm giving you a taste. Givin' you a taste of me, tell me what you want from me. Every little inch of me, I'm giving you a taste.

Destiny's voice serenaded the entire room with the perfect lyrics at the perfect moment. Tori screamed and squirmed, moving her hips as she held on to the back of Devontae's head while he got a taste of her sweet nectar. He sucked on Tori, licked her middle, and sipped on her juices. Then he took his index and middle finger and stuck them inside Tori's anus, working them fast and hard. He told Tori before he wasn't a soft-ass nigga. He wasn't with all that piano shit, but he had his ways of turning the heat up a notch. He couldn't create his own beat, but he definitely knew how to fuck to any type of beat.

Talking about loving, every time we're licking, kissing, touching, and fucking. Make me feel something. You're blessed with a gift, and you're humbled. I love how you make me feel when we're fucking. Massages got me lusting; don't stop. I'm your lady in the streets, but in the bed, I'm your thot. Start down low and work your way to the top.

Destiny sang. Her voice had Tori feeling the mood. She was saying all the right things that had Tori ready to explode.

I'm grinding real slow, patiently, maintaining the flow. As the candle and moonlight reflect off seductive eyes, making you release as the sunrise, pleasing your G-spot as your juices run down your inner thighs.

Jace brought the verse to an end.

"Devontae." Tori moaned his name. He was eating her so right.

Everything about Devontae made Tori feel like she was living on the edge. She wasn't supposed to be with this man in any type of way, but here they were, up against the wall in an intimate setting, and Tori was on her way to an orgasm. Devontae took off. His tongue game was superb. Tori had a first-class, round-trip ticket to everything the Devontae Express had to offer.

"Devontae . . . it's coming," she said.

Devontae didn't speak. He just sucked even harder—his finger dove into her ass even deeper. One would've thought he was digging for gold. Devontae needed Tori to rain down on him. His mouth was ready to receive her creamy goodness. This entire situation was so erotic and pornographic. She saw herself playing this whole scene over and over again in her mind. It felt so good, maybe too good . . . but it was all betrayal. However, neither party felt bad or guilty about what they were doing. Tori promised herself this would be the last time, but Devontae was putting in so much work that she didn't know how to ween herself off his good lovin'. She figured out of sight and out of mind would be the best route for them.

"Devontae, baby." Tori breathed heavily.

Devontae moved his head in a circular motion, making sure to lick and suck every nook and cranny of Tori's lips, yoni, and clit, even slipping his tongue near her ass. Tori's legs tensed up around his neck, and she shook uncontrollably. She could no longer hold back. Tori came—and she came *hard*. She dripped and squirted her secret extract into Devontae's mouth. He drank it all down with no problem because Tori was absolutely delicious.

With one last kiss to Tori's middle, Devontae picked her up from his shoulders. Then with their bodies still up against the wall, he cornered her.

He placed his arms up against the wall on both sides of Tori, boxing her in while he placed his cum-painted lips to hers. Intimacy was written all over them. However, Devontae was the wrong person, and this was a very wrong situation. This is something she should've been sharing with her man, Jace. After all, this *was* Valentine's Day.

"This is it, Devontae. I can't keep doing this to Jace," Tori said in between his pecks. "This baby—" Tori spoke, and Devontae kissed her again.

"Nah, I still want you. This ain't it. Fuck that soft-ass nigga. You deserve a *real* man," he said. He wrapped his hand around her throat and choked her softly. "I told you, Tori, this pussy, your body—it all belongs to me."

He lifted her effortlessly and carried her to the bed through the double doors. Tori never once protested. She liked all the rough shit Devontae dished out, and she loved how he talked crazy to her. He tossed her roughly onto the bed, then stood in front of her. Devontae stared at Tori while he began massaging his dick. He stiffened, and his dick grew in size as he pulled at it. Devontae took his bottom lip in between his teeth and smiled at Tori. She lay back, watching him. This man was so fucking sexy, and his body was muscular in all the right places. His arm flexed as he moved his hand back and forth. Tori was suddenly wet all over again. She placed an eager hand on her thigh, contemplating following Devontae's lead.

"Play in that pussy, baby," he coached her, and she did as she was told.

Tori watched him as he watched her, both arousing each other. Her sexual sighs were loud and dramatic. It was so beautiful and music to Devontae's ears. Tori played with herself with a purpose, and her sexual drive would help her reach a body-numbing orgasm. Tori went hard when it came to masturbation. She was a pro at it. So, she knew exactly where to touch, where to feel, and how deep her fingers needed to go. Using three fingers, she played with her pussy as if it was her favorite toy. Her head fell back, and her eyes rolled. She was almost there.

Devontae watched her like a hawk. She was about to be his prey. He held his erection in his hand, no longer jerking it. He instantly grew jealous at the sight before him. Tori was giving her fingers more attention than she was giving him. Suddenly, he was tired of watching. He took Tori's legs into his grasp and pulled her to him. Then he opened her legs wide and lifted her behind from the bed. It was *his* turn to put in some work. He couldn't let Tori's fingers outdo him. Devontae held Tori's legs up with his arm while forcing his way in.

"Shit," he said.

He rolled his hips and broke into Tori's walls like a fucking robber. He controlled her body with

his tight and steady grip of her legs, pulling her
to him every time he pushed forward. Tori bit
her bottom lip and helped Devontae violate her
innermost sacred parts. She moved her hips with
his, holding her waist up with her hands and moving her body like a circus freak. Tori was indeed a
freak, and with Devontae, her entire body bent and
folded in ways she never imagined.

Devontae lay on top of Tori in the missionary
position. He still held her legs up in his grasp as
he dug in, taking long, deep strokes. His animal
grunts and her feral cries seemed so loud as he lay
his head on her shoulder. The feeling of an orgasm
was so overwhelming. However, Devontae tried
his best to control himself while he beat up Tori's
insides.

So many songs played during Tori and
Devontae's carnal night. The music was no longer important at this point. Their bodies were their
own personal instruments, and their moans were
the lyrics to their long night of sexing.

"Shit, I'm tired," Devontae said. "Get on top."

He rolled onto the bed, and Tori climbed on
top of him. As she'd always done while in control,
she planned to ride the two of them into a restful
orgasm. Quick and rough, but sexy and amorous.
Her body movements were always sexy and sen-
sual. She was Devontae's perfect scenery with bent
knees and wide-open pussy lips. Tori worked her

body as Devontae moved his hips, working her middle. She felt like she was a part of an erotic dance video as she performed. Her body moved to the beat, and her hips rotated to the wave as if she were doing the perfect eight count. Tori put delicate hands to her thighs and popped her body on Devontae as he grabbed her waist. She wound her hips and stared down into her lover's satisfied face. Slowly, she brought her bottom lip into her mouth, masking her moans that threatened to escape. No strings attached, Tori gave Devontae all of her. If a taste were all he wanted, then she'd given him more than he could ever ask for.

"Jace, where's Tori?" Amelie asked. Her tears were evident as she cried out to Jace over the phone. She was hysterical and frantic. Jace was confused. He didn't know how Tori's best friend had gotten his number or why she was calling him, crying.

"What do you mean? How did you even get my number?" he asked. "Is everything OK?"

"I got it from Tori just in case of an emergency," Amelie said. "Where is she? I've been calling her for hours now. I have something really important to tell her."

"I'm on my way to her right now. What happened?"

"It's about her parents. Can you please tell her to call me as soon as you get to her? Please, Jace," Amelie said.

"Yeah, sure." Jace's voice now had a bit of worry in it. Amelie hung up, and Jace looked over at Destiny.

"What happened?" Destiny asked. He pulled in front of her house and sat close to the curb, idling the car.

"I don't know. She didn't say."

"Who is she?"

"That was Amelie, Tori's friend."

"Ole girl from the studio?"

"Yeah, her." Jace smirked.

"Mmm, well, thank you for coming to my performance and dropping me off at home. I really needed you there tonight."

"No problem. It was my pleasure," he said.

He reached his hand out to Destiny, but instead of shaking it, she leaned over and kissed his lips. Destiny caught him off guard. He quickly pulled back and began fixing his clothes.

"I have to go. I know Tori is at home waiting on me," he said, and Destiny sat smugly.

She pushed her hair behind her ears and rolled her eyes. Jace was something Destiny wanted. She needed to know what was behind all that swag. He'd allowed her to flirt all this time . . . so why stop now?

"Jace." Destiny finally spoke up. "I want you. That 'Givin' You a Taste' song just felt so personal. On stage, you said you got the ideas from me, but I know you had to be speaking from your own experiences."

"Maybe, but we can't go that route. I have a fiancée at home and a baby on the way. You *do* remember my fiancée, right? Tori. You just apologized to her earlier," he said.

"Whatever," Destiny replied. "Call me when you make it to your destination, please. And I hope everything is OK with Tori's parents."

"A'ight. I got you," he said, and Destiny climbed from the car.

Jace sat for a few minutes, making sure Destiny got into her home unharmed before he pulled off. Fifteen minutes later, he pulled in front of his home. He walked through the threshold and smirked. Jace yelled Tori's name and followed the trail of rose petals that led from the front door to the bedroom.

"Tori," Jace yelled.

He walked into the bedroom and folded his arms. He put one hand to his chin and admired Tori's hard work. Roses surrounded the bed, and on top of the blanket was a heart with the letters J&T in the middle. He walked over as the aroma of a grapefruit and Cassis-scented candle burned, giving the room a relaxing, fruity smell. The fire flickered, and Jace walked toward it. He noticed a folded card sitting next to the candle and Tori's JD necklace. He smiled knowingly. He picked up the necklace along with the card and read it.

Roses are meant for a get well soon. Violets just won't do. So if you really love me as much as you say you do, then meet me in room 3-1-2. I have a sexy surprise for you.

XOXO

Jace looked underneath the candle and picked up a hotel key card. He read the name and address. Then he placed the beautiful card in his pocket and made his way to Tori. It took him thirty minutes to reach the hotel. He sat for a few minutes thinking about everything. Jace found Tori's gesture spontaneous and romantic. This was the first time he'd ever experienced this type of treatment from a woman, and this was just another reason, amongst others, to love her. Finally, Jace pulled the key card to Tori's room from his pocket. He fisted it and read the note one last time.

Jace called Destiny as promised, and when all was well, he stepped from his car and made his way to the room. When Jace stepped from the hotel elevator, he heard music playing. The sexy music was alluring. It called his name. Jace was ready to put all bullshit aside and give Tori a night of lovemaking. He needed to romance her. That was all she needed. Jace knew that when Tori was horny, she did the most, so he figured if he fucked her real quick, all would be forgiven.

He bobbed his head to the beat of "Come Get It" by Jacquees, and he knew his baby was playing that song just for him. He was on his way to get it. He had to make up for spending Valentine's Day with another woman.

Jace slid the key card into the door and watched as the red dots turned green. He opened the door slowly and looked around. Growing a little suspicious after seeing a white towel, Tori's coat, and her underwear scattered across the floor, Jace quickly became defensive. The music was so loud that he couldn't think straight. He tried to piece it all together, but it was hard. He couldn't imagine things being what he thought they were. The shit he envisioned in his mind was causing him to become heated.

It was as if the song were pulling him in its direction. *"Come get it, come get it, come get it, come get it, come get it."* The chorus played, and Jace followed. As he got closer to the back of the room and near a set of double doors, Jace heard moaning. He frowned and pulled his pistol from his waist. He slowly cracked open the door and saw the silhouette of Tori on top of a man. Her body moved slowly to the beat, riding as if she didn't have a man that loved her. At that very moment, everything for Jace went blank. He instantly flew into a blind rage.

His heart crumbled. He became a man scorned, and his entire life began to replay. He couldn't believe he allowed Tori to play him this way. Love and pussy would absolutely make you do some crazy things. Jace was coming to get it, and this crime of passion was the end-all to everything he attempted to build with this insecure girl.

Tears blinded Jace's vision as he busted into the room, and without thinking, he pointed his gun, airing shit out. He filled the entire bed up with bullets. One shot, two shots, hell—twelve gunshots later, Jace's right mind finally came racing back to him. He fell to his knees and cried as he watched his woman slump over on top of his favorite cousin. He couldn't believe this. How could two important people in his life betray him? It was one thing seeing a video. Anything could be edited, mixed, and mastered. Hell, he did that shit for a living. Editing, mixing, and mastering were his specialties when it came to music. But to see this shit up close and personal was a whole 'nother thing.

Jace's family had taught him well. Never go any-where unprepared, not even to pull up on his bitch. Jace never expected this shit, though. Devontae knew precisely what it was between Tori and Jace. This entire thing hurt him to his core. Jace knew what type of nigga his cousin Devontae was when it came to a fight. Jace would've never won this shit going toe to toe. However, killing Tori and

Devontae was the furthest thing from his mind. This right here was a terrible crime of passion.

Jace stood and walked over to Tori's still moving body. She breathed in and out slowly as she tried to gasp for air. Blood was everywhere, and Jace cried even harder.

"Tori?" he said.

The bullet wound in her back had Jace so weak. How did shit get to this point? He rolled her body from Devontae's and shook his head. If only he knew what type of woman Tori was from the beginning. Her sex addiction caused him so much pain. He loved her. Hell, he was *addicted* to her. As he dislodged her body from Devontae's, he wept. He looked over at Devontae's still body and laughed a little through his tears. Devontae knew what Tori meant to him. He noticed the bullet wound in the side of Devontae's head and flared his nostrils. Jace damn near threw up from the sight of Devontae's bloody brain matter slowly leaking onto the bed. His eyes were wide open, and his mouth as well. He was already gone, so Jace did what he could to help Tori. Tori lay on her back, still gasping as Jace applied pressure to her chest.

"How could you do this to me?" he asked.

He looked Tori in her eyes as she looked up at him, breathing deeply. Blood leaked from the sides of her mouth and the bullet wound. Tori was only hit once, but the bullet traveled from her back to her chest.

"I loved you so much, Mocha. Why did you do this?" he said through his tears.

He pulled his phone from his pocket and called 911. Jace knew this was the end of everything he'd built. Everything in his life was going downhill thanks to a woman he thought he could trust. Maybe she should've just been one of his little hoes because she wasn't worth the trouble, and she should've never been wifed up. Tori was unworthy of a man like Jace. Everything about her told Jace to run from the beginning. Even Devontae told him to tread lightly with Tori, but he didn't listen. Now, look at him.

Tori said she wasn't going out without a nut, and in the end, maybe it was worth it. She found love and lust in a sinful situation. She allowed her addiction to get the best of her. Tori was sick, and she had no control over the things her body craved. Pain was the number one factor when it came to fulfilling her needs. Now, her life was slipping away. What about the baby that was still growing inside her womb? No one was thinking in this situation. Nothing lasts forever. Tori had to know that Jace would catch on one day, but this was so unexpected.

As Tori lay in Jace's arms gasping for air, she mouthed the words, "I love you, Jace. I'm so sorry."

Tears ran down her face. This pain right here was a different type of agony. It was more than emotional and more than physical. She'd hurt Jace terribly, and in return, he gave her his hard-core side. Although every action doesn't deserve a reaction, Tori deserved this shit. Her eyes fluttered slowly, and Jace's face became so blurry. She heard his weeping and wished she could mend it all. She was sorry, and it wasn't because she got caught. In her heart that was sluggishly beating now, she was genuinely sorry. As everything became distant, the music, Jace's cries, his handsome face, the pain from the bullet, Tori took deep, labored breaths. Her heart was stopping. Her eyes fluttered a few more times until they closed permanently, and darkness took her away.

Epilogue

One year later . . .

Live from the BET Awards Preshow, we have a live performance from Destiny and Producer Jacey on the Beat. So help us welcome them to the stage.

The crowd went wild as Jace stood on the side of Destiny with his arm around her shoulder. Dressed in a pink and white Medusa print Versace short set, with a pair of dark-colored shades covering his eyes, his head was down as he nodded to the beat. It was a whole freaky vibe. The melody of the song was slow and sexual. This little piece was written exclusively for Destiny.

"Do you want me, Jace," she sang, removing his arm from her shoulder and grabbing his hand. Destiny looked at Jace seductively, smiling as he

looked at her, smirking. Finally, she walked in front of him, with his hand now wrapped around her neck, grasping her left breast.

"Oooohs" and "aaaahs" came from the audience as the two displayed their love.

"Can I play in it, lay in it? Make your body scream?" Leaning his head back slightly, Jace crooned. His vocals came out loud and boisterous. "Baby, even if I got to beg for it, I don't mind." Live, with millions of people watching, Jace expressed how bad he wanted Destiny.

"Whew, child, slow down now," she said while laughing into the mic while fanning herself. Jace and the crowd followed Destiny's lead and laughed too.

This moment had been a long time coming. It had only been a year ago Jace feared for his freedom. After murdering both Devontae and Tori, he knew he was going to prison for the rest of his life. Luckily, he had only spent a few weeks in jail. The detectives uncovered a hidden video camera during the investigation, and after the footage was carefully reviewed, Jace was set free.

Everything from Devontae and Tori's infidelity was caught on tape, everything from when she entered the hotel suite until Jace entered the room.

So, it was understandable why Jace had done what he did. It had to be Tori or even Devontae looking out for him. It was fucked how they had played him, but in his heart, all was forgiven.

After Jace was released, he did the right thing and gave Tori a nice homegoing service. He still loved her. Honestly, she was still the love of his life. That day was very emotional for him, but he had to move on after laying Tori to rest. She was gone forever. He knew he could never bring her back, but her beautiful face was still etched in his mind. Soon after, his music career took off. Especially after he began to dedicate all his time to Destiny and the studio. They both were a distraction from everything going on in his life. Soon after, the two began dating. He didn't know if he was with her for convenience, money, or if he really felt something for her, but he made sure their relationship was public, making their music intriguing. It seemed to tell the story of their lives. And he, just like the record company, knew people were a sucker for a good ole real-life love story . . . even if it were fake.

"You don't know how you make me feel; being trapped in your love is not enough. I want to breathe your air and feel your heart beat inside mine. If only we can make this moment last forever," Destiny sang out.

Jace put his mic to his lips and ad-libbed a few words.

"Fuck the love. It ain't no love in fucking. Tonight, I'm cool with lusting. Assuming your favorite position, riding your body like a tidal wave." Destiny grinded on Jace as she swung her head to the side, put her hand on her knee, bent over, and moved her body, popping her back. She stood, turned to look at Jace, smiling as he reached into his pocket. Destiny did another turn, and Jace grabbed her hand, turning her back toward him. He got on one knee, and the audience gasped. The music volume turned down a few notches, but the beat continued to play as Destiny placed her hand to her mouth and cried. Her makeup was beautiful. She had a full face, and her highlights made her glow as her tears fell onto her exposed breast and silver-shingled crop top.

"Jace . . ."

"Destiny, I love you. After everything I been through, I never wanted to fall in love again. But with you, it's different," he said.

"I love you too," she cried into the mic.

"Will you accept my ring?" he asked, looking at her. His hands shook, and his lips quivered from nervousness.

"Yes, baby, I will."

He slid the ring on her finger and stood up. He lifted her in his arms and tongue kissed her as the music turned back up. After everything he had been through, Destiny had stayed by his side. He didn't know if he was doing the right thing, proposing to her, but something about this felt so right. It was as if his life had come in a full circle. Tori taught him how to love one woman. She helped build him into the man he planned to be for Destiny. Honestly, he always liked her, but he loved Tori, and now that she was gone, he felt her blessing. He deserved love. He deserved her love. Marriage was going to have them locked in for life.

"This whole time, Jace . . . this whole fucking time. You never loved me. I killed my parents, set my sister up to be hurt, and you still go wife up the next bitch?" Aja yelled after seeing Jace's proposal to Destiny on live television. She realized she would never be woman enough for him. Throwing a champagne bottle at the TV screen, instantly causing the screen to become distorted, she buried her face into her pillow and cried. She wanted to murder something or someone. "I hate you, Jace. I hate you." Even after her relationship with Amelie, she stalked Jace. Hell, she broke up with Amelie after finding out Tori had passed away, expecting Jace to run to her for comfort.

She had the money, the time, and she was willing to give it all to Jace. Nonetheless, he moved on to a bitch who didn't deserve him in Aja's eyes. She picked up her phone and went to Jace's name. She was sure he had blocked her. Still, she called him anyway. Of course, it went to voicemail, and she screamed out her voice messages.

"Jace, how could you do this to me?" Hanging up, she went to an unsaved phone number and called it. The voice came through in a soft but excited tone.

"Hello," the voice said, and Aja sat silently. "Helloooo." Aja still didn't say anything. She just whimpered into the phone. "Jace." Aja heard the phone being exchanged, and she waited to hear his voice.

"Yeah, hello."

"Yeah, hello, my ass," Aja yelled. "Why the fuck did you just propose to that bitch on TV? You *really* hate me that much? I'm going to kill that bitch when I catch her." Aja ranted on and on until Jace finally hung up on her. Crazy was an understatement. The fact that she had been rejected her entire life, you would think she would be used to it by now. However, this pain was something she wouldn't wish on her worst enemy. Nevertheless, she planned to do Destiny worse than what Jace had done Tori.

She stood from the bed, feeling like she had nothing left to live for. Going into the bathroom and grabbing a brand-new bottle of 600 mg painkillers, she looked at herself in the mirror. Her face was drenched with tears. Opening the bottle and pouring ten into her hand, she popped them one by one into her mouth, only using her saliva to wash them down. Instantly becoming drowsy, she lay there on the bathroom floor and closed her eyes. This was it for her. If Jace wouldn't love her, she no longer wanted to live. She was miserable with life.

Aja's eyes slowly began to flutter open six hours later as her doorbell buzzed loudly. She put one hand over her ear and the other to her stomach. She felt queasy, and she was pissed that she survived her attempt at an overdose.

"Police, open up!" she heard, which caused her to snap back to reality. However, she was weak. She could barely move. Turning to the side and rising slightly on her elbow, she pulled her way into the hallway. She wanted to get up and run but couldn't.

Hearing the door crashing down, Aja just lay on her back. Fuck it. After they realized she was trying to kill herself, they would undoubtedly lock her up in a mental institution. Footsteps rushed her way, and as they approached, they announced why they were there. Aja was being arrested and charged with the murder of her parents.